Winter's Chill
A Larry Macklin Mystery-Book 16

A. E. Howe

Books in the
Larry Macklin Mystery Series
(in order):

ISBN-13: 978-1-7346541-3-4

DEDICATION

For Dad

CHAPTER ONE

Everyone has a moment in their lives that they'll never forget—an event that is permanently etched onto their souls. Mine came on a Sunday afternoon in early December. It was my weekend on call and I was just heading back to the office after settling a minor domestic dispute when I heard Marti's voice over the radio stating that an officer was down.

I'd heard similar calls before and they always struck fear into my heart. But what made this one different was the next thing the dispatcher said: "I can't locate the sheriff."

I knew Marti well and I picked up on the tremor in his voice, a hesitation that spoke volumes. He was telling everyone who could hear him that he thought the fallen officer could be the sheriff... my father.

My heart pounded in my chest and I let out a gasp of air as I pressed my foot down on the accelerator. The speedometer was nearing ninety miles an hour before I remembered to turn on my siren and flip on the blue lights embedded in the grill of my unmarked car. All I could think about was getting to the scene as fast as I could.

Over the radio, Marti was passing information to Deputy Susan White, who had reported in as being nearest to the scene. A citizen had reported passing a van parked on the side of the road and seeing a man in a green uniform lying on the ground. For some reason, they hadn't stopped. If I ever met this person, I promised myself to have some serious words with them about their civic duty.

I was chilled at the mention of a van. Dad often drove around in his ratty old van, especially when he was going somewhere with Mauser, his Great Dane. I racked my brain, trying to remember if Dad had mentioned anything on his schedule for today. Maybe another church picnic? It was one of his jobs as sheriff, at least the way he saw it—staying in touch with the community. He would go anywhere he was invited if it meant getting a chance to listen to the people he served and having the opportunity to talk about his vision for Adams County's chief law enforcement agency.

I ran through a stop sign and calculated when I'd have to slow down to make my next turn. I heard Deputy White report that she had arrived at the scene and was not surprised to hear her confirm everything Marti had already told her. I knew from the way they were talking that it had to be my dad lying on the ground injured… or worse… and I felt only a second's relief when Marti assured Deputy White that an ambulance was already en route. I understood them being circumspect about the details. In our rural community, there were any number of people who might be listening in on the conversation via their police scanners. Whatever had happened, it would be best not to gear up the rumor mill any sooner than was absolutely necessary.

My tires skidded off the road as I made my turn and accelerated past a slow-moving pickup truck. I didn't even care about the speedometer anymore. The only factor I considered was whether or not I could keep my car on the pavement. Luckily, I was now on a stretch of road that was sparsely traveled at the busiest times.

As I came around a curve, I could see a horribly familiar van half a mile ahead on a long straightaway. One of our patrol cars was parked just behind it. I pumped the brakes and pulled over, slamming the car into park before jumping out and running past the van. I caught a glimpse of a frantic Mauser, barking and scratching at the windows, but I couldn't spare the time to worry about him. Thirty feet in front of the van, I saw Deputy White kneeling over the body of my father. I felt my heart do the impossible and begin pounding even harder.

White heard me approach, sparing me only a quick glance before turning her attention back to Dad.

"Thank the Lord, he's alive!" she shouted, keeping her hands pressed against the wound in his chest. I wanted to push her aside and take over, but I knew that she was far more competent than I was at lending medical assistance. The full-figured, dark-skinned mother of all younger deputies in our department had worked several years as an EMT before training to be a law enforcement officer.

"How bad is it?" I didn't recognize my own voice as I knelt down beside her. It sounded more like the voice of a five-year-old child than an experienced sheriff's deputy. Dad was breathing shallowly and spitting up small amounts of blood.

"His lung is punctured," she told me. "We need the ambulan—" She stopped as we heard a siren coming around the bend.

Seconds later, I heard a familiar voice tell dispatch that he was on scene. Alejandro Valdez was one of the best EMTs I knew and I was grateful that he was answering this call. He leaped out of the vehicle and didn't waste any time taking over from White while another EMT ran to the back to fetch a stretcher.

"Make sure no one runs up on us!" he shouted to me.

He'd stopped the ambulance in the eastbound lane. Luckily, it was on a long straightaway, but Hondo was right. You could never trust another driver to be paying attention. I stepped into the road, keeping an eye on Hondo as he gave Dad a quick examination, then helped load him onto the stretcher.

"We'll have him at the hospital in fifteen minutes if you

can clear the way," Hondo said, pushing the stretcher past me.

"Go as fast as you can and don't worry about the intersections, they'll be clear!" I shouted back to him on the way to my car.

"I got this!" White yelled, already folding herself into her patrol car. The flashing lights were joined by the siren as she pulled onto the road. I started my car as Hondo took off in the ambulance.

"We need all intersections covered between here and the hospital in Tallahassee," I told dispatch, pulling around the ambulance and catching up to White. Both of us had our pedals pressed to the floor.

Dispatch began to coordinate the effort to make sure Dad's ambulance didn't have to slow down for even a second at the many intersections it would have to blow through to get to the hospital. White blocked the first intersection while I covered the second. Several Florida Highway Patrol cars joined us as we hopscotched our way into Tallahassee. We slowed a little as we entered the metro area, but not by much. A trip that normally would have taken forty minutes took less than half that time.

Brakes squealed at the entrance to the emergency room, where a doctor was standing at the curb waiting for us. He gave Dad a once-over, confirming everything he'd already been told, then a team of nurses and aides rushed the stretcher through the ER and straight to the hospital's surgical wing.

I tried to follow, but hands grasped at my clothes and pulled at my arms. A wall of blue scrubs and surgical masks blocked my progress.

"You can't go through there."

"We have him now. He's in the best hands."

"We'll tell you as soon as we know anything."

I allowed myself to be pulled into a small alcove with chairs and other anxious people waiting on their loved ones. I tried to catch my breath, then remembered poor Mauser going crazy in the van. I grabbed my phone and called Pete Henley, my best friend and fellow investigator.

"I'm at the scene," he answered. "And I've already put in a call to Cara. She's coming to get Mauser. How's your dad?"

"He's in surgery. I don't... What about..." I couldn't think straight, but Pete was able to read my mind.

"The crime scene? I've got it locked down and we're taking measurements now. And White's on her way back. She'll be able to tell us exactly what she did and what she saw when she got here."

"Thanks."

"We'll catch the guy that did this." Pete's voice was fierce "We have to."

"Stay with your dad," he instructed, then hung up.

I called Cara. "Sorry you heard it from Pete," I said, after explaining everything I *didn't* know.

"How are you? I know that's a stupid question." Her voice was tense.

"I'm holding it together."

"Have you called Genie?"

My heart sank at the thought of Dad's fiancée. "Damn it, no. I haven't had time to think about anything. I'll call her as soon as we get done."

"I'm on my way to get Mauser now. Do you want me to come to the hospital once I've taken him home?"

I hesitated. Part of me desperately wanted Cara by my side, but my rational brain took over. One more person pacing the halls wouldn't help Dad, and she could do something that would mean much more to him if she stayed in Adams County. "No. Just take care of Mauser. I'll call you later."

My conversation with Genie was short. She was in her car before I'd finished telling her what had happened, and she joined me in the waiting room within twenty minutes. Genie was normally an island of calm in the sea of my father's more volatile nature, but as soon as she walked in I could tell that her emotions were frayed.

Two hours later, a short man who wasn't much older than me, wearing scrubs and a serious expression, came into the waiting room. After surveying the half dozen other people sitting near us, he came straight over to me.

"Deputy Macklin?" he asked without smiling, which caused my stomach to lurch.

"I am," I said, standing nervously.

"I'm Dr. Osman, thoracic surgery. The good news is that we were able to repair the damage to your dad's lung. The wound was clean and should heal well. The bigger concern is the traumatic brain injury he suffered."

"What?" No one had mentioned any damage to his head.

"He took a bad hit to the back of the head. Maybe when he fell backward after being stabbed, he hit it on the ground or some other object as he was falling. That's why he was unconscious when he was brought in and there's still bleeding on his brain. We're monitoring it closely and, if it reaches a critical point, we'll need to operate to relieve the pressure. That won't be me. I've called in a neurosurgeon. He's on his way now and he's already reviewed the scans we sent him. I'll let him explain the benchmarks he'll be looking for."

"I... I guess you can't answer any questions about his prognosis." I shook my head, thoroughly overwhelmed.

"Like I said, the prognosis for the stab wound is very good. There's always a risk of infection, but it's small. He'll be on a course of antibiotics and he'll have some pain, plus he'll need some respiratory therapy. But I won't attempt to make any predictions about the concussion. I've seen people with worse blows to the head make a complete recovery, but any cranial bleeding is bad. I understand that your father is the sheriff of Adams County?"

"That's right," I said, surprised at the apparent change of topic.

"And I imagine you all are keen on catching whoever did this. Unfortunately, I feel confident in telling you that your father won't have any memory leading up to the attack. He'll be lucky to remember anything that happened today. This is very common with severe concussions. For right now, we have him in an induced coma to help control the swelling and to give his brain time to rest and repair itself."

I hadn't considered that. With Dad being the only eyewitness we had, if he couldn't remember anything about the crime, how would we be able to catch his attacker, let alone prosecute them?

"I appreciate you being honest with me," I told the surgeon.

"When can we see him?" said a voice beside me. I'd almost forgotten about Genie.

"He'll be in ICU. You'll be able to see him in about half an hour."

"Thank you." Genie reached out and took the doctor's hand. He looked surprised, but relaxed and smiled reassuringly.

"I'll have a nurse escort you up to the ICU."

"I don't know what I'll tell Jimmy," Genie said, wiping tears from her eyes as the doctor walked away. Genie's son, who was about my age, had been born with Down's Syndrome and now lived in a group home in Tallahassee. He loved Dad and was very excited about the upcoming wedding. "I don't think I'll tell him until we know a bit more."

At a loss for words, I just nodded. I was doing everything I could not to think of the worst case scenarios. The more I tried to redirect my thoughts away from Dad's injuries, the more I focused on my desire to see that whoever did this was brought to justice.

"What happened?" Genie asked, as though she had read my thoughts.

"We don't know. From what I can tell, Dad must have pulled up behind someone and gotten out of the van. At some point after that, the person stabbed him. It must have been a surprise attack for Dad to have fallen backward like that." I was trying to picture the event in my mind. "It would have to have been someone who didn't appear to be a threat."

"Ted's given me his situational awareness lecture a few times. Be aware of your surroundings and the people who are close by," Genie said, falling into Dad's cadences as she recited his words. "Don't trust strangers in isolated circumstances."

"Being cautious can mean life or death for anyone. But whoever did this couldn't have rung any of Dad's alarm bells."

"Maybe it was someone whose car had broken down?" Genie suggested, a thought I'd already had.

"If they were broken down, then how did they drive off?"

"Could they have been pretending?"

"It's possible. That stretch of road isn't well traveled. Not the worst place for an ambush. There's a long straightaway which would give a crook a good line of sight if anyone was coming. Maybe they were planning to abduct someone, but instead of someone they could jump, it was Dad who stopped. Maybe something alerted Dad or caused the bad guy to get nervous and he attacked, then drove off. That's not a bad theory."

"Do things like that happen?" Genie's voice was incredulous.

"Not normally in the middle of the afternoon. Though there have been serial rapists and killers who were bold or crazy enough to try something like that in broad daylight. Ted Bundy, for one."

"This is insane." Genie's voice shook. "I know that he's the sheriff and that there's always some danger, but this... I just thought something like this would be for the younger deputies, the ones who are on the road, to worry about."

"Dad isn't one to sit back and send others into harm's way without being willing to go there himself. Besides, this looks like the type of crime that could have happened to anyone. You stop to help someone and... things go bad."

"He has to be okay." Genie's hands trembled and tears rolled down her cheeks. As gently as I could, I guided her back to one of the chairs. A few minutes later, a nurse came up to us.

"Sheriff Macklin is in the ICU. Dr. Osman asked me to escort you up there," she said. The nurse had large, kind eyes and looked ready to help Genie to her feet if she needed it. Genie gave her a brief, sad smile and stood up.

On the next floor up, we were led down a hallway and through a set of doors into the ICU. Inside the unit were a dozen small cubicles where patients lay hooked up to tubes and wires. The digital readouts showing heartbeats and respiratory rates produced an eerie glow, a high-tech reflection of our oldest fear.

I'd had more than my share of time in the ICU. I could vividly recall the hours Dad and I had spent there before finally admitting that an aneurysm had taken my mother away from us. And I knew that Dad and Cara had kept a vigil over me after I'd had my own encounter with the sharp end of a knife. But somehow this was worse. Seeing Dad so grey and shrunken, hooked up to machines, flew in the face of my belief that he was an unstoppable force of nature.

They would only let one of us in at a time, so I stepped back and let Genie go in with him first. I watched through the glass as she moved to his side and took his hand. Tears streamed down her face as she talked to him. I couldn't hear the words, but I felt her love for him.

After a short while, Genie came out and touched my arm gently as I slipped past her and into the small room. For a moment I just stood there and looked at him, not knowing what to say. I couldn't stop my inner voice from running through all the painful and meaningless questions: *Why did this happen? Why now? And how can I make this right?*

Finally, I took his hand and said softly, "Please come back to us. I promise never to take you for granted again. Just come back. I love you." I squeezed his hand. It was warm, but lifeless, making me think of Purgatory. "I promise you, I'll find whoever did this to you so we can stand together and watch him be dragged off to jail after the jury declares him guilty."

My words were an oath to Dad, God and anyone else who was listening. I looked at the bandages across my father's chest and felt rage at the fact that someone had knowingly inflicted pain on a man who had spent most of his life trying to right the wrongs of the world. I gripped his hand tightly as hot tears stained my cheeks, then I turned and walked out of the room with a single mission—to find the person responsible for this.

CHAPTER TWO

As I rejoined Genie outside, a tall man in an expensive suit came striding down the hall toward us.

"Would y'all be the family of Sheriff Macklin?" he asked in an accent straight out of the Carolinas.

I nodded. "I'm his son, Larry, and this is his fiancée, Genie Anderson."

"I'm Dr. Titus. I'm ordering more scans of your father's skull and brain." He looked at his watch. "I should have a better idea of his situation in two hours. Leave your contact information with my assistant and we'll discuss his prognosis and treatment options then." His tone was clinical, but softened by the cadences of the Lowcountry. He handed me a card bearing his assistant's phone number.

"Of course." I took the card, but before I could say anything else, he was already opening the door to the ICU and leaving us behind.

Genie gave me an uncertain look.

"Let's go down to the cafeteria and get something to eat," I suggested, though only to kill some time. Neither of us had much of an appetite. We found a quiet table in a corner where Genie nursed a hot coffee and I played with the straw in a cup of soda.

My phone rang as we were heading back upstairs. When I saw that it was Cara, I excused myself to Genie and walked a few steps away to answer it.

"I'm sorry. I know you said you'd call, but I couldn't wait any longer."

I told her what we knew about Dad's condition.

"My God, Larry." She sounded stunned. "I wish I could be there with you."

"Me too. How's Mauser?"

"He tore up his front paws clawing at the door of the van. Luckily, it's not too bad. I've cleaned them and put some salve on them. But he's so... upset. Kind of mopey and whining. He didn't even want his dinner."

"Really?" I couldn't remember the big guy ever turning his nose up at food.

"He was barking when I got to the van. I felt so bad for him." I could hear a slight tremble in Cara's voice. "It was only after I talked to him and stroked him a bit that he kind of came back to himself. He finally calmed down enough that I could put a leash on him and get him into Terry's van."

"He drove you out there?" I asked. Terry was one of Cara's friends and co-workers from the veterinary clinic.

"He let me trade cars with him for a couple of days. I just thought I needed something bigger than my car. You know it's a tight squeeze to get Mauser in it. I thought if he was upset, it would be easier with Terry's van. I knew Pete wouldn't let me take your dad's. When I got there, Shantel and Marcus were already going over everything, collecting evidence. I almost lost it when I saw the blood." Her voice faded.

"Genie is taking it pretty hard," I said after a minute.

"What about you?"

"I... It's tough. I just have to believe that he'll be fine."

"He'll make it through this... We'll *all* be fine." I could almost see Cara close her eyes and make the wish. "Do you think the person who did this knew who he was?"

I shrugged. "He was in his uniform. They knew he was the sheriff. I think it was an ambush."

"They *meant* to attack him?"

"That's the part that I don't know. Probably not. If they had wanted to kill him, then they certainly could have. He was knocked out as soon as he hit the ground. And they didn't just run off because they took the knife, or whatever they used to stab him, away with them. If they had wanted him dead, all they'd have needed to do was plunge the knife into his heart. Another second or two would have been all it took." I felt a chill in my veins thinking about how easy it would have been. "I don't think they were expecting him to stop. Maybe something spooked them, they lashed out and then took off."

"Can you hear him?" Cara asked. In the background, Mauser was whining pitifully.

"Poor guy. I wish he'd had a chance to get at the person who did this. For such a big wuss, he can be protective when he wants to be."

"He loves your dad. I did think to call Jamie and asked him to feed the horses for the next few days."

"Damn, I forgot about them. Thank you." We hadn't yet been married a year, but every day we seemed to be getting better at picking up the slack for each other.

"Are you coming home tonight?" Cara asked gently.

"I don't think I can." I couldn't imagine leaving Dad in the hospital, unconscious and vulnerable. "I'll try to get some sleep here and then, depending on what the doctors have to say, head straight to the office in the morning."

"All right. I love you."

Genie was waiting for me when I got off the phone. As we headed for the elevator, Dr. Titus's assistant called to let us know that he'd meet us at the ICU desk.

"The bleeding appears to be slowing," the doctor reported. "That's good. However, the pressure on the brain is very close to the threshold where I'd recommend immediate surgery. I'm going to monitor the situation, but what I'd like to have from you is a signed authorization to perform surgery if I deem it necessary." He looked at me with eyes that suggested I was just smart enough to understand what he was saying.

"So he might be taken into surgery at any time?" Genie asked.

"If it's necessary," Dr. Titus said with only a glance at her.

I had no option and there was no reason to pretend that I did. "I'll sign it."

"Good. I'm going to remain in the hospital and will be ready to do the operation at any time. My assistant will get the papers ready for you." He gave me a brief nod before turning on his heel and striding off.

"He's an arrogant prick," I growled, all of my pain and anger rising to the surface.

"I don't think you want a surgeon who doesn't think he's part god operating on someone you care for," Genie said, her voice oddly solemn.

"Maybe." I knew it was stupid to want to kick the man in the shins when he could be operating on my father's brain at any moment. I reminded myself that I didn't need to *like* him; I just needed for him to be the best neurosurgeon in the country. *At least* he *seems to think he is*, I consoled myself.

After a long night in the ICU waiting room, we were given another five minutes with Dad early the next morning. A nurse reported that his condition had remained stable and that Dr. Titus had decided to wait another twelve hours to reassess the need for surgery.

"Are you going home?" I asked Genie.

She shook her head. "Even though I can't do anything, I'd just go crazy not being here. I've told the assistant manager at Bon Temps that she's in charge for the foreseeable future," Genie said, referring to the upscale restaurant she managed.

"I'm heading to the office to check in with the

investigation." I'd exchanged several texts with Pete, but that wasn't the best way to be brought up to speed. Besides, I wanted to personally get in on the hunt.

Genie fiddled with the end of her long braid of brown hair, which showed only a few streaks of grey. "I've never seen myself as the type of person who'd seek revenge for a wrong. But now, right this minute, there are two things I want more than anything in the world. First, I want your Dad to wake up. Then I want to see his attacker in chains." Genie's voice was low and I saw a fire in her eyes that had never been there before.

"I couldn't agree more." I gave her a quick hug, then headed for my car.

"Major Parks wants to talk to you," Pete said as soon as I walked up to my desk in the criminal investigations department.

"Dill already told me." Our semi-retired desk sergeant had been very insistent about it.

"I've been ordered not to say a word to you until you've see him," Pete added.

I sighed, not looking forward to the conversation. Major Sam Parks always served as acting sheriff whenever Dad was out of town. He was a good guy, older, conservative. His main job was maintaining the department's budget and Dad relied heavily on the major to keep the department solvent. At county commission meetings, Dad would always let Parks do the talking when it came to money. Parks would get so deep into the numbers and had such a command of the facts that the commissioners wouldn't push him because they didn't want to show everyone how ignorant they were regarding fiscal issues. I could sympathize with them. I'd been present six months earlier when Parks had been explaining to Dad the depreciation of every piece of equipment owned by the sheriff's office. It was mind-numbing stuff.

I stood outside the door to his office for a five-count before knocking.

"Come in!"

Major Parks stood behind his desk, his brow furrowed. "How's your dad doing?" he asked kindly and I explained what little I knew.

Parks picked up an envelope from his desk. *Instructions for Major Parks* was scrawled across the front in Dad's handwriting.

"Ted gave this to me a year ago. It is to be opened if he's rendered incapacitated for any reason." He glanced at me before breaking the seal. "To be clear, I want you present not in your capacity as an employee of this department, but rather as your father's son. I feel you have a right to know your father's wishes."

I flinched a little, gritting my teeth. Parks's words made it sound like Dad was dead. I wanted to tell him to tear up the damn envelope. A part of me refused to see the reality of the situation and argued that Dad would be back sitting at his desk in a couple of weeks. But the image seared in my brain of Dad lying in his hospital bed forced me to nod grimly at the major.

He unfolded the document and read it out loud. Not surprisingly, it stated that Dad wanted Major Parks to serve as the interim sheriff until such a time that Dad could return to duty… or until the governor felt it necessary to appoint a new sheriff.

"Dad has a lot of faith in you," I said.

"This is not a situation I'm happy with. I much prefer to be in a supporting role. That being said, I will do everything in my power to carry out the duties of sheriff as your father would wish." Parks paused and took a deep breath. "Which brings me to the next order of business. I don't want you to have anything to do with the investigation into your father's case."

Every muscle in my body tensed. "You can't do that," I said, even as I realized that he had set this up so that the first part of our meeting would show me that not only *could* he do it, but that he could do it with my father's blessing.

"You know better," Parks said with a disappointed shake of his head. "Any involvement by you would give a defense lawyer a club that he could use to beat down a prosecutor's case by claiming prejudicial conduct." He paused. "Tell me I'm wrong."

"I won't be able to focus on anything else," I argued.

"Then I'll have to put you on leave." Parks sounded so matter-of-fact that I knew he wasn't bluffing.

I stood there trying to think of a rational argument for me being involved in the investigation while Parks patiently waited. I had nothing. Of course he was right. Defense attorneys made mincemeat out of cases where an investigator had a demonstrable bias.

"I'll stay away from my father's case," I finally muttered, wondering if I was telling the truth or not.

"I'm going to help you keep your word by promising to watch over you. Now, I'll tell you what you already know. I will use every resource this department has, and can beg and borrow from other agencies, to find the person who did this to your dad, my friend and the sheriff of this county. Do you doubt me?"

"No." And I didn't. Major Parks had law enforcement in his DNA. The thought of a villain attacking his commanding officer must have been gnawing away at him almost as badly as it was eating at me.

"You will still be instrumental in helping us solve this," he said, making me wonder if I'd heard him right.

"But didn't you just say…"

"I'm putting both Pete and Julio on the case. You know we're already short-handed, so I'm going to need you to cover their caseloads."

That all made sense and I hated it. "Yes, sir," I said, trying to sound enthusiastic. I would have to work harder than I ever had for Pete and Julio to be able to put in the type of effort I wanted them to.

As I turned to leave, Parks said, "If you overhear other officers talking about the case, or if you voice your opinions about it, I wouldn't consider that a violation of my directive. But to be clear, if you so much as touch a piece of evidence or talk to a potential witness, then you will be driving a patrol car on the night shift for as long as I can make it happen. Understood? Now, send Julio and Pete in here."

I left his office with my mind trying to wrap itself around the idea that the way I was going to help catch Dad's assailant was to work my ass off on dozens of *other* cases. At least Parks had given me permission to keep up with the investigation.

When I was halfway back to CID, I saw a familiar face coming down the hall. Before I could stop her, Calhoun's chief of police and my ex-partner, Darlene Marks, pulled me into a savage, but thankfully brief, bear hug.

"Whole thing sucks. How's he doing?" she asked, backing away and giving me a couple of feet of personal space.

I repeated what I'd told Parks earlier.

"I came down here to tell the major that my department is ready to help in any way we can to catch this bastard."

I grinned. "I'm the one who might need your help. Parks is going to put Julio and Pete on the case full time, so I'm going to be picking up their slack. I'm sure there's more than a few of their cases that fall within the city limits."

"I can help you with those. Batman and Robin, back together again." She punched my arm.

"Thanks, Batman." I rubbed my arm, wincing.

"Anytime, Robin. Now get out of my way. I'm going to talk to Parks." I thought she was done, but as she walked away, she said in a serious voice, "Anything I can do for you or your family, just let me know."

I found Pete and told him that Parks wanted to see him and Julio right away.

"He better be clearing the decks for us to go full hammers on this case," Pete growled.

"He is, and I'm doing the deck clearing." I shared what Parks had told me.

"Excellent. I'll put all my cases in your folder," he said in his usual, good-natured way before a dark cloud crossed his face. "We're going to need all the manpower we can get to find this bastard. I've got an order in with a company in Tallahassee already, printing up a billboard asking anyone with information to come forward. We're going to put it up where the attack took place." He put up his hand to stop me when I started to speak. "Don't worry, we aren't going to be that passive. I've already got two patrol deputies manning a checkpoint there this morning, talking to everyone who drives past. The sign is for when we don't have the checkpoint."

"With the road being out in the middle of the woods, you'd think someone would have noticed the car stopped on the side of the road," I said, hoping I was right. Right now we needed something, anything, before we could even start looking for the suspect.

"Maybe Shantel will find some DNA. I'll tell you, I've never seen her and Marcus so determined to come up with something. Your dad's van is in the compound out back. After they spent four hours scouring the roadside looking for evidence, the two of them spent the rest of the night going over every bit of that van."

Shantel Williams and Marcus Brown were our best crime scene techs. I didn't doubt that they, and everyone at the sheriff's office, would be putting their hearts and souls into finding the perpetrator. Dad pissed people off sometimes, but I didn't know many people who didn't respect him. Certainly every deputy knew that Dad had their back. He'd proved it time and again. Everyone also knew that he held the reputation of the department as a sacred trust. If he knew about a bad officer, he would work night and day to see that the bad apple found itself rotting in some other barrel. No good cop wants to work beside a bad one.

"What's your next move?" I asked.

Pete shrugged. "Without a good lead to follow? Long and tedious footwork, what else? We'll go door-to-door for a couple of miles in each direction from the scene."

"That can't be more than thirty houses."

"About that. We'll also start digging into reports looking for similar MOs, stabbings where cars were involved, or that occurred on the side of the road, or parking lots, or gas stations. We'll be looking for similar victims too—first responders, older men. Of course, there's always the possibility that your dad was specifically targeted."

"I thought about that. Being the sheriff makes him a target for all types of bad guys and nutjobs."

"Exactly, so we'll have to go through his correspondence for the last six months."

"And interview friends and family," I said with a little irony.

"Don't worry, we won't overlook anything. I better get up to Parks's office and get my marching orders."

"Where's Julio?" Julio Ortiz was a young deputy who'd recently been promoted to investigator. Nothing like being thrown into the deep end.

"I think he went down to records," Pete said. "He's asking them to search some of the older cases that your dad was personally involved with."

I nodded and texted Julio to let him know he was expected in Major Parks's office sooner rather than later. Once Pete was gone, I was left sitting at my desk and feeling like a grounded kid watching the rest of his friends leave on a field trip. Before I turned to my suddenly larger pile of cases, I texted Genie, but there had been no change in Dad's condition that she was aware of. Thinking about that, I called Dad's lawyer.

"HIPPA is non-negotiable," he told me. "Ted could have told the hospital to keep Genie informed, but you can't do it. Only the patient."

"I have Dad's power of attorney, right?"

"Yes, that's true."

"So I'm authorized to act for him, correct?"

"I'll give you two answers. One, I'm not sure if HIPPA recognizes that distinction. Two, you can try it on the hospital and see. They probably aren't sure what the law is either and you might just bluff your way through."

"You look into it for sure. Meanwhile, I'll trying bluffing them."

CHAPTER THREE

I called Cara and told her about my new marching orders from Major Parks.

"I didn't get any sleep last night," Cara said, exhaustion clear in her voice. "Mauser just kept whining and going back and forth to the door. At one point, he was clawing at the door frame. But when I took him out, he just went over to Terri's van and whimpered."

"He *did* see Dad get attacked," I said, hardly believing that I was making excuses for Mauser's behavior.

"I know. But he hasn't been much better since we got to work. Dr. Barnhill isn't very pleased with the situation. We've talked about giving him something to calm him down."

"Barnhill or Mauser?" It was a poor joke, but I tried.

"Stop it. I'm too tired between worrying about your dad and Mauser."

"Sorry," I said contritely.

"I don't want to give him a sedative, but we have to do something. Do you think Jamie could come and get him?"

Jamie was a local college student who Dad frequently used as a babysitter for Mauser. He'd also done a better job of training the dog than Dad had ever managed. "I can check with him."

"I think he'll need your dad's van. Jamie only has a little truck."

"Shantel might be done with the van by now. I'll check on it and give Jamie a call."

"Thank you. I hate to put more on your plate."

"A little more isn't going to make a difference."

I called Jamie as soon as I hung up with Cara, but the call went straight to voicemail. I left a message, then turned reluctantly to the files on my computer.

What I really wanted to do was go down to the evidence room and go over everything that Shantel and Marcus had brought in. Instead I put my head down and settled in to work. I needed to clear out as many of my own cases as I could so I'd be ready to take on Pete's and Julio's. As I went through them, I found a couple that couldn't be closed right away, but which had conveniently occurred within the city limits. I saved them into a new folder I'd called: *For Darlene.*

After a while, Julio came up to my desk. "How's your dad?"

"The doctors are keeping him in a coma while they monitor the swelling in his brain."

"Pete and I will find the asshole who did this." Julio's tone was hard as steel.

"I know you will."

"I transferred all my current cases to a shared file."

"Yeah, I got the notice."

"I hate to do it, but if I'm going to be working with Pete full time on your dad's case…."

I waved my hand to dismiss his apology. "I'm on board with the plan. I'll go over the files this afternoon."

"There's half a dozen on the front burner and another dozen simmering," he told me. "We can go over my notes on them anytime. The older ones are mostly complete, it's just the more recent ones where I haven't added all my notes to the files."

"I'll get with you," I told him. Julio was assigned mostly

auto theft and burglary cases and I wasn't looking forward to working on them. I'd never liked dealing with either one. The perps were usually kids or drug addicts and neither made for very satisfying arrests. Of course, what I liked or didn't like didn't matter now. I didn't want Julio to be distracted from following any leads on Dad's stabbing.

"The major said we could keep you updated on our progress. Probably 'cause he knew we'd do that anyway, no matter what he said." Julio's words were defiant. "I think he should let you work the case."

"Parks is right. I can't be involved," I mumbled, irritated at having to support my own exile from the investigation.

"I'm heading out to where it happened to do some door-to-doors. Pete's going over the old cases I pulled from records." Julio paused and looked a little embarrassed before adding, "My wife is lighting a candle for your dad and we've asked our church to pray for him."

"Thank you." I meant it. The gesture carried weight coming from Julio and his family. I knew that they took their faith to heart and their entreaties to God would be met if anyone's were.

Once Julio was gone, I dealt with the top of my inbox, which included an interview with a domestic abuse victim that I had to conduct via Zoom. The girlfriend was willing to give me a full statement, but she was leery of coming out of hiding for a face-to-face interview. Technology came to our rescue, as the recording of the conversation would be enough to proceed with an arrest warrant.

"Should I get a restraining order?" the girl asked me near the end of the interview.

This was always a tough question for me to answer. A lot of deputies urged victims to file for one, but I had three major problems with restraining orders. First, depending on the lawyer, they didn't come cheap. Second, they required that the victim inform their abuser of their current residence and location of employment, which just seemed insane to me because, third, they only stopped the rational creeps. In my experience, less than half of abusers fell into that category.

"I think you should move closer to your family," I finally said. She was twenty-five and didn't have a job, so it wouldn't be hard for her to pick up stakes and move to North Georgia where her folks were.

"That's what my dad and mom want. But I don't want to be dependent on them again."

"Right now, I think it'd be a good idea to be close to some folks who can look after you."

She let out a heavy sigh and wiped away a tear as I watched her on my laptop. "I think I'd kind of like that," she said softly.

Feeling hopeful that I'd helped at least one person today, I moved on to Pete's cases. I was familiar with most of them since Pete and I both worked violent crimes and backed each other up when we needed help. The only case I didn't know much about was a beating that had taken place near an ATM in town.

According to the original report taken at one in the morning a few days ago by Deputy Robbie Sykes, an ambulance had been called to take a man with severe injuries to the hospital. The victim had been seen trying to crawl down the sidewalk away from the ATM. When the ambulance arrived on the scene, the EMTs had radioed in that the man was the victim of an assault. The EMT made it clear that the man would probably pull through, but that the assailant couldn't have known that. Bam! The case became an attempted homicide and Pete had been the investigator on call.

Eduardo Alverez, the victim, had been uncooperative when Pete questioned him. He claimed to have fallen down and hit his head on the sidewalk. The ER doctor was adamant that Alvarez had received half a dozen blows to the top and back of his head, but the patient insisted that he had been trying to get money from the ATM when he tripped and fell. Pete's report from that first interview included the very diplomatic: "Suspect's statement does not match up with his injuries."

Alverez was from Guatemala and lived in a small community on the far edge of Adams County. He was a large equipment operator and was employed at Southeast Express as a forklift operator. Pete had run a check and all his INS paperwork was in order.

A review of the camera footage from the ATM clearly showed a hooded man throw Alverez against the machine and strike him repeatedly with a pipe. After seeing this, Pete asked Alverez if he wanted to change his story, but he refused to say anything else. Pete informed him that he was moving forward with the investigation with or without his help.

Other security cameras had picked up the man wearing the hoodie emerging from a light-colored SUV in the bank's parking lot. The tag on the car belonged to a different vehicle that had been stolen from Panama City International Airport. Pete's report concluded that, without more cooperation from the victim, there wasn't much chance of discovering the identity of the attacker. On the off chance new evidence might be found, such as the SUV itself, the case was going to remain open for now.

I looked at the report thoughtfully. There were several interesting tidbits, including the fact that Pete had noted that the victim did not appear to be a user of controlled substances. Still, a drug deal gone bad was a possibility, especially with a victim who refused to admit that an attack had happened at all. I decided I'd take a shot at talking to Mr. Alverez, then I moved the file into the folder I was saving for Darlene. After all, the ATM had been inside the city limits. Maybe she could help me get through to Alverez.

When I moved on to the files that Julio had sent me, I wondered if I might find a link with the Alverez case since it had included a stolen tag and probably a stolen car. Julio had identified a pattern in five of his open cases. All of the cars were high-end and had been stolen late at night from residences where the victims were not at home. Two of them had involved breaking into the garage in order to gain access to the cars, which implied that the thief had known that the car would be there.

My phone rang with a call from Jamie. Before I could begin to explain about Mauser, he asked me about Dad. "I can't believe this," he said.

"In the last few weeks, when you've been over at Dad's house, have you seen anyone hanging around?" I didn't think asking Jamie a few questions was really breaking Major Parks's rule about talking to witnesses.

"No. It's always pretty quiet around there."

"Anything unusual? Something missing or moved around?"

"I don't think so. Between your dad and Mauser, things always move around and get broken. So I might not notice."

"Understood. Speaking of Mauser…"

"Mauser's a lot more sensitive than you'd think, being such a big fella," Jamie said once I'd filled him in. "I'm not surprised. I'll be glad to pick him up. I only have a couple of exams this week, then I'm out until after New Year's. But Cara's right. I can't get him in my truck."

"Hang on a second." I picked up my desk phone and made a quick call down to the evidence room. Shantel confirmed that Dad's van was free to go.

"I'll pick up the van in half an hour," Jamie told me.

With the Mauser situation taken care of, I decided to pack up my laptop and head back to the hospital. I would be able to get an update from the doctors and check on Dad. The truth was, I knew I'd feel better just being near him.

I was climbing out of my car in the hospital's parking garage when I got a call from Cara. She was fighting back tears as she explained the wrench that Mauser had thrown into our plans.

"He won't get in the van. Every time that Jamie or I try to get him into it, he starts barking and pulling away." I could hear the obvious strain of the past twenty-four hours in her voice.

"Don't worry, we'll figure this out." I had to fight hard not to vent my own frustration. I couldn't believe that, even now, I was having to deal with the antics of my father's spoiled damn dog. "Have you tried throwing a treat into to the van?"

"I'm not stupid!" Cara yelled, her voice cracking. After an awkward silence she added, "I'm sorry, but we've tried everything." She sounded a little calmer.

I doubted that Terry wanted to loan out his van long term. Terry was pretty fastidious and it had been very generous of him to give us his van for moose transport in the first place. I thought about suggesting that Jamie take Cara's car and leave Dad's van with her, but my new husband radar told me that I probably shouldn't suggest that Cara give up her car right then.

"What about Bernadette Santos? She has a van for Cleo." Cleo was a female Great Dane that Mauser was smitten with, and I was a large part of the reason that Bernadette had her.

"I don't know," Cara said hesitantly, thinking about it.

"I'll call her."

"Are you sure?" Cara argued half-heartedly.

"Yes, it's fine. I'll call you right back."

Bernadette had heard about the attack on Dad and was willing to do anything she could to help. A quick call back to Cara assured her that another van was on the way and everything was settled as long as Mauser approved of the plan.

It was just after one o'clock and I was already exhausted. Not even the cool north wind that hit me as I headed for the hospital doors did much to revive me. Of course, the sense of dread that I felt approaching the building didn't help. *He'll be fine*, I told myself over and over. It was impossible to imagine a world without my dad in it. He was the type who filled up a room when he entered and commanded everyone's attention when he spoke, and the room felt very empty when he wasn't there.

Genie looked haggard. Her usual disposition was so energetic and sunny that I barely recognized her sitting slumped in a chair and shaking slightly, pushing back her unkempt hair.

"I finally got one of the nurses to at least acknowledge that he's still alive." She stood up as I came over to her.

"I'm going to get you on the list," I told her, gently rubbing her shoulder. "Wait here."

I didn't like the stubborn expression on the first nurse I saw behind the main ICU station, so I went over to a bulletin board and mindlessly scanned the numerous public service announcements tacked up on it. In less than five minutes, the nurse picked up a tablet and hurried down the hall and she was quickly replaced behind the computer monitors by a male nurse with soft eyes and unruly hair.

I walked up to him with the brisk air of someone who was needed elsewhere. Shamelessly, I pulled out my bifold and showed him my badge. "Hi, I wonder if you can help me?"

The badge clearly startled him. "What's going on?"

"My dad's in the ICU…"

"The sheriff?"

"That's right. I'm an investigator myself. Look, I just want to make sure that Dad's fiancée has access to any information relevant to his condition."

"Fiancée?" He sounded like he'd never heard the word before.

"Yes. I have my dad's power of attorney and I'm giving you authorization to list her as a member of the family with all the rights that entails." I rattled this off with as much authority as I could muster.

"I don't know…" The nurse frowned, turning his head right and left, no doubt looking for someone higher up the food chain.

"I can have my lawyer call the hospital's administrator if that would help," I said innocently.

"No!" he yelped. His hand was already reaching for the large-ring binder where they kept all patient notes.

A few minutes later, I was telling Genie that she could ask for whatever information she wanted about Dad's condition. Her eyes were sad and grateful at the same time. "He's going to be fine," she told me, echoing the mantra in my own head.

Not long after, Dr. Titus met with us again. He reported that the bleeding had stopped and that the swelling in Dad's brain appeared to be going down. He looked over our shoulders while reciting the details of Dad's progress, and I figured that he was already looking for the next patient since Dad didn't seem to need his top-notch surgical skills.

"I won't recommend easing him out of his coma for another day or two until we can be sure that the swelling is down."

"Will there be any side effects?" I asked, and received a disdainful look in return.

"Of course there will be side effects. With TBI, there will be short-term memory loss at the very least. Headaches too. More severe long-term issues? We'll have to wait and find out." His cold, clinical air made me want to punch him in the face.

I spent ten minutes in the room with Dad. I held his hand and, as an intermittent church-goer at best, felt like a hypocrite as I begged God to restore Dad to the man he'd been a week ago.

I left the room feeling frustrated and helpless. I talked Genie into taking a break and going home for a while, then I sat down and tried to concentrate on reviewing all the cases I had to work on. My biggest problem was keeping my mind focused. Eventually, I gave up and called Pete because I just couldn't stand being in the dark when it came to the only investigation I cared about.

"I'm doing everything I can," Pete said, sounding almost as tired as I felt. "We've had three people come forward with descriptions of the other car that was probably involved.

They all saw the vehicle parked on the side of the road with your dad's van behind it. That's the good news."

"Let me guess what the bad news is. None of their descriptions agree."

"I bet you've done this before. According to the witnesses, it was either a small green car, a medium-size blue car or a medium-size silver car. One of them thinks he saw a guy in a hoodie sitting in the driver's seat and another is sure it was a woman. I think some of the problem is that your dad's van drew most of their attention."

I sighed. "Which do you think is closest to the truth?"

"You know the game. The guy who thinks he saw a man in a hoodie also had the most detailed description of the car. He claims it was a silver BMW, maybe five years old with a Florida tag and pretty heavy tinting on the windows."

"If the windows were heavily tinted, then how could he see the driver?"

"Funny, that was my first question. He claimed the driver's window was part way down. But I didn't like the way he got defensive and tossed out the answer."

"Like he was just saying the first thing that came to his mind."

"Exactly. I think we can be sure that there was a car there. Why it was stopped? Who knows? Being as rural as the area is, all the houses are set back from the road so we haven't got any security footage yet. We've mapped out all of the possible routes that lead to the scene and we're going to pull footage from any cameras with a view of the road."

"I was looking through your cases. When you mentioned the guy in the hoodie, I thought of the attack at the ATM."

Pete chuckled. "We've been working together too long. That came to my mind too. Could this be our guy with the stolen car who's going around attacking people? Which brings up a question that I have. Why didn't your dad call in the tag? That could have changed his whole approach."

"Something must have made him drop his guard. My guess would be that the car appeared to be broken down."

"Julio and I figured that too. Then how did the perpetrator drive away?"

"I keep coming back to it being a set-up."

"But that gives us another paradox. If it was an ambush, then why didn't the attacker finish the job?"

"Yeah…" I mulled it over. "None of it adds up."

"There's an answer and we're going to find it," Pete said forcefully. "Tell me your dad's doing better."

I assured him that Dad was stable and that things at least appeared to be heading in the right direction. Then I thanked him for everything he was doing and hung up, alone again with my fears.

CHAPTER FOUR

Genie came back around four o'clock, looking refreshed.

"I feel much better," she told me. "A hot shower and knowing that Ted is improving has lifted my spirits a bit."

I smiled. "If you're sure, then I'm gonna head back to the office."

Genie gave me a little push toward the door of the waiting room. "Go on. I'll be fine now."

I wanted to talk to the ATM victim, Eduardo Alverez. Maybe there was a connection to Dad's case. Even if there wasn't, it was a case I could look into easily and decide if it was going to be permanently relegated to the back burner where Pete had already put it.

Alverez's current address was in a small community that had grown up several decades ago when a family had subdivided a large farm. The lots varied in size and featured almost as many mobile homes as site-built houses. Thinking about some of the notes Pete had made in his report, I decided that it wasn't a place I wanted to visit without letting someone know where I was. I called Pete as I drove.

"If you don't hear from me in an hour, send out the cavalry," I told him.

"10-4," he said. I could tell that he was distracted and let it go at that.

When I saw Alverez's trailer, I was glad that I'd called Pete. The run-down mobile home with several cars in various states of disrepair in the front yard sent all of my Spidey senses to tingling. In contrast, a fairly new truck with fancy rims was parked in the driveway. I pulled onto the lawn with the derelict vehicles and parked so I could get out of my car while still having it between me and the trailer. I got out cautiously and sniffed the air for any hint of cooking chemicals. Nothing.

For a moment I stood with my car door open, looking over the hood at the beat-up door and broken windows of the trailer. The truck in the driveway was worth twice what the house was. I was wishing that I'd put on my ballistic vest, but it was too late. If I did it now, anyone watching from inside would be sure that I was there to serve a warrant. I probably should have thought twice about going out there, but I needed to take some sort of action, even if it had nothing to do with finding Dad's assailant. Making up my mind, I slammed my car door.

When I was halfway to the trailer, a voice yelled at me: "Who the hell are you?" The man spoke clearly with a distinct accent that made his words sound soft and rich.

"I'm with the Adams County Sheriff's Office and I want to talk to Eduardo Alverez about the assault at the ATM."

"I told that fat man I don't want no trouble. That's over, man."

"I'm Deputy Macklin and I just want to follow up on a few things. Would it be okay if we talked face to face?" I asked in my most non-threatening tone.

I tried to keep my breathing steady as I waited to see how the scene would play out. I found it comforting when the front door opened and a man wearing jeans and a dirty bandage wrapped around his head waved me forward.

Once I'd climbed the rickety iron stairs, I was surprised at how short the man was. He couldn't have been much more than 5'3" and my six-foot frame towered over him. He sported a dozen tattoos on his arms and bare chest that looked homemade. He stood firmly in the doorway, blocking any further progress.

"So why are you here? I said I didn't want to do nothin' about gettin' hit." His dark green eyes challenged me.

"Someone beats the hell out of you and you're just going to let them get away with it?" I gave him stare for stare.

"It's all bullshit! You ain't gonna catch him so why waste my time?"

"You haven't given us a chance."

"Nah, we're done, man." He hitched up his jeans and looked ready to close the door.

"You know who did this to you, don't you?" I said.

He hesitated for just a second before shaking his head. "You're wrong."

"You know who did it and you're scared."

His lips curled and fire burned in his eyes. "I'm not scared of no one."

"Then tell me who attacked you."

He just stood there.

"What if I told you that I don't care what you did to him. I don't care if you stole from him, took his drugs, screwed his wife or said something mean about his mother. I just want to know who he is."

I'd gotten it into my head that there could be a connection between the hoodie-wearing perp at the ATM and the hoodie-wearing driver of the car seen where Dad was stabbed. My rational mind told me that this was stupid, but rational thought had taken a backseat to my fear and hope.

"Forget it," Alverez said, and stepped back inside the trailer before banging the door closed. "I don't got to talk to you!" he shouted from the other side of the door.

I considered my options. I didn't think that threatening him with arrest or harassment was going to get me anywhere, at least not right away. The best thing I could do was to back off and come at him in a day or two after I'd found some real leverage. *You were going to put this one on the back burner,* I reminded myself. *There's something here,* myself argued back as I walked to my car.

I called Cara during the drive back to Calhoun. "I'm working late tonight."

"You need to get some rest," she told me, though I could tell from her voice that she knew lecturing me wouldn't do any good.

"If I can at least prioritize all these cases, I'll sleep better. There's going to be more piling up every day while Julio and Pete are working on Dad's case."

"Major Parks has to get you some help."

"I'm going to shift some of the work onto Darlene and her people. And I'll get some deputies from patrol to help out with the footwork. But first I have to get them sorted and decide who I need to do what."

"Just promise me you'll get home early enough so you can get a full night's sleep."

"I'll be home by nine."

When I pulled up to the office, I saw a familiar blue Dodge Dakota in the parking lot. Jessie Gilmore, a young woman who had been instrumental in a couple of recent cases, was due to start law enforcement training at the public safety academy in January. For the last couple of months, she'd been working for the department as an intern. As soon as I saw her truck, I decided that she could help me out with some of the background on my cases. She'd already proved herself adept at reviewing security camera footage and searching the archives, skills that could come in handy. Unfortunately, she had a different agenda.

"Pete said you're handling his cases," Jessie said as I got out of my car. "And I'm really, really sorry about your dad. Are there any leads?"

"Let's go inside," I suggested. The wind had picked up and the temperature was dropping as the sun slipped below the horizon.

"I found more people who've seen her," Jessie said as I

held the office door open for her.

I didn't have to ask who she was talking about. Five years earlier, Terri Miller, a young woman Jessie was acquainted with, had disappeared. Pete had been working the case, but the leads had dried up early. Even with Jessie and the woman's mother papering the town with flyers, nothing had turned up. At least not until this fall, when a hoodie-wearing figure had appeared on a convenience store's security camera. It had been impossible to see her face clearly, but based on similar features and mannerisms, Jessie had been convinced that it was Terri. However, our efforts to find the woman on the video had been as fruitless as the original search.

"Jessie, I don't have time for this right now." We'd already had more than one conversation about her bashing her head against this particular brick wall.

"I've talked to a few people who are sure that they saw her recently."

"Did they know her personally?" The chance of misidentifying someone was much higher if the witness had never known them.

"No. I know, I know. But these are good witnesses," Jessie insisted. "One of them used to be in law enforcement."

"Cops can be wrong too."

"You've got to at least interview them and put the information in her case file. Maybe you could put out another flyer for the patrol officers. These people said they saw her out by the interstate."

I sat down at my desk, the weight of the last couple of days heavy on my shoulders. Jessie looked at me with pleading eyes and, as much as I wanted to tell her I didn't have the time, I found myself nodding.

"Okay, I'll interview them, just not today… or tomorrow, or even this week. As for the flyers, our deputies are well aware of Terri Miller and what she looks like. However, since these sightings were out by the interstate, I'll make sure that the highway patrol gets another round of flyers. Will that make you happy?"

"I know that you're having a tough time. I don't want to be a pain in the ass." She paused for a second before adding, "But I just am."

"You get an A-plus for self-awareness." I gave her a slight smile, the best I could manage.

"But she's alive, I know it."

"There's another side to this. Terri was an adult who, by all reports, was in complete control of her faculties when she went missing. If she's walking around free, then there hasn't been a crime committed. She has a right to her privacy."

"I don't believe she'd just walk away from her life like that," Jessie started to argue, but then she must have seen the frustration and fatigue on my face. "But I'll let it go for now. I *do* want to help find the guy who attacked your dad."

I explained that I'd been designated to clear the way so that Pete and Julio could take on that particular task.

"Then I'll do whatever I can to help you. I've got lots of time before my classes start," she said with resolve.

"Let's get to work right now."

We spent the next hour going through the rest of the cases that had been added to my plate. When we were done, there were twenty-five cases in my active file. Eight had taken place within, or partially within, Calhoun city limits, so I could get some assistance from Darlene and her officers on those. The other seventeen were all mine to deal with.

Luckily, Major Parks had issued a decree that any new cases that didn't rise to the level of a first-degree felony would be handled by patrol. This was a great idea on two levels. It would give me some breathing room and, since we had a couple of positions to fill in CID, it would give Parks a chance to evaluate how the patrol officers handled cases and who might be a candidate for promotion.

I went back over Julio's stolen car files and had Jessie map them for me on a program called KrimeMap. The program highlighted probable locations of security cameras within the vicinity of the crimes. Of course, most of the thefts had taken place in neighborhoods and the map couldn't know about cameras on individual homes, but it covered the main streets leading in and out. Julio had already secured footage from the homes near where the cars had been stolen, as well as from cameras on some of the main feeder streets, but not all of them. Collecting additional footage was going to be high on my list. It would go a long way if we could get a shot, no matter how blurry, of our car thief on camera.

"I can guess who'll be going through all that footage," Jessie groaned.

"At least we have a timeframe for most of the thefts," I said encouragingly, looking at my watch. It was already after six and the office was mostly deserted. "I know it's late, but if you have time, I've got something you can get started on right now."

"As long as it's something like real police work," Jessie said with a frown.

"It's as real as police work gets." I pulled up the footage of the attack on Eduardo Alverez. "See that SUV? It's got stolen tags, so odds are the vehicle is stolen too. Pete *thinks* it's a white 2016 Toyota Highlander, but he couldn't find any stolen cars reported around here fitting that description. I think you should double-check the make. I want you to search stolen cars in Florida, Georgia and Alabama from the... Let's see, the attack happened on November 30... so cars stolen from November 25 to November 30."

"You said to make sure it was a 2016 Highlander. How?" She seemed genuinely puzzled.

I pulled up the best image of the SUV, which showed just the right quarter panel and the bumper. It had been pure luck that the camera had picked up the tag.

"You'll have to Google images of SUVs and compare the back panel and bumper to this one until you get a match. You can start with Pete's guess and go from there."

"I *do* have to go to work tomorrow. I've got another

week before I'm done at the library."

"Just do what you can." I wasn't worried. Once Jessie dug her teeth into a task, she was like a Pitbull.

"Think I can use Pete's computer?"

"Use mine. I'll work off my laptop."

"Who wants to use my computer?" Pete's voice boomed out from down the hall before he and Julio appeared in the doorway. They were both smiling.

"We've got it covered," I told him. "I hope you have a reason for those smiles."

"We do, Larry boy." Pete did a little fist pump. "Shantel got a tire impression from the scene."

I stood up. "She didn't mention that."

"She wanted to make sure that the casting went well. She'd taken the best pictures she could while we were at the scene, but you can't hardly make the details out with a photo. If the cast hadn't come out well, we'd have had to get someone to look at the photos and video of the print and do an artist's rendition. Of course, the jury, when we get to a jury, wouldn't have been nearly as impressed. A plaster cast is much more convincing."

"Have you looked for a match?"

"Done and done. The car was a Nissan Sentra, though we still don't know the color since our witnesses were all over the map."

"That's great!" I felt the first tingle of hope. "Which means you know what you're looking for when talking to people or looking at surveillance camera footage."

"Not more footage!" Jessie yelled.

"Still a needle in a haystack, but at least we've narrowed it down to which haystack," Pete said.

"Or which needle," Julio joked.

"I thought about that, but it didn't really work."

"Unless the haystack was full of needles," Julio argued.

"How does that make any sense?"

"You guys need to get to work," I told them.

"Don't worry." Pete smiled. "Dinner and then an all-nighter if we have to. Want to join us at the Palmetto?"

"No. I'm putting in—" I looked at my watch. "—two more hours, then heading home."

My phone went off with a text from Genie. The doctor had reported that the swelling in Dad's brain was continuing to go down and that they might be able to bring him out of the coma by Tuesday afternoon. I passed the news on to the others, making Pete's smile grow larger.

Once they were gone, I made more than a dozen calls, generating solid suspects in two of my cases. I was able to close a third case because the stolen items, including a valuable watch and a box of expensive jewelry, had been discovered in the victim's son's room. Needless to say, they wouldn't be prosecuting.

"Pete had the right SUV, just the wrong year," Jessie said as I was packing up to head home. She had a dozen windows open on the monitor and was flipping back and forth between images that she'd pulled off the Internet and the still image from the ATM's camera. "See that light over the tag? It's a little different between the 2016 and 2017 models. Our Highlander is a 2017."

"Nice. Now you know what your next job is."

"Wish we could be sure of the color. I can't tell if it's white or silver," she mused.

"You can ask Lionel if there's any way to enhance the image or determine the color. Visually, I just don't know." I'd watched the video a dozen times and, at night with the sodium vapor street lamps providing most of the illumination, the color of the car was just washed out. "It's a light color, but I couldn't swear to anything else."

"I'll ask him in the morning."

"How are you and Eddie doing?" I asked. Eddie Thompson was my old, drug-abusing, crossdressing confidential informant turned respectable citizen. He worked with Jessie at the library and they had been casually going out for a couple of months. They were a bit of an odd couple, but they were also both outsiders who marched to the sound of their own drums.

"Eddie's a nice guy." I could almost see her blush.

"Y'all serious?"

Jessie was very quiet as she looked at my monitor and started to close the different windows. "I don't think we can be."

"You know, if it's the crossdressing thing…" It was my turn to blush.

"It's not that, stupid. I just mean with him getting clean and me going into the academy. We're just… not ready to be serious."

I nodded. "It's probably best to go at your own pace. Come on, I'll walk you out to your truck."

The cold north wind hit us as soon as we got outside. It was the beautiful, crisp winter weather that I always looked forward to when it was ninety-eight degrees outside, but I couldn't enjoy it now. I was too tired and too concerned about my father to relax and breathe in the holiday air. Even the Christmas lights and decorations along the street just depressed me. All I wanted right now was to go back to the way things had been two days ago.

I had to shake myself awake a couple of times during the short drive down dark country roads to our twenty acres in the woods. When I got to our drive, I saw that Cara had left the gate open for me. I thought about leaving it open, but something niggled at the back of my mind. What if the attack had been directed at Dad? Was it possible that whoever it was might follow up with an attack on me or Cara? Sighing, I got out of the car and shut the gate, making a mental note to tell Cara to be extra vigilant and not leave the gate open again.

Cara met me at the door and she wasn't alone. Dad's black-and-white house moose was standing behind her, looking pathetic. He greeted me with a lethargic bump and whimper instead of his usual painful exuberance.

"I'm sorry he's here," Cara explained. "Jamie thought he might settle down at your dad's house, but he was even worse over there, so he brought him back to me."

I knelt down beside the dog and looked into his sad brown eyes. "Dad's going to be fine, big guy," I told him. For a moment I felt a real connection with him… then he tried to climb on top of me. I managed to push him off before he broke something. "Dad would want you to be a brave boy."

In answer, he dropped to the carpet in front of the couch like a felled ox. Our other housemates, Ivy the tabby cat and Alvin the Pug, watched him suspiciously from the back of the couch.

"I don't know what we're going to do with him. He only ate half his dinner, and even Ghost couldn't distract him," Cara said, her brow furrowed. The kitten in question peered at us from one of his favorite perches on top of the refrigerator.

"He'll be fine," I said optimistically.

Cara turned her concern to me, pulling me into a fierce hug. For a long moment we just held each other, sharing the weight of our anxieties and fear. Finally I pulled away.

"I'm gonna grab a warm shower."

"There's some of the stew I made this weekend in the refrigerator. I can heat it up for you."

"That would be nice." I headed for the bathroom, trailed by a whining Mauser.

At midnight, we both lay awake listening to Mauser whimper and occasionally paw at the bedroom door. We'd already tried letting him into the bedroom, but all that had done was allow his restlessness to be right on top of us.

"I can't take this," I said, sitting up.

Cara pushed me back down. "Stay here. I'll take him and sleep in the guestroom. It's on the other end of the house, so maybe you won't hear him. You need sleep."

"So do you," I said, but I wasn't going to argue with her. Our old mobile home wasn't that big and there wasn't a chance in hell that I wouldn't still hear Mauser's whining, but I was willing to try anything.

CHAPTER FIVE

Cara must have snuck out of the house very quietly with Mauser Tuesday morning, because I woke up after eight alone except for Alvin and the cats. I'd spent a restless night filled with strange dreams, so I was grateful that she'd let me sleep in. I called Genie before I rolled out of bed.

"Ted did well during the night. Dr. Titus wants to run more scans this morning before making a decision about letting him come out of the coma."

"I'll come over before noon and give you a chance to get out of the hospital," I promised.

"Don't worry about me. One of my friends brought me a change of clothes and a decent breakfast. And if they move him out of ICU, then I'll be able to be in the room with him."

My next call was to Cara.

"I let Mauser up on the bed with me," she told me. "It wasn't too bad except that he was *so* restless. About every half hour, he'd get up and turn in circles for five minutes."

"That sounds painful."

"I've got some bruises that could land you in jail as a wife-beater," Cara said with a tired laugh. "He can't go on like this."

"We'll figure something out," I said, not having a clue what that something would be.

"Thank goodness Jamie is basically done with school. He's going to entertain Mauser today. We'll owe him a very big thank you."

"Dad can give him a bonus." Talking about Dad doing something in the future felt odd. I wondered if I was being too hopeful, or running the risk of jinxing his recovery.

I headed to the office, determined to spend the morning making calls and setting up interviews so I could make some real progress on my cases. Though I was trying hard not to think about the one case that wasn't mine, I couldn't help wondering if Pete and Julio were having any luck tracing the car from the tire tracks.

Pete had his phone in one hand and a donut in the other as I walked by his desk. He was nodding vigorously.

"Thank you, Doc. That helps a lot. Please send me a report when you get the chance. I'll be in touch." He clicked off the call and gave me an ear-to-ear grin that warmed me more than a cup of coffee.

"Good news?" I asked, trying not to sound too eager.

"Twenty to thirty thousand miles."

"What?"

"The car that left the tracks. A specialist who consults with FDLE looked at the cast and did some measurements. The wear patterns are consistent with a tire that has somewhere between twenty to thirty thousand miles on it. And the tires are the ones that came with the car."

"How the hell could he know that?"

"Tread pattern. They were a short run. Only fifty thousand were produced and they all went on Nissan Sentras. The following year the tread was changed slightly. According to our expert, there was a rumor that the tire could lose traction under the right, or I should say the *wrong* conditions, so the tire company quietly changed the tread pattern to resolve the issue."

"How did you get him to look at it so fast?" I asked,

impressed.

"I've done a few favors for him over the years. Besides, he'd heard about your father and looked at it first thing this morning."

"Nice." Not only could this help to identify the car if it was found, but it was circumstantial evidence that could put a suspect at the scene.

"I swear I can smell the rat who stabbed your dad." Pete had the look of a hunting dog who's finally seen the deer he's been chasing. "Jessie's going over some of the video we picked up last night."

"Last night?"

"I told you we were pulling an all-nighter. Julio and I hassled the two Fast Marts until the owner made his son come out at midnight and pull the footage for us. Hey, we didn't want to lose it."

"We're lucky that this isn't the days of VHS when they reused the tapes every other day. Most stores now keep stuff going back six months."

"We just need a little luck." Pete held up crossed fingers.

"Jessie has an eye for cam footage."

"Lionel set her up with a pretty sweet monitor. I've also asked him to analyze the ping data from your dad's phone so we'll know exactly where he was prior to the attack."

"Did you get any sleep?" I asked.

"Four hours on a cot in back. I'm fine, showered and shaved and everything. I just want to find this asshole. Julio's dragging a bit. He spent most of the night going through old cases where your dad played a significant role."

"Did he find anything?"

"One case where your dad had a complaint filed against him. The perp he slugged just got out of jail three months ago."

"Dad hit someone?" I asked, incredulous.

"I haven't read the report. This was back when your dad was still on patrol. Apparently, he pulled this car over for speeding. While he was writing the ticket, the husband and wife got into an argument in front of their ten-year-old daughter outside the car. One thing led to another and the man shoved his daughter, who stumbled into traffic and was almost hit by another car. Julio said that the medical report indicated the husband had suffered a blow to his head and injuries to his neck."

"How'd Dad get out of that?" I was astonished. Dad was one of the most even-tempered law enforcement officers I'd ever known. Though he was easy to anger if a child or animal was involved in a crime, I'd never heard of him resorting to unnecessary violence.

"You'll have to ask Julio. He just told me that your dad came out smelling like a rose."

"Neat trick. You say the guy is out of jail? Why was he *in* jail?"

"Turned out it wasn't the first time he'd hit his daughter; or his son who'd been removed from the home a year earlier."

"Damn!"

"Gets better. The guy had his sentence lengthened because he stabbed another prisoner."

"I like that." I felt a flicker of hope. "What kind of car does he drive?"

Pete shook his head. "It's not going to be tied up that neatly. He drives a 2010 Ford F-150."

"Time to check on his friends and relatives."

"His name is Fred Durrell. Luckily he's still on parole and he's been a good boy about keeping in touch with his parole officer. Lives in Marianna. Little over an hour is all it would take for him to get here."

"Gives him a fair chance for an alibi," I said, feeling some of my hope dim. "That's almost a three-hour round trip."

Pete shrugged. "If he's not our man, he's not our man." He was trying to be an even-keeled investigator, but his eyes gave him away. He wanted this to be our man. I wanted it too. Tying the investigation up in a neat little package would put us all on the road to normalcy.

"Let me know as soon as you find out anything."

Pete frowned. "Do you have any doubt that you'd be the first one I'd call… with good or bad news?"

"I'm just… going a little crazy." I explained the situation with Mauser.

"He needs to know that his dad's okay."

I sighed. "Me too." I'd made the mistake of reading about induced comas. There was a significant chance of brain damage.

Pete left to go find Julio. I stared at my computer screen and couldn't help thinking about one of my more disturbing dreams from the night before. I'd been walking through town and kept running into people I knew, but they were all wearing hoodies. Even people like Pete and Cara seemed ominous with hoods pulled up over their heads. At one point I had been surrounded by a dozen people, all with their backs to me. I'd reached out to them until they'd faced me, one by one. Except they didn't have any faces… there was nothing under the hoods. Finally, the last person I touched had whirled around and stabbed me—once, twice, three times—before I started running. The faster I ran, the closer the figure in the hoodie came to me.

The nightmare still made me shudder, and I wondered if it meant anything. Was my subconscious trying to tell me that the man who had assaulted Eduardo Alverez was the same man who had attacked my father? Or was I just making connections that weren't really there?

Shaking my head, I got up from my desk and wandered down the hall to Lionel West's technology corner in our evidence lab. I wanted to see how Jessie was coming along with the video footage. I found her dividing her attention between two sets of videos.

"Lionel suggested that I watch some of the footage Pete and Julio brought in last night, then switch to the stolen car stuff for a while."

"That way she's less likely to just zone out and miss

catching something," Lionel said, not turning his head from his own monitor.

"Sorry I haven't found anything interesting yet," Jessie told me with a sad smile.

"I'll try to get some more for you." Thinking about Alverez, I wanted to expand the search out to a mile from the ATM machine. I knew of a dozen possible locations for security cameras along that route.

"I'll be here," she said with a sigh, turning back to the monitor. "Julio just dropped off another USB with a gig of data."

"When do you have to be at work?"

"I told Eddie what I was doing and he talked to Mrs. Vila, the head librarian, who said I should take the day off. She's a big fan of your dad."

"I may go by and see Eddie today. If I do, I'll make sure to thank Mrs. Vila." Eddie was on my short list of people to talk to about the auto thefts. Even though he'd been clean for more than a year, he could still give me names of guys he'd known who were into stealing cars.

Back at my desk, I dug into my pile of cases. I had one new one from the night before that I decided to prioritize since it involved a minor. A fifteen-year-old girl had hit another girl with a brick a few days before at school. The victim hadn't wanted to tell her parents, but she'd ultimately been unable to hide the large purple bruise on her shoulder.

According to the report taken by Deputy Matti Sanderson, the attack had been a result of passions that had been building since October. I visited the victim and her family to get a feel for what had actually taken place. As I talked to them, it became clear to me that the victim wasn't at all interested in pressing the issue, despite her parents' insistence. It was obvious that there were secrets she wanted to keep. A case like this was full of subtleties, and a wrong decision could result in one or both of the girls not getting the help or support they needed.

After assuring the parents that there would be

consequences for the girl who threw the brick, I called Sandy and asked if she would be interested in pursuing the investigation. I thought she'd be a better fit than I for dealing with the families. She eagerly agreed, so I called Major Parks to receive his approval. With luck, the charges would be minor and more educational than punitive.

With that settled, I headed over to the library.

"I know you don't hang out with those kind of people anymore," I told Eddie as he shook his head.

"It's not that I don't want to help," Eddie assured me. "I hate that your dad got hurt. Does this case have something to do with the stabbing?"

"No. I don't think so." I explained how I was taking over things for Pete and Julio.

"I think you should be solving your own dad's case." Eddie frowned.

"Not the way it works, unfortunately. Look, I could really use some names from you."

"I don't run in those—"

I held up my hand. "I hear you. But please try. Think of anyone you know who's stolen a car, bought a stolen car or dismantled a stolen car."

After a long pause, Eddie finally said, "Pisser, I guess."

"Who?"

"Come on. You've got to know Pisser. Every time he gets drunk he gets arrested for peeing in public." Eddie looked around nervously, realizing that he'd let his voice get loud enough to be heard by an elderly man scanning the books in a nearby re-shelving cart.

"Tall, blond-haired guy about thirty-five, always wears a worn old dress coat?" I asked.

"Yep, that's Pisser. He'd steal a car if you asked him. Very mechanical."

"Who knew? I'm pretty sure his name is Mark Something, something that begins with an S." I'd arrested him myself once for drunk and disorderly. "Okay, anyone else?"

"Maybe Ty. He's a short guy. About this tall." Eddie held his hand at his shoulder, making Ty only about five feet tall.

"Black man in his late twenties?"

"Yeah, that's him. He's always loved cars. He'd sometimes scout them out for... Hey, you were involved in busting that gang! They were shipping the cars to Jacksonville."

I remembered it well. The Carlsons were hardly a "gang," but it had been how Dad had ended up with Mauser. I swallowed the sudden lump that formed in my throat.

I thanked Eddie for the names.

"Remember, you didn't hear about them from me."

"Have I ever sold you out?" I asked with a crooked smile.

I called one of the deputies on patrol to get a line on Pisser's current location. Finding him was easier than I thought. Turned out he was serving thirty days for an open container violation and vandalism. I hurried to the jail and had him brought into one of the interview rooms.

"I haven't stolen a car in years," Pisser said in a way that suggested there was more to the story.

"Thirty days is a long time for open container and vandalism," I commented. Pisser had eaten up a good many brain cells over the years and I hoped that by bouncing between topics, I might confuse him enough that he'd forget what secrets he was trying to keep.

"My fourth time in front of Judge Ridgeway. She was pretty angry."

"I can see that. She doesn't have much of a sense of humor."

"You got that right."

"What was the last car you stole?"

"Hey! I'm not going to incarcerate myself," he said indignantly.

I chuckled darkly. "I think you mean incriminate, though incarcerate could still be the case. Look, I don't care about anything you've done in the past. If it's more than a year old, I'm not going to bring a case against you. I just need some information."

"Then why are you asking me?"

"People say you're good at snatching cars."

"What people?"

"You like fast cars?"

"No way. I like luxurious cars. The first car I ever stole was a Cadillac. A beautiful golden Seville. A lot of kids my age would steal a car and rag it out as fast as they could before the cops caught them. Not me. I rode around like a king." Pisser leaned back and put one hand out like he was steering a car, while the other waved out of an imaginary window.

"Where did you find the cars you stole?"

"Driveways. I'd get a friend to drive me around until I saw one I liked. Then he'd drop me off." He shrugged.

"At night?"

"Yeah. Rich neighborhoods are the best. Lots of room between houses, so you can get in the car and get out without anyone seeing you. Besides, no one knows anyone else. So even if someone sees you, they don't know if it's your car or not. The only time you're in real danger is the minute or two it takes to jack the door open." He had leaned forward, his eyes showing life for the first time since I'd entered the room. He was reliving the excitement that came from stealing cars.

"Take a look at these pictures," I said, laying out photos of the five cars and the garages or driveways they'd been stolen from.

Pisser leaned in for a close look. "Not my style. Luxury sedans were my ride, not the sporty stuff. Though I will say, these *are* expensive." He picked up two of the photos. "If these were stolen from a closed garage, then the thief would need to have known that the car was there and that the owner wasn't going to be home. Garage doors can make a lot of noise. That's bad. I never wanted to meet the owner 'cause people get mean when you steal their car."

"Gee, imagine that," I said, letting the sarcasm drip from the words. "Who would want cars like this?"

"Someone's probably selling them. Overseas, most likely. Maybe parts in this country, though that'd be hard. This one—an Audi R8—even used, it's worth over a hundred-thousand dollars. But how many are there in this country? Who needs the parts? No, someone has a market for these. They wouldn't be that hard to sell, but you'd have to move them overseas. There would be too many headaches getting a legit tag in this country."

"If you wanted to steal cars like this, how would you find the owners?"

"Easy. High-end detail shop."

"Is there one around here?" Adams County didn't seem the market for that type of service.

"There must be one in Tallahassee. You think all those people with cars worth hundreds of thousands clean them themselves? You think they trust the local suds-and-rinse carwash to do it?"

I made some notes, then showed him a picture of Eduardo Alverez and the Toyota Highlander that had been used in the attack at the ATM.

"So?"

"Do you know him?"

"Nope."

"What's your impression of the car? Hard to steal? Fit in with the other cars?" I pointed to the other photos.

"Obviously not in the same class. The SUV would be easier to steal than the fancy cars. Its anti-theft devices wouldn't be that hard to disable. The high-end ones, you got to have some know-how. Be tech savvy, as they say. You got to get in and reprogram them."

"How do you do that?" Since most cars were half computer these days, it didn't surprise me that thieves would need some hacking skills to steal the expensive ones. I'd dealt with a case a couple of months ago where someone had hacked into a car to murder the occupant.

"You can buy gadgets on the dark web," Pisser told me. "Which is why these thefts had to be carefully planned." He tapped his skull. "You need a plan, at least for the high-end market. That's another way your snake could have found out which nests to rob. He could have gone on the dark web and bought lists of car owners. Any information that can be hacked can get bought these days. Hell, someone at the DMV could be selling the information."

Pisser had nothing else to tell me, so I sent him back to his cell and headed for my car.

I wondered if there was a way I could get out in front of my car thief. He'd been stealing about one a month. How many cars valued at more than a hundred-thousand could there be in a rural county like ours? If I could get a list of all of the ones that hadn't been stolen and figure out which ones were probable targets, then I could set up some surveillance cameras and catch him in the act. Maybe.

Finding Ty proved to be a little harder than finding Pisser. Using my laptop, I pulled up the files from the Carlson case and found a guy named Ty Woodson listed as a witness in the trial. He'd given testimony that had helped to put a nail in the lid of the prosecutor's case, so he'd walked out of court with a suspended sentence and parole that had ended this past July. I knocked on wood that he hadn't moved since his last meeting with his parole officer.

"He's moved." The manager of the fifty-unit Section 8 housing complex on the edge of town dashed my hopes. "I liked Ty. He was one of the good ones. Paid his rent on time, had his apartment neat and clean on inspection days. He even helped a couple of the older residents fix up their cars. He can't have done anything bad."

"I just want his help with a case I'm working," I assured her. "There's no reason to believe that he's involved. Can you tell me where he's living now?"

"No," she said, and I thought for a minute she was going to leave it at that, but then she added, "I *do* know where he works. He's an aide at the Palms Nursing Home."

CHAPTER SIX

I found Ty Woodson assisting a resident back into her bed.

"I can take a break," he told me. "Just give me a second with Mrs. Wistron."

I stood outside the room, listening as the small man patiently showed the woman where all of her personal items were laid out on her nightstand. After a few minutes, he joined me in the hall.

"We can go out back to the smoking patio."

Two hardy nurses and three residents huddled behind a trellis that was covered in the monstrous tentacles of a dormant wisteria vine, trying to keep their cigarettes lit in the cold wind.

"You mind being out in the wind?" Ty asked me.

"I'd prefer it," I said, trying not to cough.

We went to the sunniest spot in the small yard, out of earshot of the smokers.

"I haven't done anything wrong," Ty said defensively.

"I told you, I just want to talk to you. I'm working some auto thefts and wondered if you'd give me your thoughts on them."

"And names?"

"If you have any, yes."

He pursed his lips. "I'm still getting crap about testifying at that trial."

"I'm not talking about anything official."

"It's been years since I've had anything to do with... that kind of thing."

"Understood." I handed him the pictures of the stolen cars.

"Nice! Better than the cars we were dealing in. These would be harder to peddle and a lot less demand for parts. They would almost certainly have to go directly to ships."

"Carlson did some of that."

"I was a kid. I didn't see anything above the street. He thought it was funny to use the short kid to go around and spot for him." His voice was bitter.

"How did you do it?"

"He'd give me a sheet with makes and models and told me to go find them. I always figured he was getting requests from somewhere else."

"Did he care where the cars were?"

"Driveways were best."

"What if people were home?"

"Didn't matter. Most of the thefts were done between two and five in the morning. I went along a couple of times. Carlson had some fast mother... guys working for him. They could get into the cars faster than someone with keys."

I pointed at the pictures of the fancy cars he still held in his hand. "Who do you think would be stealing cars like this?"

"Man, I told you, I was a nobody. Had a little habit and working for Carlson filled it. I never saw nothin' like this." He handed the photos back to me.

"I hear you." I pulled out my card. "If you think of anything or anyone, give me a call. Maybe someone who talked about moving up to more expensive cars. Something like that."

Ty nodded in an un-encouraging way and I knew I'd never hear from him again.

I was almost to my car when I got a call from Genie.

"They've stopped the barbiturates that were keeping him in the coma. The doctor thinks he'll start coming around in a few hours."

"I'll be there soon," I told her.

Hanging up, I noticed a text from one of our newer deputies, Todd Snider. At the most, he'd had a year on the job. I called him back.

"Todd, what's up?"

"Sorry to bother you. Julio told me that you were taking on the auto theft cases."

His voice sounded nervous, like he was talking to a superior. Had I ever been that green? Of course, having grown up with my father and most of the deputies and supervisors I came to work with, I hadn't really been intimidated by any of them. Well, maybe by Lt. Johnson whenever he'd put on his drill sergeant impression.

"What's going on?" I asked.

"I just caught an auto theft and wasn't sure if I was supposed to handle it or not. Major Parks sent out an email that said we should do our own investigations if it's not a serious crime."

Clueless, I thought. The email had actually said that patrol would investigate any crimes that didn't rise to the level of a first-degree felony until further notice. Theft of a car valued at less than twenty-thousand dollars was a third-degree felony.

"How much was the car worth?" I asked. A small part of me hoped that it would be a fresh case for my cluster of expensive thefts. No such luck.

"Ummm, I don't know. It's a 2016 silver Nissan Sentra."

I thought about telling him to handle it, but decided to take pity on the victim. "Send me your report. I'll take it from here."

"I don't want to… burden you… with your father in the hospital and all. By the way, I think your dad is a great sheriff."

"Thanks, Todd. Send the report." I'd barely ended the call before my laptop dinged with the addition to my inbox.

I called Jessie on the off-chance that she had any leads from the surveillance footage for me to follow up with. Her answer was not encouraging.

"You sound zoned out," I said sympathetically.

"My eyeballs are going to fall out."

"Put Lionel on." I heard her pass the phone to the other side of the office. "Y'all grab something to eat. I'll reimburse you."

"Does that include wine and dessert?" Lionel asked eagerly.

"Tacos, chips and a drink at the food truck."

"Good enough. And we are grateful."

I hung up and looked at my watch. I had time to do some more work before heading over to the hospital, so I pulled up the email from Deputy Snider. At least his report was written in clear and concise English. The car had been stolen from the parking lot of the AmMex Trucking Company sometime in the past forty-eight hours. That seemed like a long lag time in reporting it, but maybe it belonged to a trucker who'd been on the road. Whoever had stolen it, we'd probably never see it again, at least not in Adams County. AmMex wasn't far from the interstate and I was sure the thief was long gone. Still, I headed over there to see if there were any leads to follow or anything unusual about the case. With a car like that, it almost certainly was not a part of my serial car thefts.

Inside the main office, the receptionist looked at me with a bored expression. She stood behind a large front desk with a couple of doors behind it. One was obviously an office. Through a window in the door I could see the back of a man sitting at a computer. After I told her who I was and why I was there, the she called her boss, Glen Shaw, who had been listed as the victim on Snider's report. Within minutes, a tall man in his late forties with a neatly trimmed beard and smiling eyes came down the hallway. He had his hand out when he was still six feet away.

"Great service!" he said with a smile. "I thought I might have to call that deputy back. Patti said you're an investigator? I heard about the sheriff getting stabbed. That must be tough on the department." His delivery was rapid-fire.

"Thank you. It has been," I managed to say as he pumped my hand up and down.

"We found some security footage of the theft. That's what I was going to tell that deputy when I called him back. Come on, I'll show you." Glen glanced at the front desk and into the office beyond for a moment, as though looking for someone, before leading me toward the back of the building. I had to walk quickly to keep up with his long strides.

"The video would be helpful," I said as I followed him down a corridor that was strictly utilitarian. The polished floor was wide enough to accommodate a forklift, and stainless steel panels protected the walls from whatever vehicles or dollies might be navigating the halls.

"Our security office is down this way," Glen said, making a right turn before stopping at a door. He rapped three times and went inside.

The room was about fifteen-by-twenty feet, with a bank of monitors taking up one corner while lockers and equipment filled the rest of the space. It was an impressive setup for a company their size.

"We haul a lot of valuable cargo. Pays to keep an eye on things," Glen explained, noticing my raised eyebrows. "Pull up that footage of my car getting swiped," he told the man sitting in front of the monitors.

For all Glen's good humor, this man could have been his sober twin. His mouth was a flat bar across his face as he nodded to his boss and looked at a monitor, clicking a mouse that moved rapidly under his hand.

"Got it."

"Play it through at regular speed first," Glen told him. We stepped up behind him and looked over his shoulder.

The video showed a half-full parking lot at night. The pole lights cast shadows around the cars and trucks. I noted the time and date on the video: it had been taken at three in the morning on Sunday. After five seconds, a figure wearing a hoodie, back to the camera, walked toward the vehicles. *What's with all the hoodies?* I thought. Something about the way the person moved made me lean forward. There was a feminine sway of the hips, nothing exaggerated, but noticeable.

The person on screen stopped at a light-colored car.

"That's my car." Glen pointed at the monitor. "Kyle, one of our drivers, had borrowed it."

My brain was setting off alarm bells, a lot of them, but I couldn't pinpoint why. I continued watching as the figure's head whipped back and forth for a second before they opened the door and got in.

"Kyle thinks it's a woman he was talking to at the truck stop."

"She stole his keys?" I asked, my eyes still glued to the screen as the car whipped out of the parking space and drove off the left side of the monitor.

"That's a long story which Kyle should probably tell you." He tapped the shoulder of the man operating the mouse. "Go at half speed now."

The cursor moved and the mouse clicked until we were watching the same scene in slow motion.

"It doesn't really help much 'cause she never looks at the camera," Glen said.

His words flipped a switch in my brain. The video reminded me of the footage from the Fast Mart that Jessie had been so sure showed Terri Miller. The comparison was ridiculous. How did it make any sense to equate one indistinguishable figure on tape with another? They were both wearing hoodies and moving the way you'd expect a woman to move, but that meant next to nothing. I had to let it go.

We watched the footage again and I asked the man at the

monitor to make me a copy to go. As he was loading the USB drive, I said to Glen, "Let me get this straight. Kyle was borrowing *your* car?"

"That's right. Kyle Whitten is one of my drivers. His own car is in the shop, and I drive my pickup most of the time, so I let him borrow this one to get back and forth to work. He drives cross-country for us, so no one noticed right away when the car went missing. It wasn't until Kyle got back from his run late last night that anyone knew it was gone."

"But you didn't report it until this morning?"

"You can understand a guy not wanting to call his boss at midnight. Besides, Kyle thought I might have taken it for some reason." Glen gave me a kindly grin.

"Makes sense," I allowed.

"Best thing would be for you to talk to Kyle."

"Is he here?" I asked, still hearing the alarm bells in my head. I'd dismissed them thinking about the Terri Miller connection, but something still nagged at me.

"Will you go ask Patti to page him?" Glen told the man at the monitor, who stood up and gave him a nod as he left.

"I guess I should have introduced you to Tindall, though he's not much more talkative when he knows you."

"Do you own the company?"

"The Manning family owns it. I'm just the manager."

We heard a voice page Kyle and tell him to report to the security office. A few minutes later, Tindall came back in, followed by another man. Kyle Whitten was the epitome of a trucker, from the soles of his boots to the dirty Great Dane Trailers ball cap on his head. Of average size and in his mid-thirties, he nodded nervously to the boss.

"Tindall said there's a detective here to talk to me."

I held out my hand and he shook it. "I'm Deputy Larry Macklin from the Adams County Sheriff's Office. I just wanted to ask you about the woman you believe stole your car."

"Sure. But it wasn't my car. I was just borrowing it from Mr. Shaw."

"I understand that. What happened?"

Kyle blushed and looked down at the floor. "Stupid. I should have known when she started talking to me that she wanted something. At first I thought she... Lots of those kind of women approach you when you drive a truck."

"You mean prostitutes?"

He looked at me like he wasn't sure how smart I was. "Always. Whenever I pull into a rest stop or a truck stop."

"I'm just trying to clarify the details."

"Anyway, that's what I thought and I told her I wasn't buying. She said she wasn't selling, which surprised me. Usually, as soon as they know you aren't a customer, they're gone. Instead she got more talkative."

"Where was this?"

"Oh, yeah, sorry. It was at the Rolling On Truck Stop right up the road. I was filling up before I headed out to Houston Saturday afternoon. She gave me a sad story while I pumped my diesel. I guess it got me to talking too. Anyway, I told her where I was headed and that I'd had a fight with my wife about getting our car fixed. Must have mentioned that I was driving the boss's Nissan."

"She got you to tell her what car you were driving?" I asked doubtfully.

"Yeah. Ever since I found out the car was stolen, I've been thinking about all of that. I'm sure she was fishing to find out where my car was. She must have seen me drive from here to the Rolling On. Figured I was heading out and tricked me into telling her which car was mine."

"And she stole your keys?"

"That wasn't hard. After filling up the truck, I went inside to buy coffee. She had plenty of time to find the boss's key."

"What did she look like?"

"I didn't get a real good look at her. She had a hoodie pulled down pretty low over her face. You know, it was kind of cold that day and the wind was blowing pretty good. I didn't think too much about it. 'Sides, she was young, maybe mid-twenties. I think her hair was brown. Not too tall or short. I don't know." Kyle shrugged.

I thought of Terri Miller again. The age, height and hair color would fit. Of course, the description would also fit thousands of other women across North Florida.

"Were there any other distinguishing features about the woman? Think. Odd gestures, movements, accent, odors? *Anything?*"

"Like I said, I was fueling up my truck, getting ready to head out on a long haul. And I'm married. I might have let her distract me a bit more than usual 'cause of the fight I'd had with Dee. Still, I wasn't in the market, free or not, if you know what I mean." He frowned. "I really don't know anything else. Mr. Shaw has been really nice not to rip me a new one for getting his car stolen."

"It's not a big deal. That's what insurance is for," Glen told him and flashed him a big, reassuring smile.

I looked at my watch, thinking that it was time to head to Tallahassee. Like a spark jumping across the positive and negative posts on a battery, the connection was finally made.

"Your car is a Nissan Sentra? Stolen early in the morning on December 3?" I felt lightheaded.

"That's what we've been talking about." Glen seemed slightly amused at my backtracking.

"I've got to make a call."

I stepped outside the office to call Pete. "I might have a lead on the car. I'm sending you an auto theft report so you can run the VIN number and see if it falls within the range of Nissan Sentras that had those tires."

"Where are you?"

"At AmMex Trucking. The car was stolen from here the night before Dad was attacked. They have surveillance video. The thief is wearing a hoodie and it was a woman."

"I guess there isn't a good shot of her face?" Pete's voice wasn't hopeful.

"Not even close. But she stole the keys from a trucker who talked with her. She's average height and weight." I considered my next words carefully. I didn't want to send

Comment [A]:

the investigation off on a wild goose chase. "This is going to sound a little crazy, but his description would fit Terri Miller. And there's something about the figure in the video that reminds me of the person Jessie saw on the tape from the Fast Mart."

"That sounds like a reach. First things first. Send me the VIN number."

CHAPTER SEVEN

"I guess you didn't need to hurry." Genie told me when I arrived at the hospital forty minutes later. "They've postponed bringing him out of the coma."

"Seriously?" I felt my heart drop into my stomach. All of the doom-laden information I'd read on traumatic brain injuries and medically induced comas flooded my mind and my anxiety red-lined again.

"The surgeon didn't think the swelling had gone down enough." Genie's hands clutched nervously at each other as she explained.

"I want to talk to him." I knew my voice sounded harsh and I saw Genie flinch. "I'm not questioning you. I'm questioning *him*."

"I read up on head trauma." Her voice trembled.

"So did I."

"I'm going to have to tell Jimmy what's happened."

I pulled her into a hug and Genie began to cry into my shoulder. I longed for Cara to be there, knowing she'd have more encouraging words for Genie than I did. I didn't even know what to tell myself.

"He'll be okay." It was the best I could come up with. "He has to be," I added for both of us.

"I called Tilly, my friend who's been helping me with the wedding, and told her we'd need to move it back. I don't see how we can have the ceremony the first week of January." She cried harder and I wiped at my own eyes.

"Sit down while I go find Dr. Titus," I said, encouraging Genie down into one of the waiting room chairs.

After leaving her, I called Cara, though I didn't have answers for any of her questions. I just wanted to hear her voice.

"Jamie is worried about Mauser. He won't eat, not even ice cream."

"I'll think of something," I said, though I had no idea what. "Let me go corner this surgeon and find out what's going on."

Hanging up, I was left with a short, purposeful to-do list: Get some answers from the surgeon and come up with a way to help Mauser so we could all get some rest.

I had to show my ass at the nurses' station to get my call put through to Dr. Titus, who had just finished making his post-surgery rounds.

"Mr. Macklin, I can only do so much. The best solution is for your father's body to heal itself. Every test indicates that it can and that it's trying. If I think that trend is changing, I will step in and operate. That time hasn't come yet."

"I've read that a medically induced coma can cause problems beyond the head trauma," I challenged him.

He sighed. "If you have more confidence in your Internet research than you do in my medical experience, I will be glad to find another doctor to look after your father. However, I'm one of the best in the country and the decisions I'm making are well within the margins of accepted medical practice. A lot of surgeons would have already operated. But in my opinion, and it's backed up by peer-reviewed studies, that's not warranted at this moment. I say moment because it could change in a heartbeat, which is why I have my own assistant monitoring your father's vitals at all times." His words had become more heated as he spoke. At the same time, I felt my faith in him increasing as I heard the passion and dedication in his tone.

"I'm just worried about my father," I said.

"Of course you are," he said, his tone slightly more gentle. "Rest assured that my team and I are also worried and will do everything we can to make the outcome one that will be acceptable to everyone. Now, unless you need any more assurances, I've got work to do."

I thanked him and let him end the call, then turned my mind to Mauser. I came to the conclusion that the canine mountain wouldn't be happy until he knew Dad was okay. That gave me an idea. The mountain would have to go to Muhammad. I thought about the long list of people who might owe my dad a favor, then hit one of the numbers I had on speed dial.

"Are you busy?" I asked when Dr. Darzi, our county coroner, answered.

"Yes, but oddly not with one of your bodies."

"I'm coming down there."

"Suit yourself."

Down in the morgue, I walked into the room where Dr. Darzi was working over the body of a petite older woman.

"Before you ask, she died of a blow to the chest. A case for the Tallahassee Police Department, by all accounts an accident. She was trying to dig up a tree in her yard and had rigged up some Rube Goldberg contraption using her son's truck. I guess it was supposed to pull the tree out of the ground. Unfortunately, when her son accelerated, the rope broke and the tree snapped back, hitting her in the chest. Collapsed her lungs and stopped her heart. She might have been saved if the paramedics had gotten to her soon enough, but her son tried to revive her for almost ten minutes before calling 911."

I whistled. "That's a tough one."

"I believe they are going to let the son go without charges." He paused before adding, "I was very sorry to hear about your father."

"That's why I'm here." I went on to explain how I wanted his help.

"Sneaking that menace up to the ICU?" Darzi wasn't a huge fan of Mauser, though Dad had brought the dog over meet Darzi's kids one day and they'd been delighted. He shook his head and chuckled. "He's a very big dog."

"I need someone with the power to make it happen. Five minutes is all we need. They let therapy dogs into the hospital all the time," I argued.

"That's true. A friend of mine brings his Standard Poodle to visit. Two big differences, though. Sari, the Poodle, has completed a great deal of training to participate in the program. And she does *not* go into the ICU."

"Come on. You have to know someone in hospital administration who has the clout and would be willing to help Dad."

Darzi studiously weighed the woman's internal organs as I waited. As he was placing a kidney on the scale, he turned to me.

"The operations manager might do it. He lives in Adams County and I believe he knows your dad. As an extra bonus, I know one of his secrets. One that is not too serious, but would be quite an embarrassment."

Half an hour later, I was in the top-floor office of Ron Brandt. He was shaking his head firmly.

"No way. I like your dad. He's done me a couple of favors over the years, but there are limits to the rules that I can break. Getting a dog, *that dog*, into the hospital's ICU? That's crazy."

"Dr. Darzi told me that, if you were dragging your feet, I should mention Antigua."

Brandt turned bright red. I thought for a moment that he was going to kick me out of his office. Instead he took some very deep breaths before he allowed himself to speak again.

"I can only do it under one condition." He paused. "Make that two conditions. One, it happens after eleven at night; and, two, he's an official law enforcement animal."

The first condition was not a problem. I wasn't so sure about the second. "What do you mean by 'official?'"

"I mean that the dog has some sort of official papers proclaiming him a K9 law enforcement dog. I need some type of cover for my ass."

My brain mulled this over. "Done." I'd figure some way to get the Dane an official title.

Brandt checked the schedule and talked to someone down in ICU.

"Tonight. Midnight. And you better have that dog looking official," Brandt warned me.

I had Major Parks on the phone almost before I was out of Brandt's office.

"What do you mean, make Mauser a member of the department?" Parks sounded appalled. He was friendly to Mauser, but he hunted birds and had much higher standards for dog training than Dad did.

"He already works for the department. This would just make it official," I argued, trying to sound completely reasonable.

"How the hell?"

"Communications. Name me anyone else who does more liaison work with the community than he does. Mauser is a great ambassador for the sheriff's office. He's our answer to McGruff the Crime Dog. He deserves a badge."

"Larry, be honest. I've heard you talk about that dog."

"I might have been… jealous, that's all. I respect what he does to promote goodwill within the community," I managed to say without choking.

Parks sighed. "What do you want?"

"A badge number and documentation of his employment with the department."

"I'll tear it up as soon as this craziness is done with."

"Dad loves that dog. This is for him as much as for Mauser."

"I know that's true. I'll have everything ready when you

get into town."

On the way back to Calhoun, I called Cara and told her what I was working on.

"You're crazy, but I love you," she said, laughing. "You'll have to use my car, though. Bernadette needed her van back for Cleo."

After swapping cars and picking up Mauser, I met our K9 sergeant, Mack Burrows, at the sheriff's office. I was a little concerned that he wouldn't approve of what I was doing, but I needn't have worried.

"Hell, he spends more time at the sheriff's office than half the deputies," Burrows told me as he petted and hugged Mauser.

Next to him, the one-hundred-and-ninety-pound Dane almost looked like an average-size dog. Burrows was the largest man in the department. He'd worked his way through college on a weightlifting scholarship and had missed the Olympic team by one slot. I'd seen him pick up his German Shepherd like it was a Yorkie. His canine partner Tornado lived up to his name. Between the two of them, they'd never lost a suspect. Tornado ran them down and Sergeant Burrows picked them up and carried them to the patrol car.

"Do you have a vest he could wear?"

Burrows stepped back and looked at Mauser thoughtfully.

"He's got a better chance of wearing mine than Tor's." Then a big grin showed on his dark face. He went to his locker and pulled out a canine vest. "I got some black duct tape. We'll make it work."

When he was done, you almost couldn't tell that he'd used duct tape to extend all the straps around Mauser's large girth.

"Not half bad, Deputy Mauser," Burrows said, admiring his own work.

"It only has to get us through tonight."

"I'll drive you in the K9 SUV."

"We'll be all right in Cara's car," I assured him.

Burrows huffed. "To hell with that. I'm going in with you. No one's going to question me and my new dog," he said, patting Mauser firmly. Together, the two of them would top the scales at almost five hundred pounds. Who would be brave enough to stop them?

"Thank you."

"Your dad is the best sheriff I've ever worked with. We aren't going to lose him now." He turned toward the door, then stopped. The look on his face told me he was deadly serious when he added, "I want you to promise that if I'm ever in the hospital, you'll make sure that Tornado can come in and see me."

"You got it, boss," I said and meant it.

A little before midnight, we pulled up to the hospital. I'd changed into my uniform so that the three of us looked as imposing as possible.

Brandt had told me to come to the entrance of the hospital's security office. Security was one of the departments that was directly under his management. As soon as we buzzed the intercom, the door opened. A uniformed woman opened the door and drew in a sharp breath when she saw Burrows and Mauser. I'm not sure she even noticed me.

We introduced ourselves.

"Mr. Brandt said to expect you. I've got orders to take you up to ICU. We can use the freight elevator." From her tone of voice and sideways glances, I figured that Brandt hadn't told her what our mission was.

At that hour, the back hallways of the hospital were dark and quiet. Once on the ICU floor, we passed by a nurse who pretended not to see us. I don't know if she had been warned or was simply unwilling to accept what her eyes were showing her.

At the nurses' station, I got a hard look from another one that I'd met on my daytime visits.

"I've been told to let you into your father's unit for five minutes."

"Thank—" Before I could finish, I heard Genie call my name. I'd warned her that the visit would be on the down-low, so her voice was a conspiratorial whisper.

"I told you, you didn't have to stay up," I said when she joined us.

"I wasn't going to miss this." She put her hand on my arm.

"I can't let all three... four of you go in," the nurse stuttered.

"I don't have to go." Burrows handed Mauser's leash to me.

I thought the nurse was going to argue that three was too many, but then she gave us a look that clearly said: *This was messed up anyway so whatever.*

"Five minutes, and then I want you out of the ICU and off my floor," she hissed.

Mauser, Genie and I made our way past the other units to Dad's. Mauser was doing a remarkable job of ignoring the sounds and smells of the machines and patients. But as soon as we opened the door and he saw Dad, I had to use every ounce of strength I possessed to keep him from charging ahead and smashing into thousands of dollars of medical equipment. He dragged me toward the bed, his eyes laser-focused on Dad as he ignored everything else in the room.

All the tension went out of the dog as soon as his black, rubbery nose touched Dad's hand. Mauser nuzzled and sniffed at him, licking his arm gently. I eased up beside him and touched Dad's shoulder.

"Mauser's here to see you."

"He knows," Genie whispered beside me.

There was no movement from Dad to indicate that he felt us there with him, yet we all were sure he did. Mauser licked Dad's hand again and made soft grunting sounds. I worried that I wouldn't be able to pull the dog away, but when our five minutes were up he came away with only a few backward glances.

Mauser stayed beside me as we went back down in the elevator. When I patted him, I felt him lean into me.

"He looks a whole lot more relaxed now," Burrows said, ruffling Mauser's ears.

"Oddly, I feel better too."

"It's because Mauser knows your dad's going to be fine." Burrows put one of his giant hands on my shoulder encouragingly.

Even though I didn't get home until almost two o'clock, I got a good night's sleep for the first time in days.

Cara let me sleep in again on Wednesday morning. Once I was up and dressed, I shared the milk from my cereal with Ivy and Ghost while Alvin watched enviously from the floor. As I ate, I thought about the lead I'd unwittingly discovered the day before. That stolen car was the key to Dad's attack. I felt sure that, even if the female thief hadn't done it, she had to know who did.

I picked up my phone and called Pete. The sound of his voice told me there was something big happening.

"I was just getting ready to call you." His dead neutral tone was so far from his normal, happy-go-lucky attitude that I just waited, afraid of what he had to tell me. "We found the Nissan Sentra."

He paused, but I knew there was more.

"And Terri Miller. She's dead."

CHAPTER EIGHT

I was speechless. Was it possible that my first thoughts about the surveillance video had been correct? Had that really been Terri stealing the Nissan? Had Jessie been right all along about the video from the convenience store?

"What happened to her?" I finally asked.

"You need to come down here. The body was reported just after sunrise. I've been at the scene for an hour and a half. There's... just a lot to take in." Pete gave me directions.

"I'm on my way."

"Bring some hot coffee."

Forty-five minutes later, with two containers of by then semi-hot coffee from the Donut Hole in my hands, I arrived at the scene. It was half a mile north of town down a dirt road that led to a large vacant tract of land used by hunters. The body had been found by a young man heading out to his deer stand.

Pete was standing by his car, talking with Julio. They were both blowing dragon breath in the cold morning air. They reached eagerly for the jugs of coffee and cups before nodding to me.

"It's freezing out here. Wouldn't be so bad if my feet weren't wet," Pete complained.

79

The ground was muddy from a line of showers that had moved through the area after I'd made it home the night before. Once the rain had passed, the wind took its place and the stiff breeze this morning felt like it was coming directly from the Arctic Circle.

"You can just see the car," Julio said, pointing about a hundred yards down a rutted track leading into the woods. I could see Marcus and Shantel walking on the east side of the car as they filmed the tracks and searched for evidence.

"Was it a homicide?" I asked.

"Looks like she killed herself," Pete said, his brow furrowed.

"But you don't think she did?"

"I don't know. The problem is, I've been looking for a woman who disappeared and who I thought might be in danger. But what I've found is a woman who apparently stole a car, stabbed my boss and then committed suicide. I'm finding it just a little difficult to reconcile the two."

"Other than the car, do we have any evidence that she was involved in Dad's case?"

Pete frowned and pulled up a picture on his phone. It showed a bloody knife lying on the passenger seat of the Nissan. "What do you think? We'll need to run a DNA check on the blood, but… There was a note too."

He pulled up another picture. This one showed a handwritten note on one of those cute notepads people keep on their refrigerator. This one featured daisies and butterflies. The note read: *Sorry I didn't mean to do it. Sorry sorry sorry!!!*

"How did she die?"

"Pills and carbon dioxide. It looks planned. A piece of hose from the tailpipe. Lots of duct tape holding the hose to the tailpipe *and* over the window to keep the gas from escaping. And there's an almost-empty bottle of Temazepam on the seat with her."

"Any chance she didn't commit suicide?"

"We'll know more when we get the body out of the car.

Though, if this was staged, it was well done. Her body and clothes look like she got in the car on her own and was relaxed when she went to sleep." Pete shrugged.

"There's a half empty bottle of water in there too," Julio said. "Probably for the pills."

"Makes some crazy sense." I was running through everything we knew in my mind. "If Dad saw her on the side of the road and recognized her, he would have certainly stopped."

"And not be on his guard," Pete said.

"Exactly. And if she was trying to hide, then seeing the sheriff, especially if he called her by name, might have caused her to strike out."

"That's not the craziest thing I've ever heard." Pete looked thoughtful.

"This is all speculation until we know if that's Dad's blood on the knife."

"We'll know pretty soon," Pete said.

"What about your other suspect? The one from Marianna?"

"We're scheduled to interview him this afternoon," Julio said.

"Are you going to postpone that now?"

"I don't know." Pete was staring down the road at the Sentra. He shook his head as if to clear it of all the questions swirling around inside. "We heard about Mauser's induction into the ranks of K9 officers."

"We had to do something. He was wearing himself down with worry and driving Cara nuts."

"Did it help?" Pete asked.

"Seems to. I'd like to think it helped Dad too."

"They say that a person in a coma can hear what's going on around them," Julio said.

The words were hardly out of his mouth before my phone rang with a call from Genie. "Dr. Titus has given the final okay for them to bring him out of the coma," she told me.

"You sound better."

"I'll *feel* better when he's conscious again. I think Mauser's visit was good him."

"I hope so." I went on to tell her that we might have found the person who attacked Dad.

"A girl? I thought it would be some... tough guy."

"We don't know anything for sure. I'll be at the hospital in a couple of hours." I hung up and thought about my own caseload. "I need to head to the office and get to work on your cases," I told Pete and Julio.

"We'll be here until afternoon at least," Pete said. "Look on the bright side. If this is your dad's attacker, we'll be done with the case and can get back to work on our own investigations."

"I hope this is the answer. Even if it's a very unsatisfactory one. Have you told her mother yet?"

"I want to wait until the body is at least on the way to the morgue. I'm sure she's going to want to see her."

"What exactly are you going to tell her?"

"Nothing until we have some answers."

I heard a truck speeding down the road and turned to see Jessie behind the wheel, weaving a little as the truck slued through the mud. She braked and jerked the wheel, coming to a stop inches from my car.

"It's not her!" Jessie said, hurrying over to us. Her anxious expression begged us to agree.

"Jessie, it's her," Pete said, stepping forward to stop her.

"It can't be!"

"I could tell you all the reasons I'm sure, but you don't have to believe any of it. As soon as Shantel gets done, you can see for yourself."

I wasn't sure that was such a great idea. Jessie had barely known Terri before she went missing, but in the intervening years Jessie had taken up the cause of finding Terri and had formed a bond with Terri's mother. She had invested so much time and hope into finding Terri that Terri had become as much a mission to Jessie as a person.

Julio, Pete and I nervously exchanged glances, each of us wondering the same thing. How were we going to tell Jessie about our suspicions that Terri had stabbed my father? Silently, we all decided to give her time to absorb the fact that Terri was dead before we hit her with the insult to injury.

Jessie was trying not to cry and failing as Pete wrapped his big bear paws around her shoulders. I wondered how this would affect her desire to be in law enforcement. Terri's disappearance had led her there. Would Terri's death and guilt in my father's attack turn Jessie toward a different path?

I decided that my other cases would have to wait. It was more important right then to support my friends and colleagues. We needed to get this right, and seeing Jessie reminded me that there was an emotional aspect for all of us. Pete was certainly having a hard time with it, and I wasn't sure how I felt about it myself. I couldn't be as angry with Terri Miller as I would have been at someone else. If she had attacked Dad, then she did it as a damaged person who struck out as much from fear as from anger. But then weren't most perpetrators wounded individuals? I wasn't sure about that. Some, yes, but others were as close to evil as we ever see on earth.

"We're done with the road and around the car," Shantel called, walking back toward us with Marcus. "And someone better have saved us some of that coffee!"

"You can't touch the car," Pete told Jessie, who was shifting from foot to foot, both anxious and scared to go look inside the car. "I already told you she's not pretty. She vomited before she died and her color… isn't natural."

"I'm not stupid," Jessie shot back, though her eyes were nervous. She'd seen dead bodies, but I was sure she hadn't seen the body of someone she cared about who had died so unnaturally.

"Okay. Stay close to me," Pete ordered.

"I'm coming too," I told them and followed behind as they made their way down the muddy track. I wondered how

Terri had even found the place.

"Why did she come out here?" Jessie asked, mirroring my thoughts.

"Where has she been for the last five years?" Pete responded. "There are still a lot of questions to be answered. I'm not saying that this ends our investigation."

We approached the car from the driver's side. The door was open and we could see Terri's left arm and her hip. I could tell that she was wearing a dark hoodie and jeans.

"The young man who found her opened the car door and turned off the engine," Pete explained.

"You said he was sixteen?" I asked.

"That's right. He comes out here during hunting season. According to him, there are three families that hunt the tract."

"How big is it?"

"Three hundred acres, with any number of other large-acre tracts surrounding it. The closest houses are a cluster of trailers a quarter mile back toward town. In the other direction, you have to go almost twice that far before coming to an old homestead. There are two or three houses there."

Jessie was shaking slightly as she looked at Terri's body. I thought it was a mercy that Terri's face was hidden from view, the body slumped over toward the passenger seat. But Jessie wasn't going to let it go. She leaned in until she was able to see Terri's face, then she stepped back, breathing hard.

"It's okay," I said, putting my hand on her back to steady her. "Take slow, deep breaths, not shallow, quick ones."

"I'm okay. It's her." Jessie's voice was cold and flat.

"I'm sorry."

"What am I going to tell her mother?" Jessie said.

"I'll tell her." Pete's voice was soft and kind.

"I have to be there with her."

"We can do that," Pete said. "I can drive you over there and we'll tell her together."

"Yes."

With Jessie composed, I looked into the car as best I could without touching anything. I could see the knife, the bottle of pills and the note as Pete had described. I noticed that the seatbelt was unfastened.

"Was the radio on?" I asked.

"The boy who found her didn't say. We'll find out when we start the car, unless he turned it off."

Was that even important? I had no idea.

"Whose case is this?" Jessie asked.

Pete and I looked at each other. "Mine and Julio's," Pete told her.

"I thought Larry was covering all of your cases, including Terri's."

I didn't want Pete to tell her why it was his case.

"We think the car was involved in another crime," Pete said quickly, with the forlorn hope that she wouldn't ask the next natural question.

"Which case? I thought you were only working on…" Then it dawned on her. "No way."

"The car is the same make and model," Pete explained.

"You can't know for sure that this is the same car." She was facing me with accusing eyes.

"No, we don't," I agreed. "Maybe it wasn't. However, this car was stolen the night before Dad was stabbed."

"She didn't steal the car!" Jessie insisted.

"We need to stop discussing this," Pete said.

"Why?"

"Because there is an open investigation and, even though you've been working as an intern with the department, I don't think it's a good idea for you to know any more than what you do…" She started to get up in his face and Pete put his hand up to stop her. "…at this time. Just at this time. You're going to talk to her mother and… other people. We just need to keep a handle on this information. Honestly, you shouldn't be here either," he added, looking at me.

"You're right," I said to Pete. "Jessie, I'll walk back with you."

She glared at both of us before turning and stalking back to the cars. Her back was stiff, and I could feel the heat of anger and frustration coming off of her as I followed.

She turned toward me when we reached the cars. "I'm not going to let you smear her name."

"I have no agenda here except to find the person who stabbed my father. I'm not even working the case."

"I bet!" She crossed her arms.

Shantel and Marcus, who had put up their cameras and video equipment and retrieved their evidence-gathering paraphernalia, kept their eyes to the ground as they walked past us on their way back to the Nissan.

I realized it wouldn't do any good to try to reason with Jessie right then, so I bit my tongue. A glance at my watch told me that I needed to head to the hospital. There wasn't much else I could do at the scene anyway. If the blood on the knife was Dad's, that's when things would get interesting.

"They're going to try bringing Dad out of his coma, so I'm heading into the hospital," I told a tight-lipped Jessie.

The silence grew and I thought she wasn't going to say anything.

"I really, really hope he's okay," she finally mumbled to my back as I headed for my car.

"Thank you," I said, and started the car.

I called Cara on the way to Tallahassee and filled her in on the latest developments.

"Do you want me to meet you at the hospital?" she asked.

"Yes, but don't. We have no idea how long it will take for him to regain consciousness. You're being a huge help taking care of Mauser."

"Jamie's doing the hard work. He said Mauser has been eating and is much more relaxed after last night."

"The poor boy saw Dad stabbed and knocked unconscious. Who can blame him for being upset? Now that he knows Dad is... if not okay, at least still... well, you know what I mean."

"Give your dad and Genie my love," Cara said and we hung up.

"He's responding." Genie smiled at me as I joined her in the waiting room.

"And the swelling is down?"

"'Improved' was the word Dr. Titus used. But one of the nurses who's been very nice said that's an understatement. She told me she overheard the surgeon talking with the radiologist. Did I tell you they did another scan? Anyway, the radiologist said the improvement was marked and the swelling should be completely gone by tomorrow if the rate of improvement continues."

I smiled for what felt like the first time in a week.

At one o'clock they let us in to see him. His eyes looked unfocused and he kept licking his lips.

"Hi, you." His voice was hoarse and his words slightly slurred. Neither Genie nor I knew which one of us he was talking to. I'm not sure he did. I urged her to step up beside his bed.

"Hello back." Genie was all smiles.

"I'm in the hospital?"

"Yes. There was… an incident." Genie clutched his hand.

"Oh." He looked puzzled.

"Larry is here," she told him, pointing to me.

"Who?"

"Hey, Dad." I stepped up beside Genie.

"Larry. What happened? Was anyone else hurt?" Dad looked around as though he expected to still be at the scene of some sort of carnage.

"No, Dad. Just you, and you're going to be okay."

"Good. My head feels like it's full of molasses," he muttered. "I think I'd better sleep."

"We'll let you rest." Genie patted his hand and turned away, her initial happiness tempered by the reality of seeing Dad.

A nurse met us at the door to his unit. "He's really doing very well," she told us encouragingly. "It's just going to take a day or so for him to get oriented."

"Do they think he'll make a full recovery?" Genie asked.

"I can't say anything about that. But I've seen people who came out of comas in much worse shape than he is, and they were fine after they recovered." She patted Genie on the arm and gave her a reassuring smile. "Y'all don't need to wait up here. He'll probably sleep for twelve hours. We'll continually check in on him to make sure he's doing okay, but he won't be in any shape to talk to visitors until tomorrow."

Genie promised to go home and get a little rest, then I headed down to the morgue. I wanted to talk to Dr. Darzi about Terri Miller's autopsy.

CHAPTER NINE

I found Darzi in his office, which was filled with ghoulish models, drawings and sealed containers holding all manner of the macabre.

"No bodies to chop up?" I asked him.

"Very droll, Deputy Macklin. Even a dedicated public servant such as myself needs a break now and then." He waved his hand for me to sit down, not taking his eyes off of the two computer monitors in front of him, both of which were larger than the TV we'd had when I was a kid.

"Am I bothering you?"

"I'm just comparing an X-ray taken last year with one I took during a recent autopsy. It's a question of how much force it would have taken to break the man's back. He was sixty-six years old and suffering from back problems. You can see the bone loss along his spine, here and here." Darzi pointed at the screen on his left. "Now here's where the fracture occurred when his brother either forcefully hit him and knocked him down or accidentally bumped him, causing him to fall."

"The fall killed him?"

"He suffered a stroke that was a complication of the broken spine." Darzi leaned back in his chair. "I'm guessing you came here to talk about the body your colleagues are sending me."

"I just want to make sure that you look at all the possibilities." As soon as I said it, I knew it sounded foolish.

"So you want me to do a good job on this autopsy." He smiled. "Unlike my usual half-assed efforts."

"You know what I mean."

"Yes, I know. I'm also planning to do a forensic analysis of the knife they found to determine whether it could have inflicted the wound that your father sustained. I've already assembled a file with your father's medical notes."

"*Mea culpa* for doubting you," I said.

"Ron called and told me I owe him one for talking him into letting you and your—I believe he called it a *dogiphant*— into the hospital."

"I had to resort to blackmail. What *did* happen in Antiqua?"

"Not as much as he thinks." Darzi laughed. "When the woman left his room, she made some very disparaging remarks about his performance." He paused for a moment, smiling at the memory. "I hear your father is doing better. I'm glad to hear it."

"Yes. Thank you."

Darzi gave a little bow. "Now you owe *me*." His smile widened.

"That sounds ominous."

"It's worse because I have nothing I need from you now. But one day I will call and you will answer."

"I knew what I was getting myself into. It was worth it."

"Now what do you suspect about the young woman?"

I shrugged. "Honestly, I don't have a clue. Something."

"You're flailing. I will do my best. Linda has already given me her general impressions from the scene. Assuming she took an overdose of pills before the carbon monoxide overcame her, a case like this will be tricky because everyone reacts differently to an overdose. Assuming that this is actually a suicide. Assuming, assuming, assuming. Until I have the young woman's body on the table and can examine her, I won't know anything." Darzi looked directly at me. "I know this is a special case for you. Your father is a very fine man and you care for him like the good son you are. But now you will have to trust me. I will take all of the evidence found at the scene, and all of the evidence that the body can give to me, and then—and only then—I will be able to give you my best evaluation."

I stood up. "Of course. Pete or Julio will attend. This isn't officially my case."

He gave me a fatherly smile. "Get some rest. We'll know more in a few days."

After checking on Dad one more time, I headed back to Adams County, though with no intention of resting. There was too much work waiting for me. I still had my cluster of high-end car thefts to work on, as well as a dozen other cases that needed attention.

When I got to the office, I saw Pete getting out of his car in the parking lot. He waved me over, his expression grim.

"Jessie and I just informed Mrs. Miller of her daughter's death."

"Fun times," I said with gallows humor.

"This was one of the worst. Jessie tried to help, but she was in almost as bad a shape as Mrs. Miller. I don't know. I feel like I failed them." Pete was clearly taking it hard.

"You did all you can with a missing person case."

"I know. They just get under my skin. You don't have a solid crime to get your hook into. More than half the time there's no crime to investigate. A person walks off and... that's it... they walked off. No law against it. And in a case like Terri's, I felt sure that there were only two options. Either she walked off and would be back, or she was dead. Turns out both were probably true. She walked off and now she's dead." I could tell that his frustration wanted to turn into anger or self-pity, but he couldn't seem to decide which.

"I don't know if I want her to be guilty of stabbing your dad or not. If she's guilty, then we can move on. But on the other hand, to think that your dad came this close to dying because of a distraught young woman that he stopped to help… it's just kind of crazy. But I'll follow this wherever it leads me, if she's guilty or not."

"What about the kid who found her? Anything there?" I asked, opening the door to the building and trying to distract Pete from his dark thoughts.

"Nice young man. Goes to high school. Helps out at his dad's business. Polite. A little shaken up about finding a body. I'm going to check up on his timeline, make sure there aren't any gaps he can't account for… but I think he's clean."

"*Could* she have been killed?" I was asking myself as much as Pete.

"Maybe. Someone gets her to drink a cocktail of sleeping pills and then sits her up in the car with the engine running."

"I'd be more confident no one else was involved if we had her face on camera stealing that car."

Pete nodded. "We should try to get that truck driver, Kyle, into the office. See if he can pick her out of a photo lineup."

"Can I be there?"

"I don't see why not. Either she stabbed your father, in which case there will never be a trial so what harm can it do if you're there? Or she wasn't involved, in which case this is your investigation anyway."

"There's a third option. She might not have actually stabbed Dad, but she was somehow involved."

"It's possible. I wish our witness hadn't driven down the road to her car. If there were tracks from another car, he wiped them out. I can't see someone setting her up on that dirt road a quarter mile into the woods without a vehicle to get them home. They would have had to drive the car back there and have someone else pick them up. Which means there'd have to be two more people involved. Seems a bit of a stretch," Pete said.

"And what would be their motive for killing her if she stabbed my dad?"

"That brings us back to the question, was your dad set up or was it just a coincidence that he was stabbed?"

"Maybe he drove up on something else going down and was attacked because he'd witnessed it, or it was a trap set for *anyone* who stopped."

Pete shook his head. "I think if it was Terri, then it was just happenstance. She panicked when she knew she'd been recognized."

"What was she running from?"

"Good question. When I was doing all the background on her as a missing person, I never saw any reason why she would take a runner. That was why I was so sure she'd been abducted."

"Secrets can be well hidden."

"But if she'd stolen money from her employer or anything like that, it would have surfaced by now. There was no hint that anyone was harassing her. She had a boyfriend, but the relationship seemed casual on both sides. There was no indication that drugs were a factor." Pete shrugged.

"She was hiding for some reason."

"But why the long gap and then she all of a sudden pops up?"

"We wouldn't have known she was around at all if it hadn't been for us pulling the security footage from the Fast Mart a couple of months ago."

"True. I still feel like if she'd been in town when she first went missing, then we would have found her."

"Maybe she left town for a while and then came back," I suggested.

"I like that explanation better than believing that we searched the county high and low and she was here the whole time."

Pete headed for his desk, still looking dejected. I settled down to work on some of my own cases, trying not to think about Dad lying in that hospital bed looking drained of all his vitality.

I managed to get a hot lead on one of Julio's burglaries. A pawnshop in Tallahassee had accepted some very specialized woodworking tools that had been stolen from a truck in Adams County. The suspect was a crack addict who hadn't even tried to hide his identity when he'd brought the stolen goods in to be pawned. The perp's last known address was in Tallahassee, so I called a friend with TPD who was more than glad to go pick him up for me.

Savoring one small victory, I grabbed a Coke from the vending machine, then sat back down at my desk. The file on the high-end auto thefts taunted me. Wanting to take a more proactive approach on that one, I picked up the phone and called Darlene.

"How's your dad doing?" she asked.

"He's out of the coma. We're hoping for the best."

"I've got my grandmother sending prayers up for him. She's closer to the Big Guy than anyone else I know."

"Thanks. Hey, I want to come up with a plan to catch this car thief."

"Funny, I've been thinking about that. I've identified cameras on every road into and out of town. It's not perfect, just a mix of our city cameras and privately owned ones. But most of the thefts have taken place within the city, so if he steals another one, we should be able to review all the footage."

"That might work, 'cause I doubt he's keeping these cars in town. Probably heading out of Dodge as soon as he gets them running."

"Exactly. We might at least get a fuzzy image of our thief."

"Might do better than that. If he runs true to form for most professional car thieves, he's got at least one accomplice who's dropping him off at the site of the crime."

"And following him out of town. If any of the cameras I have on my list can pick up a license plate, the plate on his accomplice's car are probably legit."

"Exactly. He wouldn't want some cop running his plates and pulling him over."

Darlene signed. "I miss this. We work well together, Sancho."

"I think I'm Quixote," I corrected her.

"You *are* Adams County's Tilt-at-Windmills champion."

"This is good. I like having a plan. Now we just have to wait until the bad boys make their next move."

"I'll alert all my officers to inform me immediately if they catch a car theft."

"I'll do the same with our deputies."

We patted ourselves on the back a couple more times before hanging up. With that plan in place, I turned to the other thorn in my side, the ATM attack, and headed down to Lionel's office.

"Have you seen Jessie?" I asked him. Though after what Pete had told me, I didn't really expect to find her working.

"Not since this morning, when she went flying out of here like a bat out of hell." Lionel turned away from his monitor and looked at me. "Was the woman y'all found this morning the one she's been looking for?"

I told him what we knew.

"Damn, that's rough."

"I'm not really surprised that she hasn't been back. Do you know how far she'd gotten on the surveillance video?"

"She's been through all of the footage you'd given her and about half of the USB from Julio."

"I called a few more places downtown that are going to pull footage from the time of the ATM attack. I might be going through that video myself."

"Get one of the patrol officers who wants to move into investigations to go through it," Lionel suggested.

"Good idea, but we're so shorthanded right now that I don't think we can pull anyone off the road for that long." We'd recently received some of the federal reimbursement money we'd been promised after the hurricane a year ago, and could finally see a bit of light at the end of the tunnel, but Dad still had several positions to fill. There were at least three in patrol and one in CID, not to mention the command hole left by Lt. Johnson's departure in November.

"Major Parks isn't going to hire anyone without your dad's okay."

"Like I said, I might be sitting here with you before the week's over."

I left Lionel and decided to call Eddie. Truth was, I was more than a little worried about Jessie.

"She called me all upset," Eddie told me. "I tried to get her to come to the library, but she didn't want to."

"You don't think she'll do anything crazy, do you?"

"We're talking about Jessie," he reminded me. We both knew that she could be impulsive with a capital "I" when she got up a head of steam.

"Yeah, that's exactly what I'm worried about. What did she say to you?"

"Not much. I could tell she'd been crying, so I didn't want to stir things up too much. All she said was that she didn't believe Terri had done anything wrong and that her mother was all tore up."

"Terri's mother is a good lead. I'll call her and see if Jessie went back there."

"That's possible. They've gotten pretty close."

I made Eddie promise to let me know if he heard anything from Jessie, then I hung up. Taking a deep breath, I thought about what I would say to Terri's mother. I didn't want to do anything that would cause her more pain. Was it even possible for a grieving parent to feel *more* pain? *Yeah, if you accuse her dead child of having committed murder*, I thought. If we settled on Terri as Dad's attacker, would we be able to keep it quiet? Dead people never got their day in court and, if she was openly accused, there would be no way for her mother to remove that stain from her memory. With all of those thoughts circulating in my brain, I dialed her number.

"No, she's sleeping," said the voice that answered the

phone. "I'm her cousin. We finally got her to take a mild sedative and lay down."

"Has a young woman named Jessie Gilmore come by the house?"

"Jessie? I know Jessie. She helped out with the searches. I haven't seen her."

I gave the cousin my number and asked her to call if she heard from Jessie.

Where is she? One more person to be worried about, I grumbled to myself.

It was time to call it a day. But before heading home, I decided to stop and pick up some of the security camera footage from the stores downtown that had promised to download it for me. Getting the footage was always easier said than done. Half the time they wound up giving you the wrong day or time. Driving around, I could also keep an eye out for Jessie's truck.

Most of the USBs were waiting for me, though two stores had to be reminded. I didn't see any sign of Jessie, so I widened my search, driving past her place and the garage apartment where Eddie lived. Finally heading for home, I called Genie and wasn't surprised to learn that she'd gone back to the hospital.

"I know there isn't any reason for me to be here. I just want to stay close. I did go by Jimmy's place and tell him a little of what's been going on. He thought it was cool that you took Mauser to see your dad. I just hope Ted will be able to talk to Jimmy when I bring him to the hospital."

"Jimmy can handle this." He often seemed to have insights into life that a lot of us couldn't see. I'd also noticed that, while he wore his emotions on his sleeve, his ability to internalize and move on was better than most of the people I knew. "Call me if there's any news."

"You know I will. Your father would want you out doing your job."

"Truer words were never spoken. Still, I'll be there if you need me."

"I promise I'll call."

CHAPTER TEN

Mauser met me at the door while Ghost did flips on the arm of the couch. Ivy and Alvin simply stared at me from beside their food bowls in the kitchen. I could hear the shower running. Cara usually liked to clean off the medicinal smell of the clinic when she got home. As for me, it depended on what I'd had to deal with at work. Today, I wanted to clean off the memories of seeing Terri slumped over in the car and Dad helpless in his hospital bed. I met Cara coming out of the bathroom as I was going in and we exchanged a quick kiss.

After dinner, I brought my laptop to the kitchen table and tried to do a little bit of work. In reality, I spent most of the time repeatedly glancing at my phone to see if I had somehow missed a call or text with information about Dad or Jessie.

"It's sweet of you to be so worried about her," Cara said from the couch after she saw me check my phone for the tenth time. "She sure pissed you off when you first met her."

"Jessie's like Eddie: they're both so crazy they grow on you. The trouble is, she'd gotten a picture of Terri fixed in her head and everything she saw today flipped that over. I don't want her doing anything rash."

"Do you think she might?"

"I don't know. She's just made some off-the-wall moves in the past. I'd hate to see her lose focus on her law enforcement career."

"You weren't too keen on that when she first told you she wanted to be a cop," Cara observed.

"She's put in a lot of hours since then. I hope she can see this as a learning experience. Keeping an emotional distance from your victim and your suspects is important."

"Ha! Pot, meet kettle," Cara guffawed.

"Yeah, yeah. I hear you."

Mauser got up from the floor at Cara's feet and came into the kitchen, dropping his big head onto the table. He looked at me with his big brown eyes, his raised eyebrows making it clear it wasn't me he was coming to see. His eyes shifted to the treat jar on the counter.

"Damn it, you've been through too much lately to ignore you." I got up and retrieved one of the special dog cookies that one of the vet techs made for all of the clients at Christmas. Two chomps and the biscuit was gone. I started to sit back down, but then Ghost hopped onto the table.

"What have I told you about being on the table?" I lectured him before picking him up and giving him a treat in his food bowl.

At eleven, I got a text from Eddie. Unfortunately, it wasn't the news I wanted. *I haven't heard from her. Very worried.* The text was followed by half a dozen sad emojis. My hand hovered over the phone, wanting to just text him back, but in the end I gave him a call. Eddie didn't need this stress either.

"She'll be fine," I tried to console him, after spending the first five minutes of the call trying to stop him from hyperventilating.

"This isn't like her. I know she's really upset."

"People get upset, but they get over it. You know she's a strong, independent-minded person." There was silence from the other end of the phone. "Isn't she?" I pushed.

"Yes." His voice was sulky.

"Have you talked with her roommates?"

"Duh! They're worried too."

"If we haven't heard from her by morning, I'll issue a health and safety check BOLO for her and her truck. I'd do it now, but you know that if she's okay it would just piss her off and make her feel worse."

"*If* she's okay," Eddie grumbled.

"Have you talked to your sponsor?" More silence. "Eddie?"

"Yes."

"What did he say?"

"Don't fall back on drugs."

"Good advice."

"He also said that Jessie's probably just taking some time for herself."

"That makes sense, doesn't it?"

"Yes."

"Did your sponsor say you could call him later if you needed to?"

"Of course. That's what they're there for."

"You can call me too."

"Even if it's really late?"

I wanted more than anything to say no. Instead, "Sure."

"How's your dad?"

"Doing better."

"I'm glad."

"Get some rest, Eddie."

Cara and I both had a restless night. There was too much to worry about. In the end, I got up before dawn on Thursday morning. I wanted to get moving, whether it was in the right direction or not.

After walking the dogs and feeding everyone, I said goodbye to Cara and headed into the office. The rising sun was casting a cold blue light over the parking lot as I drove in. To my intense relief, I spotted Jessie's truck parked near the back. My text alert went off as I parked beside her. She looked up from her phone and gave me an uncertain smile before looking back at her screen. With a quick glance at my own phone, I found a message from Eddie, saying that he had finally heard from her.

By the time I got out of my car, Jessie was coming toward me with her head down.

"We've been wondering where you were," I told her, trying hard to keep from sounding judgmental. Yes, I was irritated that she'd worried us all, but she was an autonomous adult who felt things deeply. If going off on her own for a while helped her clear her head and deal with her grief, then so be it.

"Sorry." She still wouldn't look at me.

"Don't be," I said, causing her to raise her eyes. "You've had a lot to deal with. How was Eddie?"

"I think he's angry with me."

"He's a big boy. He'll get over it. But there's a reason why they don't want folks in the twelve-step program getting involved in relationships too soon."

"We're not in…" She stopped. "Funny, I never thought of it as a relationship."

"Why are you here?"

"I still want to know what happened to Terri."

"When did you realize that your mission hadn't changed?"

"I *don't* think she killed herself or did anything to your dad." Her eyes were stubborn.

"Can you put what you think behind you and follow the evidence?"

Jessie took a deep breath and looked up into the branches of the live oak tree that covered the corner of the parking area. "I don't know."

"That, young lady, is the right answer. Every case I work, I have to suppress some impression or bias."

"I don't understand the difference between having a

hunch and being… biased in one direction."

"The hunch… Come on, let's get in out of the cold." I waved her toward the building and held the door open for her. "A hunch is based on your experience as an investigator, or at least your life experiences. You're fine to say that you have a hunch Terri didn't kill herself or stab Dad. The difference comes with how willing you are to give up your hunch when it's proven wrong. I've had to eat my hunches more than once."

Jessie looked thoughtful. "I've read true crime books where the case went off in a wrong direction because the detective didn't follow the evidence."

"That's all I'm saying. Making sure you aren't holding onto a hunch for the wrong reasons. For those detectives who can't let go of an idea or suspect, even when they're proven wrong, it's often pride that's keeping them from moving onto the right track."

I opened the door to Lionel's office and turned on the lights. A glance at my watch told me he wouldn't be in for at least another half hour. "Can you get started without Lionel?"

Jessie nodded. "He gave me my own password to the computer I'm using."

"Good, 'cause I've got a lot more footage for you to go over." I smiled and pulled out the additional USBs I'd collected the night before.

"Great," she said, trying to sound irritated, but I could hear the relief in her voice. Relief that the world wasn't going to end even though she'd had the wind knocked out of her.

As I turned to leave, she said, "I'd like to know what they find during the autopsy."

"I'll tell you what I can," I promised.

I was pleasantly surprised to find the inbox on my desk empty of any new reports from the night before. Major Parks had doubled down on having patrol cover cases by asking the watch commanders to contact him directly if there was a shooting or a murder. He'd been assigning the few of those we'd had to sergeants.

Parks might have occasionally come across as a bit of a stodgy pencil-pusher, but I couldn't fault him for the way he'd stepped up since Dad's attack. With no new reports to deal with, I opened the files and went back to work clearing the old ones.

I was surprised when my phone rang with Dad's distinctive gunshot ringtone.

"Larry?" His voice was hoarse but recognizable.

"Dad! How are you feeling?" Getting this call from Dad warmed my heart, which was a very new experience.

"Fine," he said and I almost laughed out loud.

"Bullshit!" I responded.

"Yeah, yeah, okay. I feel like I got run over by a herd of buffalo. Is that what you wanted to hear?"

"You know I'm just playing with you. We've been worried."

"I know. I wish I could tell you what happened."

"The neurologist said you'd lose at least a day."

"I've been trying hard to think…"

"Don't tire yourself out," I heard Genie say in the background.

"You should rest. I'll be over around lunch," I told him.

"You're probably slammed with work."

"I've got some things I can do in Tallahassee."

"Oh, okay. I've got a list of things I need you to do at the house. I'll text it to you when I hang up." His voice was becoming weaker.

"Hang up now. Larry told you he'll be here around noon," Genie told him.

"Okay, bye," Dad told me. Before he managed to disconnect the call, I heard him telling Genie, "He needs to be working. We were shorthanded before—"

I sighed and smiled. The smile lasted until I received the promised text listing a dozen things he wanted me to do at his house while he was in the hospital. They included turning off the water to the barn if the temperature was going to fall below thirty degrees, make sure there was feed for the horses, starting his truck and running it around, and even to ride Finn and Mac. I sighed again and went back to work.

I was able to add a few things to my to-do list while I was in Tallahassee, including attending Terri Miller's autopsy. I hadn't planned on going until I got a text from Pete telling me that the autopsy would take place at one o'clock. I took the timing to mean that I was meant to be there, though I didn't really know what I hoped to learn.

I checked in with Jessie before I headed out.

"I think I've found something," she said somberly.

I came around behind her and looked at the monitor. She switched windows and clicked a video. "This is a clip from the Shell station at the corner of Georgia Street and Lorring Avenue. It's about three miles from where your dad was stabbed, but it's a straight shot." She stopped the video when a blur crossed the upper right-hand corner of the screen. She slowed it down before stopping it at a frame that contained the left half of a vehicle that looked much like a silver Nissan Sentra.

I looked closely at the image. "Run it back and then forward at half speed."

"We can probably enhance it some," Lionel called over to us.

"You can't see if anyone is in the passenger seat," I said. The camera was on the roof that covered the station's gas pumps and was focused on the islands where the pumps were located. It was just happenstance that it also picked up the eastbound lane of Lorring Avenue. Unfortunately, the angle only showed the driver's side of the car.

"I think that's her," Jessie said flatly.

"I'd have to agree."

The woman driving was wearing a hoodie, but the hood was down so you could see her hair. She was focused on the road with her hands at the ten-and-two position.

"What's on the other side of the street?" Jessie asked as much to herself as to me. "That's the old flower shop. No cameras there. But now that I've got a time stamp and the name of a street, if I can find any footage from the other side of the street, I might be able to see if anyone's in the passenger seat."

I was impressed to hear her thinking like an investigator.

"Does the car have any GPS data?" I asked Lionel.

"No such luck. There were plenty of cars built that year that would have had an uplink or onboard that stored information, but not that one. Good news is that there was a cell phone in the car. Just a cheap, pay-as-you-go kind, but Pete should be able to get the ping data for it."

"Any luck with the ATM attack?" I asked Jessie as she stopped to make notes of places she wanted to check for camera footage.

"Sorry, I've spent most... all of my time this morning going over Pete's and Julio's stuff."

"I understand."

"But I plan on working all day. Promise I'll get to it this afternoon." She continued to make notes as she talked.

The sky was clear blue and the sun bright as I walked out of the sheriff's office. I was feeling optimistic for the first time in days. Everything seemed to be pulling together. Dad was on the road to recovery. Jessie had gotten her balance back after taking a hard knock. I could see my workload start to return to a manageable level. Of course, the way Dad's case was ending wasn't the way I would have wished. I'd envisioned a clear-cut case of someone who was out to get Dad having ambushed him on the road. Though the more I thought about that, it just didn't make sense that the person wouldn't have finished him off. However, I was confident that only a few days would show us where the evidence was pointing.

When I got up to the ICU, I was told they'd moved Dad down to a regular room. *Better and better*, I thought.

"I'm sorry I didn't tell you they'd moved him," Genie said when I ran into her outside of his room.

"No worries, this is great," I said, and then saw her face.

"What's wrong?"

She bit her lip. "The doctor said to expect some memory loss. I guess I was just thinking it would be from the day he was attacked, not..."

"What?"

"Like words. I don't... Just come in. I think you'll see."

Dad was fiddling with his phone when we entered the room.

"Larry, did you get the list I texted you?"

"I'm on it." I smiled and walked over to the bed.

"This thing is driving me crazy." His words were a little slurred.

"What are you trying to do?"

"Just find my messages." He held the phone out to me. "Stupid..." He got a puzzled look on his face. "Ah... tea... whatever you call it."

I felt all the anxiety I'd shed over the last few hours come crashing back. I pressed the message icon and pulled up his texts before handing the phone back to him. For a second I wondered if we should be letting him text. But what could I do, take the phone away from him?

I glanced over at Genie, who knew what I was thinking and understood my concern. With a frown, she shrugged.

"What's Major..." Dad furrowed his brow. "...you know, what's-his-name. How's it going?" There was frustration bordering on anger in his eyes.

"You know you don't have to worry about Major Parks. We're doing what we need to do to cover all the bases."

"Who the hell stabbed me?" He put his hand over his chest.

"We aren't sure yet. Pete and Julio are working on the case. There was a suicide that could be linked to it." I didn't think I should tell him too much at this point.

"Makes me crazy that the attack and the events leading up to it are a blank. Last thing I can remember is the night before, coming home in my rake and doing some chores," Dad said, unaware that he'd used the wrong word for truck.

Thinking of his slightly slurred speech and forgotten words, I wondered if he'd had a stroke. Or were they just missing pieces caused by the trauma to his brain? I wanted to talk with the doctor again.

"Can you think of anyone who might have wanted to hurt you?"

"I've made a few enemies in the past. I've been in law enforcement for over... ten or something years." In truth it had been over thirty years. How much had he lost?

Dad pressed his hand against his head and Genie stepped toward him. "Are you all right?"

"What do you think?" he snapped. Then he grimaced and apologized. "Sorry, my head is pounding."

She squeezed his hand and gave me a pained looked.

"Can I get you something?" I asked, feeling helpless.

"Get the nurse. Some water and... if I can have a pill or anything for the headache." His eyes were closed and there was a sheen of sweat on his forehead.

"I'll find someone."

I left with the intention of finding a nurse to send back to the room before I went looking for a doctor who could tell me if the memory problems and pain would pass. The nurse was easy. The doctor took a little longer. A neurologist who was consulting on Dad's case, Dr. Stella Burke, agreed to meet me in the cafeteria.

"Sorry, but I haven't had a bite to eat since I got here at five."

"You always come in that early?" I asked her.

She squared her broad shoulders and picked up her tray. Her eyes were both soft and serious. "I do when I get called in. Nasty motorcycle accident." She had piled her tray with carbs and a large tea from the soda fountain. "Let's go over by the window. I like to at least look out on the real world occasionally." Despite what she had recently seen, she had a perpetual smile on her face. It was a nice change from Dr. Titus.

"He's as good as he thinks he is. If your dad needs

surgery, you couldn't do any better," Burke assured me when I mentioned the surgeon.

"*Will* Dad need surgery?"

"No. Okay, I shouldn't give you a flat answer. At least that's what the liability seminars always tell us," she said, picking up some of fries from her plate and dipping them liberally in ketchup.

"We get told stuff like that too. I appreciate your honesty. I also appreciate hearing the good news. What's worrying me is his memory loss and slurred words."

"He might have had a small stroke. I noticed the slur, but it's slight. I'd expect that to go away in a couple of days. The memory loss is to be expected. TBI can have serious effects."

"I understood that he'd forget the time around the attack. I've seen that in other victims. What's bothering me is his misuse of words and confusion about time."

"His brain has undergone a lot of punishment. He's going to have to work through it. The more he gets back to real life, the better. He should read out loud, that will help."

"But he doesn't have any permanent brain damage?" I knew I was begging to be reassured.

"Of course he has damage. The good news is that the brain will work around it." Burke put her gyro down and looked me in the eye. "What you want to know is if your dad will be okay. The answer is yes, with my grandmother's caveat that the good Lord is willing and the creek don't rise. I'm going to tell you what I told him and his fiancée. He cannot take another blow to the head for at least six months. A year would be better."

"He's pretty active," I said, trying to sound her out on what she was actually saying. "Are you talking about... I don't know. What are you saying? What activities would you limit?"

"Physically, he won't feel like doing much for a week or two. He'll have the headaches for a while. Once he's feeling better, he should refrain from doing anything that has a higher than normal chance of giving himself another concussion."

"He rides horses."

"I'd suggest that he not. Or at least be very careful. In a few months, he could ride a calm horse at a walk. And he should certainly wear a helmet. Same thing goes for bike riding. Slow and careful. Another blow like that and he'll see permanent, long-term damage."

I thanked her and left her to finish her lunch. I felt marginally better having leeched some positive news off the doctor and headed back upstairs to share it with Genie. I thought about

trying to question Dad again about possible enemies, but decided that Pete or Julio should probably ask the questions. Instead, I listened as Dad added half a dozen more items to my to-do list before I left for the autopsy.

CHAPTER ELEVEN

I found Pete waiting outside the morgue.

"Julio didn't make it?" I asked.

"We can't all have fun," Pete said grimly. He wasn't a fan of autopsies. "He won the toss, so he's going to Marianna to check on Fred Durrell's alibi. We've postponed interviewing him, but it'd be nice to know if we can eliminate him altogether."

"And if the blood on the knife comes back as a match for Dad's?"

"I'm still going to look under the bushes. Though if it's the knife used in the attack, and we have the car, and it looks like Terri was driving it within the timeframe of the attack, it becomes hard to move her out of the suspect-number-one chair." Pete shrugged.

"Maybe the autopsy will change things," I suggested.

We found Dr. Darzi already working over Terri's body, assisted by his newest intern, Andre. The man dwarfed everyone else in the room other than Pete, and that was due more to weight than height. He'd told me that he'd earned the nickname Andre the Giant by the time he was ten.

"We've already taken X-rays," Darzi said, pointing to the monitors above the examination table. "An old injury to her leg which looks like it occurred years before her disappearance." He indicated a line across her right femur. "She also has two fewer ribs than most women. Everything else looks average for a female of her age, size and reported health."

Darzi began a detailed examination of Terri's body, starting at the bottom.

"Her feet are dirty and the toenails haven't been trimmed recently." He continued making notes on the body's condition, reaching the opinion that Terri had been in good health, though she hadn't been paying much attention to her personal hygiene. "That's typical of a homeless person, or someone who's being abused or has a mental health problem that is not being treated."

"Collect what you can from under her fingernails and toenails," Pete said. "We still don't know where she's spent the last five years."

"Linda collected what she could at the scene and we vacuumed the body before you arrived," Darzi told us.

"When you were looking her over, you said she showed signs of being sexually active. Would you say that the activity was consensual?" I asked.

"There's no sign of bruising or injuries that you would expect to see if the victim fought an attacker. That doesn't exclude the possibility that she was drugged or held at knife-point."

They turned the body onto its stomach.

"Do you see the color of the lividity in the buttocks? Bright red is a sign of carbon monoxide poisoning. This can also occur in the case of hypothermia or cyanide poisoning. I've already sent blood samples for a full analysis. The level of carboxyhemoglobin in her blood will most likely be a determinate in this case."

Finished with the external examination, they turned the body again and Darzi began the Y-incision across Terri's chest. Out of the corner of my eye, I saw Pete look away. I didn't blame him. All the weighing and measuring of organs always reminded me of some sort of pagan ritual.

"Here's the part you're interested in," Darzi said as he carefully began to exam the esophagus. "She did vomit shortly before her death, as you had noted. I looked at the contents, which included five partially digested sleeping tablets. I think what is most interesting is that she was at least partially conscious when she vomited. Her esophagus is almost completely clear of the bile and stomach contents, as was her mouth. Which leads one to assume that she bent over and expelled the contents that rose up from her stomach."

"It looked like she'd at least made an attempt to throw up into a cup in the car," Pete said.

"It's possible that someone might have held her up and helped her to clear her mouth and throat," Darzi suggested.

"But if she was conscious, that would imply it was a suicide." Pete looked like he was trying to keep from barfing himself.

Darzi collected the contents from Terri's stomach into a bag that he sealed and labeled. "I see pieces of partially digested pills and bits of food. Ground meat and French fries, I think… some sort of fast food."

"Maybe the truck stop," Pete said.

"There isn't anywhere else around there to get a hamburger and fries at night," I agreed.

"We didn't find any fast food bags in the car."

According to Darzi, the condition of Terri's lungs was also consistent with carbon monoxide poisoning.

"When the bloodwork comes back, I'll be able to give you a definitive answer as to cause of death. For now, I think you can take carbon monoxide poisoning as a running hypothesis. Your job is to decide if it was deliberate or not. Suicide, accident or homicide?" Darzi smiled at us as Andre rolled Terri's body back to the cooler.

"We're going over every detail of the scene and the car to determine if it could have been an accident," Pete said.

"It's not unknown. I've read case files of people who

were just trying to stay warm in their cars. If the tailpipe is blocked or there are holes in the exhaust system allowing fumes to enter the interior of the car… they just slowly pass out and die."

"What about homicide?" I interjected.

"So far, the evidence for that is lacking," Pete said. "Strangely, I'd feel better if it was murder."

"Though that would bring up a whole host of other questions," I admitted.

"That's for you gumshoes to figure out. And you can do it somewhere other than my autopsy room. You best get out of here." Darzi looked at Pete and his smile grew a little wider. "Our next client was found in a dumpster. Homeless fellow. Unfortunately, he was badly bitten by rats and insects. The responding officers didn't want to check the body for possible wounds, though it's unlikely it was a homicide."

We were both out the door before Darzi finished. The coroner's gentle laughter followed us.

"Would your dad like a visitor?" Pete asked as we got in the elevator.

"Sure! He can give you a list of chores," I told him. I punched the button for Dad's floor, then the one for the lobby. "I'll let you go. I want to try getting some leverage on Alverez."

"Good luck. It's irritating when you have to convince a victim to help solve their case."

"Those are the type of crap cases that you and Julio tossed off on me." I paused, then asked, "Are you going to ask Dad any questions?"

"I know he doesn't remember the attack, but I haven't stopped looking into other possible suspects," Pete said. "I'll be gentle."

"Good deal," I said, waving to Pete as the doors opened into the lobby.

After leaving the hospital, I checked one thing off of Dad's list by stopping at the feed store to pick up chow for the horses. Loaded down with bags of feed in the trunk of my car and having assured everyone at the store that Dad was doing much better, I headed back to the office.

I called Marti in dispatch as soon as I got to my desk and asked him to pull any calls for service in Alverez's neighborhood over the last six months. He promised to get the information to me as soon as he could.

After spending an hour on paperwork and phone calls, I took a break to check on Jessie. She had found more footage of the car Terri had been driving. This time the angle showed the passenger side, but no one else was in the car.

"I guess that's it," Jessie said, frowning at the computer.

"I'm sorry I can't make this feel better," I said.

"I don't understand how…" Her hand moved quickly to wipe at her eyes.

"You can try to find out where she's been for the last several years. That might give you some answers."

"That won't change what she did." She was avoiding looking at me.

"All you can hope for is to come to terms with what happened. But nothing is written in stone yet."

"I just don't know how I can tell her mother that Terri… stabbed someone." The video evidence had obviously convinced her of Terri's guilt.

"The footage is just part of the story. Terri didn't look like someone who'd been living on the street, but she did look like she hadn't been taking care with her appearance," I said.

Jessie gave me a sharp look. "She was always, like, made up. Nothing tacky, just… nice."

I shrugged. "Her fingernails were dirty and her hair didn't look like she'd done much to it other than wash it occasionally."

"She'd changed then."

"Look, Pete's on it. He made sure they collected the dirt

from under her nails for analysis. That could give us some clues as to where she'd been spending time."

I left after an awkward silence. I could see that Jessie had an emotional hill to climb and platitudes from me weren't going to help.

Back at my desk, I got a call from Deputy Sanderson.

"I hate to bother you, but I've got a case I could use some help with." She didn't sound like her usual confident self.

"What's up?"

"It's a child abuse case. The father and I had a little personality clash. Being that a juvenile is involved, I just want the investigation to be as clean as possible."

I understood where she was coming from. That was part of the reason that an investigator usually took over a case from the responding officer. During the heat of the service call, feelings could run high, establishing a dynamic between the responding officer and the people involved that was hard to overcome. First impressions and all that. A fresh start and fresh eyes were often best for doing a thorough investigation.

"No problem. Just email me your report and I'll look into it ASAP."

The case involved a thirteen-year-old boy who had accused his stepfather of hitting him. I read through the report and understood why Sanderson wanted me to look into the case. There was little evidence to back up the boy's story. His stepdad said nothing happened, while the boy swore that the man had tried to kill him. The boy's mother and sister both said that the males had been slapping at each other, but not seriously. The only physical evidence of a fight, other than a broken lamp and some dishes, was a bad bruise on the stepson's head that the other three all said he'd caused himself by running full-tilt into a wall. Sanderson had sorted it all out at the time by taking the boy to stay with his grandparents, but now the stepfather wanted to file a complaint against her—apparently just for listening to his stepson.

I needed to talk with the boy now that he'd had time to cool off. I was able to arrange a meeting that afternoon and took our best social worker with me. She acted as an advocate for the young people who ended up in our jail and was very good at separating the sincerely troubled from the truly bad seeds.

After an hour with the boy, we'd worked out a plan to take to the rest of his family. I scheduled a meeting for the following week with his parents and sister. If people could just get along with their own families, law enforcement would have their workload cut in half.

I headed for Dad's place after the meeting and called Darlene on the way. "All quiet on the auto theft front?"

"You'll be the first to know when I hear something," she said. "Your dad?"

"Doing better. He's able to order me around again," I said with a laugh.

"Good for him... And good for you."

"Kinda is," I agreed. No matter what lasting problems Dad might have, I was grateful that it hadn't turned out worse.

As I dropped off the feed, I ran into Jamie bringing Finn and Mac into the barn for dinner. I thought I'd have to fill him in on how Dad was doing, but I was wrong.

"He's called me three times today." Jamie gave me a smile that faded a little when he added, "He had a few... I mean, I guess it's normal to still have some memory problems?"

"The doctor says he'll improve. Just needs to let the brain rest."

Jamie rolled his eyes. "I don't know how much of that he's doing. He gave me half a dozen projects."

"If you don't have the time, just let me know. I'll tell Dad to lay off."

"No, it's fine. He's paying me. I'd feed the horses and take care of Mauser for nothing while he's in the hospital, but… Let's just say that some of the stuff, like cleaning the gutters, I sorta *want* to be paid for."

"If I can do anything—"

"Ha! One of the things he asked me to do is to check up on you to see if you're doing *your* chores." He looked at the feed in the back of my car. "I guess I can tell him you are. I'll help you unload it."

After we'd put the feed into the bins in the barn, Jamie asked, "Have you found the guy that stabbed him yet?"

"We've got a strong lead."

"Hope you catch him soon."

"If it's who we think it is, they don't pose a threat to anyone else."

I got home to find Cara and the gang waiting for me. Cara, Alvin and Mauser met me at the door. Ivy didn't even look up from her post-dinner bath to acknowledge my presence. She still hadn't fully accepted Ghost's integration into the household and she was holding me accountable for the whole disagreeable experience. Ghost, on the other hand, was too involved with shredding a magazine to greet me.

"I bet I know which ones have already been fed," I said, looking down at the eager dogs.

"Yep. I held off feeding Mauser and Alvin so we'd have at least five minutes to eat our meal in peace before Mauser starts begging."

"I bet if we timed it, it would be less than five minutes," I said, ruffling the monster's ears as I walked to the kitchen.

I was clearing the table when my phone rang.

"Convenient," Cara kidded, taking the plates out of my hand so I could answer.

"I put the report of calls on your desk," Marti told me. "But I thought you might want a heads-up. A neighbor called us a couple of weeks ago complaining about the noise that Alverez's friends were making coming and going from his house at night. We sent a car around to have a chat with Alverez and he got his tailfeathers ruffled up over it."

"Was he abusive?"

"According to the report, no. Just pissed off at his neighbor."

"That's not much."

"I was saving the best for last. An hour after our car left, we got another call from the neighbor that Alverez was over there pounding on the door and threatening to kill him."

"I like this."

"Five minutes later, and Deputy White arrived to find Alverez still in a snit, but calmer. Considerably calmer when he saw her. The neighbor, Lenny Morales, wasn't having any of it and wanted Alverez arrested. White decided to pour oil on troubled waters instead of escalating tensions with an arrest. As you know, if you drag a guy off to jail for a wrist-slap offense, the community starts taking sides until we're going out there every night. Anyway, like I said, she talked everyone off the ledge and got agreement from Alverez that his friends will be quieter and drive slower. She also promised to check with the neighbor to keep Alverez honest. So the neighbor agreed to let the charges go for the time being."

"This is good. I'll talk to the neighbor."

"Thought you might like it. Just don't stir the pot to the point it boils over. We're having enough trouble covering all the calls these days."

"Promise. I'll let you know if it works."

"Tell Cara I'll expect y'all to babysit if this pays off." Marti and his wife had three kids.

"We'll bring Mauser."

"Works for us. Bobby calls him Godzilla." Marti gave me contact information for Lenny Morales, including the fact that he worked at the hospital in Tallahassee as an orderly, then I let him go.

The rest of the evening felt almost normal. Dad was recovering, Mauser wasn't moping and, while it had flaws, we seemed to be nearing closure on Dad's case. After watching Ghost stalk Mauser's tail and climb on his head for a while, Cara and I snuck away to the bedroom for a little fun and a much needed good night's sleep.

CHAPTER TWELVE

Pete met me at my desk the next morning wearing a serious expression.

"I just gave Major Parks an interim report on your dad's case... which is also now Terri Miller's case."

"You know that for sure?"

"Got an email from Dr. Darzi's office this morning with the preliminary analysis of the blood and trace evidence on the knife. The report confirms that the blood is your dad's. The clincher is that they found a strand of Terri's hair imbedded in the blood. Darzi says it had to have gotten there while the blood was still fluid. Hard to see how that could be anything less than conclusive, barring some wild set of coincidences or a clever conspiracy."

Julio walked in, a lightness in his step. "Did he tell you?"

"I was just going over—" Pete started, before he was interrupted by all our text alerts going off simultaneously. Major Parks wanted to see us.

He had an odd look on his face when we entered his office. His office was much smaller than Dad's, so we crammed in, elbow to elbow, in front of his desk.

"Are you satisfied with this?" Parks asked, tapping the monitor on his desk.

"It is what it is," Pete responded.

"That's not what I'm asking. I know that you've been working on Terri Miller's disappearance for years. An attachment to the case is natural." He looked at me. "Obviously, you have emotions where your father's case is concerned." Parks pointed a Julio. "You're the one who can be most objective. What are your thoughts?"

Julio looked a little startled to be the one in the spotlight.

"Well, I... just..." He stood straighter, composed himself and started again. "The evidence is clear, though it's a result that leaves us with questions." He looked at Pete. "Motive being the big one. Of course, there won't be a trial so we don't *need* to know what motive drove her to stab Sheriff Macklin, but not knowing feels like unfinished business." He glanced at Pete and me to see how his comments were being received. "If you know what I mean," he added.

"I think we've all had cases that we closed even though they left us with a good deal of unanswered questions," Parks said. "So that's what I want to know. Are these cases, both of them, solved?"

The three of us exchanged looks.

"Yes," Pete finally said, raising his eyes to the ceiling as though looking for a sign from God as to whether he was right or not.

"This is my first stabbing and death investigation." Julio's brow was furrowed. "But I know that, if these were any other two cases, the evidence would be good enough for a prosecutor."

"He's right about that," I chimed in. "But I don't think you're talking about whether the case is ready for a jury or not." I looked directly at Parks, admiring the way he was handling this. Anyone else would have seen these cases as ones to clear up as fast as possible, yet his main concern from the beginning had been to get it right.

"No, I think both cases are too important for us to rush to judgment. I want us settled in our own minds. Sheriff

Macklin's life could be on the line if we get it wrong in his case, and anytime that a young woman's life is cut short we need to do our best to get the answer right."

"I'll tell you one thing," Pete said. "If this isn't the right answer, then we're in trouble. If we were to arrest someone else tomorrow, even with good evidence, a defense attorney could use everything pointing to Terri to get their client free."

"Are you talking about the stabbing or Terri's death?" Julio asked.

"Both. There might not be a mountain of evidence pointing toward suicide, but there's at least a good-size hill. And with the blood and the hair on the knife. Well…" Pete shook his head.

"I'd agree," Parks said. "So we have a solution that will stand unless we receive even more conclusive evidence pointing somewhere else."

"Which is where we always find ourselves with a murder-suicide," I pointed out.

"So do we still have a problem?" Julio asked.

"No. We have to consider the cases closed." Pete surprised me a little. "And if they're closed, then there's no harm in having Larry or anyone else look at both of them. What do they call it in the tech world? When you've got a program and everyone can work on it?"

"Open source?" Julio answered, though he made it more a question than an answer. There wasn't one of us in the room who didn't have a hard time figuring out a new phone when we got it, let alone know how to program anything.

"Yeah, that's it. I think we accept that, to anyone in the real world, these are both closed cases, pending final reports. Still, speaking for myself, I'd like to follow any other leads that I see, to try to tie up as many loose threads as I can."

Julio and I were nodding along with Pete.

"I'm satisfied with that," Parks said. "I'll put both cases in the pending file until we get all the reports from Shantel, Lionel and Dr. Darzi's office. What I won't do is give any of you official time to do any more work on either case. We're too shorthanded."

We all agreed that we could live with that.

"I'm going down to Lionel's office," I said as we left Parks's office.

"Jessie there?" Pete asked.

"That's what I want to find out."

"I'll go with you. She's not going to take this well."

"Give her a chance. She's known which way the wind was blowing ever since she found that footage showing Terri alone in the car."

"Why do you think Terri did it?" Pete asked.

I shrugged. "Maybe she developed schizophrenia. Her age, apparent paranoia, erratic behavior, unkempt appearance. It all fits."

"Unfortunately, there's no postmortem way to be sure."

"And I'm just guessing anyway," I admitted as we approached the open door of Lionel's office. We could see Jessie working at her monitor.

"Lionel, could we use your office for a moment?" I asked after we'd said our good mornings.

"Sure, kick me out of my own office," he grumbled good-naturedly, grabbing a mug and heading for the break room.

Jessie looked glum. "I guess it isn't good news."

Pete and I explained Major Parks's decision on the two cases.

"So we can still look into Terri's disappearance and what might have happened?" she asked, her voice hopeful.

"Of course," Pete said. "Just not on official time."

"Okay." She looked at the floor and bit her lip. "I want to help. Even if I'm in the academy or have a new job."

"I promise we'll keep you in the loop," I said.

"And let me help."

"And make you do all the drudgework that Pete and I don't want to do."

"Okay." This time she looked at us when she said it.

We left her and let Lionel have his office back.

"I'm heading out to see if I can dig up some information on Eduardo Alverez," I told Pete, and filled him in on the altercation with Lenny Morales.

"You want me to take the case back?" he asked.

"Nope, I've kinda got my teeth in it now. You're welcome to come along if you want."

"Actually, that's not a bad idea," he said, looking thoughtful. "You said Morales works at the hospital? We can swing by and see your dad when we're done. We need to let him know where the investigation stands."

I let Pete drive so I could call Morales. He agreed to meet us for lunch at a café across the street from the hospital, and was already waiting for us when we arrived. Morales was forty-five years old and just over five feet tall, with dark hair and a jaunty attitude.

"That Alverez." He gritted his teeth and shook his head. "He promised to keep his hombres from driving through our neighborhood in the middle of the night. My children have to sleep!" I was glad we were sitting at an outside table as his voice rose. "No respect for us who own homes there. He's a renter." His distaste for people renting their homes seemed a bit out of proportion.

"We think he might have information on a case we're working. We just want to put a little pressure on him to cooperate," I said.

"Good! I agreed not to press charges because the lady officer wanted us to cooperate. Does he do what he says? No!" This was punctuated with his fist coming down on the table. "I'm glad you are taking this seriously. My family means everything to me. How am I supposed to be happy in my own house when my children and wife can't get a good night's sleep? How?"

"When was the last time they woke you?" I asked.

"Well…" He waved his hand dismissively. "It has been quiet since we agreed."

I was confused and could see my own confusion

reflected in Pete's expression. "You made it sound like he was still disturbing the neighborhood," I said.

Morales leaned forward and whispered conspiratorially. "He will. I know he's just being good 'cause he thinks the cops are watching."

"So he's doing what he said he would?" Pete asked, raising one eyebrow.

"Wait, wait, that's not all. His yard, it's like a trash heap. A dump. Dangerous. I bet there are rats in there."

I was suddenly feeling sorry for Eduardo Alverez. Yes, there was some junk in his yard. Still, compared to other yards in the neighborhood, his was not bringing down the average.

"Are you sure that he hasn't woken you up lately?"

"Wait! Yes. Not cars. But there was a party at his house the other night. We heard it going on until after midnight. I would have called the police, but my wife, she started nagging that she didn't want any more trouble. Women! They don't understand. A man needs to stand up for his property."

We ordered sandwiches from a waiter who knew Morales. They had a brief chat in Spanish before the waiter left to put our orders in.

"My cousin from Nicaragua," Morales explained. "I helped get him this job. When he first came here, he was working the tomato fields."

"Tell us about this party," I urged, hoping it would give us at least a little pretense for pushing Alverez to cooperate on the ATM attack. Though I had to admit that my idea was feeling lamer by the moment.

"He had a couple of guys over. They were laughing and drinking. You know, partying," Morales said with venom. I don't know how I managed to keep from rolling my eyes.

We spent another half hour listening to Morales outline one lame complaint after another. At least my sandwich was good.

"We'll check up on him," I promised Morales as I paid

the tab, hopeful that I'd be reimbursed for his lunch. Not that I'd gotten much for my eleven dollars. I handed him one of my cards, hoping he wouldn't decide that I was his go-to person in local law enforcement.

"What a waste of time," I muttered to Pete as we headed back to the car.

"You could have gotten him to press the original charges."

"I just wanted something with a little sting."

"You're really reaching here," Pete observed.

"Maybe a little."

"Let's go see your dad."

When we got up to his room, I was surprised to find Jimmy there with Genie. "What do you want for Christmas?" was the first thing he said to me.

"Dad to come home." I smiled and Jimmy gave me a big smile back.

"Me too! I want Uncle Ted to come home so we can have a super great Christmas with you, Mauser, Mom, Cara and everyone. I also wouldn't mind too much if I got a new phone. One with a bigger screen and more memory."

"It's Jimmy's day off. Once I told him about Ted, all he wanted to do was come up to the hospital," Genie explained. "Looks like y'all might want to talk. Jimmy, why don't we go get lunch and do some Christmas shopping?"

"Can we come back?"

"We will, and we'll bring Ted some peppermint ice cream from Bruster's."

"I'd like that a lot," Dad told them, and was just able to fend off Jimmy's hug, which must have put quite a bit of pressure on his knife wound.

"What's the word?" Dad asked when Genie and Jimmy had left.

"Julio eliminated Fred Durrell based on his alibi," Pete said. He went on to tell him about the preliminary report from the coroner's office.

"Major Parks filled me in." Dad put his hand up to his

forehead and closed his eyes for a moment, making me wonder how bad his headaches still were. We waited to hear his pronouncement on our decision. After a couple of minutes, he put his hand down and seemed lost.

"What do you think?" I prompted.

His green eyes cleared when he looked at me. "You can't imagine how frustrating it is to be the victim and not remember the attack, or even the events leading up to it. But considering the evidence you've collected, I have to agree that there's a high probability Terri Miller did this."

"We'll follow any remaining leads until we can't go any further," Pete assured him.

"I'm less concerned about the attack on me than the death of Terri Miller. It seems like a failure of our department. That young woman has been missing for over a year," he said.

Pete looked down at his feet, politely ignoring Dad's fumble on how long Terri had been gone.

"You know that I'm not questioning you, or the efforts you made to find her. Our department has had a lot of challenges lately. We're shorthanded and low on funds. I just want to make sure that she gets justice in the end."

"Not everyone can be that magnanimous toward someone who plunged a knife into their chest," I joked.

"I'm certain I'd feel different if I remembered her doing it." Dad gave me a brief smile, then his hands clenched as I watched another wave of pain wash over him. "I think I need to take a minute." He forced the words out through gritted teeth.

"We'll go now. I'll get the nurse," I told him.

"No. Just text me later." His eyes were closed.

Pete and I left as quietly as we could and neither of us spoke on the way down in the elevator. Dad's vulnerability seemed so alien to who he was.

"What now?" Pete asked, unlocking the car.

"You tell me. I'm striking out every time I come up to bat."

"And you're using baseball analogies, which you know very little about," he groused. "Life runs in cycles. You're in a slump. That's all."

"Now who's talking baseball?"

"Slump is a term that can be used for any downturn in luck," Pete argued.

"So, where to now?" I asked when we were in the car.

"You sure you don't want to go hit up Alverez? You could try bluffing him."

"I'm beginning to think I've put too much time into the ATM attack as it is. If he wants to get beaten up and let the guy get away with it, it's no skin off my back."

"That's the spirit. What about those overpriced auto thefts?"

"We—that is, Darlene and I—are waiting for another one so we can try to get some fresh evidence." I explained about Darlene's plan to monitor all major cameras pointing in and out of town. "Nothing's happening right now. The last one was over a month ago, and they've been occurring every four weeks or less."

"So the next one is overdue."

"Could be. Maybe the crook met their quota. Or they got nailed for something else. Or they're off visiting their grandma for Christmas. Who the hell knows?" I threw up my hands.

"What you need is some time at the range." Pete smiled and turned toward Adams County and the department's gun range.

CHAPTER THIRTEEN

The sheriff's office had a small gun range on ten acres near the county's landfill. When we got to the range, we were the only ones there. The bays had once been shady before Hurricane Marcy had taken out a lot of the larger trees, but it didn't matter on a cool, breezy day like this. The extra sunlight was a bonus. Pete popped open his trunk and began pulling out bags.

"We'll practice on a little of everything. Don't you have an evaluation coming up?"

"I do, and don't think it escaped my notice that you talked Dad into upping the department's standards." Pete was the department's firearms instructor, as well as the SWAT team's go-to sniper.

"Bad things happen when officers don't get the training they need. I'm proud of your father for not cutting back on training, even with the department's budget in shambles after the storm." He handed me two bags, each of which must have weighed forty pounds.

"He *is* making us pay for half our own ammo."

"These days, some departments are making their officers pay for *all* their ammo. Besides, we've got the co-op up and running."

The co-op was an idea that several of our deputies had come up with. They'd pooled their money together to purchase a couple of Dillon reloading machines and to buy up bullets and powder in bulk. Dad wouldn't let us use the reloads for carry ammo, but it was saving a lot of money on practice ammunition.

"I told you I'd come take some lessons on running the machines." I frowned, wondering when I'd find the time for that. Pete had been after me for over a month. Learning the machines was part of the deal. We all chipped in money for powder and primers, as well as time to clean brass and load cartridges.

We spent the next hour going from shotguns to rifles to handguns. I preferred working with my Glock 17, mostly because I was used to it. But there was something about the new Mossberg shotguns that made them particularly cathartic to shoot.

"You should join the SWAT team," Pete suggested.

"Ha! Like I have the time."

"I've got two daughters and still find the time."

"This is your hobby. Plus you don't have to be at your father's beck and call."

"Guess that's going to be even rougher now that he'll be on short duty for a while," Pete observed as we packed up our gear. The bags were lighter after we'd sent four or five hundred rounds down range.

"I'm not even going to complain about it."

"It was a near thing. I saw his X-rays. Pretty scary," Pete sympathized.

"I don't know what I'd do if he..."

"Hell, we'd all be up the creek without a paddle. Your dad holds all this together on a shoestring budget."

Back in the car, I saw that I had a missed call from Jessie. Wearing ear protection and with rounds going off, it was almost impossible to hear a phone ring.

I called her back. "What's up?"

"I need to talk to you." There was a tremble in her voice.

"I'm headed to the office."

"I'm at Mr. Griffin's house."

"I'll pick up my car and be there in twenty minutes," I told her, wondering what was wrong now.

Albert Griffin was the head of the Adams County Historical Society and a wealth of knowledge on all things about the area. He rented his garage apartment to Eddie, who helped with odd jobs around the old Victorian house in return. I wondered why Jessie hadn't said she was at Eddie's.

I pulled into the driveway and saw Jessie's truck. I was debating whether to go around to the back door as I usually did, when I saw Jessie stand up from the swing on the front porch. She had her arms crossed in front of her chest and looked cold.

"What's up?" I asked as I mounted the stairs to the wide, wraparound porch.

"It's my fault," she told me.

"What's… Never mind, let's go in the house. You're turning blue out here."

We went inside and I saw Mr. Griffin for just a second before he disappeared into the kitchen. I figured he had some idea of what was going on and didn't want to intrude.

"Sit down," I told Jessie after leading her into the living room.

When she dropped onto the sofa, I sat down in the chair across from her and leaned forward. She was keeping her eyes down, her shoulders folded in and tense. "Tell me what's going on," I urged.

"Eddie's been drinking. He may even have scored some drugs. I don't know and it's all my fault." She pounded her thighs with her fists.

"Why do you say it's your fault?" I didn't have any idea how to unpack this.

"'Cause it started the night I was gone. The next day I thought I smelled alcohol in the kitchen of his apartment. When he wasn't around, I looked in the trashcan and found an empty pint of gin."

"Have you talked to him about it?"

"He was drunk last night too. Well, a little drunk. I could tell. I confronted him this morning and he admitted it."

"When people are trying to get sober, they can backslide. You hope they don't, but…"

I felt bad for Eddie and Jessie, but I couldn't pretend to be shocked or outraged. Eddie had had a tough life and had every right to have abandonment issues. He had imbued Jessie, his first sober adult relationship, with trust and importance beyond a casual romantic hookup. For her to disappear on him for almost twenty-four hours would naturally strain his hold on sobriety. But I didn't blame Jessie and wasn't going to put any more guilt on her shoulders.

"I shouldn't have been gone for so long without even texting him."

"Eddie's a big guy. He knew the risks when he got involved with you." I heard my words and cringed. "I don't mean that there were risks because it was you. I mean that getting into a relationship *always* has emotional risks." I was fumbling for the right words.

"I know what you're trying to say." Her eyes remained downcast.

"How do you feel about him?" I couldn't believe I was playing couple's counselor.

"I like him. I don't know if it goes any further than that. But I really want to help him."

"Even if it means leaving him alone for now?"

"Yeah."

"What if it means staying with him?"

"Sure."

"Where is he?"

"In his apartment. He's sleeping."

"Not for long." I got up and headed for the back door out of the kitchen. Mr. Griffin was sitting at the table, looking concerned.

"Have you talked to him?" I asked.

"Briefly. He wasn't in the mood to talk. Guilt and shame coming out as anger."

"I'm feeling a little pissed off myself," I said, which was only half true. I had sympathy for the battle that Eddie had to wage with himself. On the other hand, he had gone into this relationship with open eyes and I resented being called in to help clean up a situation that he'd let get out of his control.

I grumbled to myself all the way up the stairs alongside the garage to the door of Eddie's apartment. I rapped on the door hard enough to make the glass rattle. No answer.

I pounded a little harder. "Get up! It's cold out here."

I could hear someone moving around inside.

"Sooner rather than later," I encouraged him.

The door opened to show a sad example of a human being. Eddie's hair wasn't combed, he hadn't shaved and he smelled of self-pity. The embarrassing part for me was that he was wearing a black dress with a rabbit-fur coat. He stood at the door, looking past me.

"Really?"

"You know I'm a crossdresser."

"Knowing and seeing are two different things," I sighed.

"So what do you want?" he asked, making it clear that he didn't want to be talking to me.

"Aren't you going to invite me in?"

There was a long enough pause that I thought he might shut the door in my face. Finally, he walked back inside, leaving the door open behind him.

I followed him inside to find the apartment surprisingly neat. I had half expected to find it littered with beer cans and pizza boxes.

"I know I screwed up," Eddie grumbled.

"Everybody makes an ass of themselves from time to time. Question is, what are you going to do about it?"

He dropped down on the couch. "How the hell do I know?"

"You better find out. You've got people who care about

you. But you don't have so many friends that you can afford to lose any," I warned him. "Have you talked to your sponsor?"

"No."

"That sounds like a good place to start."

"Easy for you to say." Eddie fell over on his side and hugged a pillow.

"You're acting pathetic. Give me your phone and I'll make the call for you." I was pacing the room while I berated him.

"I got to get my head on straight first."

"I thought that's exactly the sort of thing your sponsor is supposed to help with."

"You don't know shit!" he said with real venom in the words.

"I know that you faced down your whole damn family of drug-dealing maniacs. Are you going to fall apart now just because you made a fool of yourself?"

"Maybe I am." He sounded like a petulant child.

"Fine. Lose all of the new life you've built." I started to walk toward the door, but stopped short of the threshold. My stubbornness wouldn't let me leave. I had helped Eddie climb up out of the gutter, and I wasn't going to let him throw his new life away. I went back to the sofa and shoved him off of it. "Get up!"

He hit the floor with a thud. "What the hell are you doing?"

"Doing what you should be doing to yourself," I said, coming around the couch and giving his ass a good kick.

"Hey! You can't do that!" he yelped. Shock and pain had replaced his self-pity.

"If you don't like it, then get up and fight me."

"You're crazy." Eddie squirmed away from my next kick.

"You don't like being kicked? Do you remember what it was like when you were running around town trying to score?"

"I'm not using again."

"Yet," I shot back.

"I only drank, like, half a bottle."

"Then act like you just made a little mistake and get back on your feet." He had gotten up on his hands and knees, but I planted another light kick to his ass. He flopped back down on his belly.

"Stop that! I mean it," Eddie insisted. I came at him again and this time he managed to scramble to his feet.

"Good. Now stand on your own two feet like a man. Call your sponsor. Get some advice. Talk to Jessie and make that right. Fix all this now," I said, wondering if that should be my exit line. I decided that dramatic parting words were for movies, not real life.

"You can be such a jerk," Eddie told me.

"I get it from my dad's side of the family."

His expression changed immediately. "Oh, shit. Your dad. How is he?"

"Doing better," I said.

"Glad to hear it." Eddie looked like he was going to sit down on the couch again.

"Your sponsor," I reminded him.

"Yeah." He looked around for a minute before finding his phone in the kitchen. I stopped him before he could dial.

"When you're done talking to your sponsor, you need to make it right with Jessie," I said, then walked out the door.

"He's all yours," I told Jessie, who was waiting for me at the foot of the stairs.

"You think he'll get sober again?"

I stopped and faced her.

"Predicting whether an addict will stay sober is a fool's game." I thought that sounded too harsh, so I took a deep breath and tried again. "Life is tough. He's not going to be zooming along on a straightaway. Few people are. But are you willing to ride along with him through all the ups, downs and curves?"

"He's my friend."

"Perfect answer. I am too. So we stand by him."

"He'll be fine," Mr. Griffin said from the back door to the house. "I've seen scores of real hardcase drunks. I've been one. Eddie isn't."

"There," I said. "If you don't trust me, then take Mr. Griffin's word for it."

I headed back to the office, feeling like I'd done my duty to help steer the ship of sobriety back on course.

CHAPTER FOURTEEN

"What's the plan for the weekend?" I asked Cara as we were cleaning up the dinner dishes that night.

"I thought we'd go see your dad."

"That's a given. We can have lunch in Tallahassee."

"Maybe do a little shopping? I've still got to get gifts for Mom and Dad. What about your dad and Genie?"

"And don't forget Jimmy. I haven't thought of a thing. What do you want?"

"I'm good."

"No. Don't be like that. You have to give me a goal of some sort."

"Hmmmm. Really, there isn't anything I need." She handed me a plate to put in the dishwasher.

"Christmas isn't about need. What do you *want?*"

"What about you?" she deflected.

"I want lots of stuff, but it's all too expensive."

"Like what?"

"A tractor would be nice. Then I could finally do some of the work I've been planning to do since I bought this place."

"Okay, you're right, that might be a little pricey." She laughed.

"Let's make a bargain," I suggested. "We'll come up with

a price point, then we'll each give the other a list of three different things that cost about that much that we'd like to receive as gifts. That way, we'll both get what we want, but it will still be a surprise to see what the other person picks."

"You've really thought this out," Cara said, sounding impressed.

"I don't want the stress of spending the next two weeks trying to figure out what to buy you for Christmas." I kissed her.

"Fair enough. So how much do we spend?"

"Two hundred each?"

"Nice! Do you think you can rein in your boyish desire for expensive toys?"

"A tractor isn't a toy. But, yeah, I can probably come up with something."

"It's Ghost's first Christmas," she said, glancing over to where the kitten was chewing on one of Mauser's ears. The Dane raised his eyes to us and moaned a little, as if he knew who Cara was talking about. The novelty of living with a kitten was quickly wearing off for him.

"He'll be happy with boxes and wrapping paper."

"When do you think your dad will be able to come home?"

"When I talked to Genie this evening, she thought he might get out of the hospital as early as Monday. Which reminds me, we need to go over and ride Finn and Mac this weekend too."

"That'll be fun. The weather should be perfect on Sunday."

"We may have to exercise them for the next six months," I said and explained what the doctor had told me about the risks of another head injury.

"That's worrisome," she said as I put the last glass in the dishwasher.

"Speaking of worrisome, your mom and dad aren't coming for Christmas, are they?"

Cara chuckled. "Don't worry. They're hosting a

community winter fest at the co-op. That's the good news."

"So…"

"The bad news is that they might make it up for New Year's."

"Great," I said with a little too much snark. In truth, Cara's parents were often very amusing to have around, but they came with a high dose of eccentricity and both of them were hanging onto their hippie lifestyle by tooth and nail.

"They aren't that bad," she said, giving me an elbow in the ribs.

"You know I love them. They're just a little tough to take as houseguests. To be fair, I wouldn't want to have Dad staying here either. It's hard enough having his domestic buffalo for a visitor." I gave Mauser a look and got his classic raised eyebrows and a big yawn in return.

The next morning, we did a few outdoor chores before getting ourselves cleaned up and heading into the hospital.

"You could have brought Mauser," Dad said after greeting us.

I grinned. "I'm pretty sure the hospital will never let that happen again. Besides, we didn't want to drag him along with us. We're going shopping after visiting with you."

"Did you really bring him up to see me when I was in ICU?" Dad had a small smile on his face.

"I didn't have a choice. The big mutt was driving us crazy."

"He must have been out of his mind when Terri attacked me." Dad shook his head. I knew he was still irritated that he couldn't remember any of it.

"Wait until you see the inside of the van. He clawed through the door panel and tore the backseat all to hell."

"I'm still trying to envision what happened. I'll think I've got a small snippet of a memory, then I'll lose the thread and it's gone." He clenched his fists.

"Every piece of evidence points to Terri Miller. I didn't

want to believe she'd stabbed you. No one did, but everything fits."

"If she's the who, what's the why?"

"I guess she was still trying to hide. But why was she hiding? And why did she run off five years ago?"

"Pete's a good investigator," Dad said. "I know that when she originally went missing, he turned over every rock he could find. So what did he miss?"

"We're not going to let this go."

"Y'all have other work to do. I've already given Major Parks the go-ahead to advertise for two new deputies so we can replenish the ranks. I've been too worried about pinching pennies. And there's still that command position to fill…"

"When do you think you'll be able to come back to work?" I asked, then hastened to add, "You shouldn't rush it."

He frowned. "My brain is still acting sluggish. I want to make sure there's no way that a defense attorney could point a finger at me and claim that I wasn't acting competently when overseeing an investigation. With that in mind…"

"You can't go back until the headaches ease up," Genie said from her seat by the window.

"That too," Dad admitted. "The doctors say that, with luck, I'll be at something close to a hundred percent within a month."

"As long as you don't get another crack to the skull," I reminded him.

"I hear you," Dad said, sounding more than a bit annoyed. I knew everyone had been warning him to be careful. The trouble was that Dad had a cavalier side that often didn't take the most cautious route.

"Cara and I are going to ride Finn and Mac tomorrow." I wanted him to acknowledge that he would have to moderate his lifestyle for a while.

"That'll be good," was all he said.

"What about the wedding?" Cara asked, trying to elevate

the mood.

"That's the great news!" Genie's face lit up. "Tilly hadn't been able to get the venue to agree to refund our deposit, but she did get them to move the date to February 12. I think it's kind of sweet, getting married a couple of days before Valentine's." She reached out and took Dad's hand, looking into his eyes. "It's going to be perfect."

Dad nodded and smiled at her.

"That's great!" Cara said.

"I think we're looking forward to it as much as you two are," I said, then remembered Cara's parents. Would they come up for the wedding? *Back-to-back visits would be challenging*, I thought.

Genie and Cara discussed wedding details while I shared all the sheriff's office gossip with Dad. Once we left, Cara and I enjoyed lunch at Harry's downtown, did a little shopping and picked out our Christmas tree.

"Is there any possibility that the woman *didn't* stab your dad?" Cara asked as we were driving home.

"There's always room for doubt. But with all the evidence, including Dad's blood on the knife and an eyewitness placing the car she was driving at the scene, that's just a lot to overcome."

"Seems so crazy."

"I hope it was her."

Cara turned her head sharply and raised her eyebrows at me.

"Don't get me wrong. I feel bad for her and her family. But the alternative is that there's still someone out there who may or may not have it in for Dad. With Terri dead, the story stops there. I find comfort in that."

"I see what you mean. Still…"

"Yeah, you can't help but have some doubt. But people can do horrible things. Even people who we don't normally think are capable of it. Remember that documentary we watched where that thirteen-year-old boy killed his younger sister?"

"Yeah, but there were signs. The family realized it… after the fact."

"Exactly. And maybe there were signs that Terri's family don't want to discuss or just dismissed at the time. If you find it hard to imagine her doing it, just think how hard it would be for her mother to admit to it."

"I guess if the evidence points that way…"

"Right now, the evidence is pretty much a large neon-red arrow pointing directly at Terri."

Sunday's weather proved perfect for riding, with a crystal-blue sky and a predicted high of seventy-three degrees. I retrieved my boots from the back of the closet and sat on the couch to pull them on, but the effort was made a little harder as Mauser plopped down on my lap.

"Get off of me, you oaf!" I pushed him away so I could get my second boot on. "Don't worry, we're taking you with us." *It'll be good to get him out of the house for a few hours so some of his dog odor can dissipate*, I thought.

"Ready?" Cara came out of the bedroom in jeans and ankle boots, looking like a model for *Practical Horseman* magazine.

"Dang! We should ride more," I said, giving her a kiss and a pat on the rump.

"You're looking manly. You should wear jeans more often," she said, winking at me.

"We're a rural county, but not rural enough for the duty uniform to include jeans." I grinned.

When we got to Dad's, the gate was open and Jamie's truck was in the driveway. We found him in the barn cleaning stalls.

"The horses are in the pasture. I'd have kept them in the paddock if I'd known you all were coming," he told us.

"No problem. We have treats." I held up a bag of carrots we'd brought from home.

The two American Quarter Horses were spoiled and got

treats more than they got worked, so when they saw us waving the carrots, they came running.

We saddled up, left Mauser with Jamie and headed out. We'd gone about two miles from the barn when my phone rang. I saw that it was Darlene and answered it.

"We got one!" She sounded like she'd just caught a record-breaking trout.

"One what?"

"One of your expensive stolen cars."

I pulled Finn to a stop and the energetic gelding pawed at the ground in irritation.

"Details," I urged.

"A BMW convertible belonging to the wife of Andrew Cargill."

"The lawyer?"

"Yep. He and his wife got home from a trip last night and discovered it missing this morning."

"When was it stolen?"

"That's the sixty-four-thousand-dollar question. They were gone for a week and when they came home last night, they left the car they were driving in front of the garage. They didn't notice the other was gone until this morning, so it could have been stolen anytime in the past week."

I looked over at Cara and gave her an apologetic look. She sighed as we turned the horses around and headed back to the barn. Darlene filled me in on the address and agreed to meet me there in an hour.

"Sorry," I told Cara, meaning it. Riding a horse on a beautiful day can be very relaxing and I had almost been able to feel my cares drift away as we rode through the dappled sunlight of the pine woods.

"With your dad on light duty, we'll have plenty more opportunities to ride."

"I just want to get this gang!" I said with feeling.

"You're sure they're a gang?"

"It has to be more than one person. Even if just one person is stealing the cars, he has to have accomplices that are helping to sell them, cut them up or whatever he's doing with them."

"I'm sure they'd be shaking in their boots if they knew that Roy Rogers was on their trail," Cara said, laughing.

"I've always thought of myself more like Maverick."

"You wish, tiger." She laughed harder.

"That's enough from you, Calamity Jane," I said, easing Finn into a trot and passing her.

"You aren't going to get away from me that easily," she said and boosted Mac into a canter, regaining the lead.

"We shouldn't be cantering them back to the barn," I yelled up to Cara when she'd pulled a couple of horse lengths in front of Finn and me.

"You're just saying that because you're losing," she said, but reined Mac in.

"I'm going to feel that," I said, sliding off of Finn's back once we got to the barn. I hadn't ridden a horse in months.

"You and me both," Cara said, rubbing her thigh but unable to keep a smile of pure enjoyment off her face.

CHAPTER FIFTEEN

I met Darlene at a house three blocks north of the sheriff's office in Calhoun's historic district. Some of the homes in the neighborhood dated back as early as the 1850s, while the latest had been built in the 1920s. Andrew and Midge Cargill's Greek revival was sandwiched between a three-story Victorian and a squat Gothic that was in need of a coat of paint.

Darlene stood in the driveway, leaning against the city's black-and-white Ford Escape, when I pulled in behind her. The garage where I assumed the theft had taken place was a beautifully restored wooden carriage house, complete with plantation shutters.

"Howdy! How's it hanging, cowboy? Get your horses back in the barn?"

"Thanks for interrupting a perfect Sunday morning," I grumbled.

"I didn't have to call you." She put her hands up.

"It's all good if we can catch these bastards."

"One of my guys took the report. All the boxes are checked. I just wish we knew what night the car had been swiped." Darlene frowned. "I told Andy that I wanted to wait for you before I talked to them."

"You're on a first-name basis with that asshole?"

"He's not a bad guy."

"Ha! You've never been cross-examined by him."

"True. How'd you end up on the stand? He's not a criminal lawyer."

"His client was suing the sheriff's office because of the treatment the little snot had received at the jail."

"Y'all shouldn't have mistreated the poor kid."

I knew Darlene was jerking my chain, but just the memory of the smirking attorney insinuating that the sheriff's office didn't care about the conditions at the jail caused my blood to boil.

"The poor kid," I said, making air quotes, "was a twenty-five-year-old who'd knocked a woman down and kicked her until she let go of her purse. His complaint about the prison was that he'd been beaten up by another prisoner. A prisoner he'd tried to cheat out of a pack of smokes. Every word that your friend Andy used in court was calculated to make us look bad."

"You win or lose?"

"The county's attorney lost his nerve halfway through the trial and settled before it went to the jury."

Darlene put her hand on my shoulder. "Come on, let's go talk to Andy. Pick a fight with him and I'll box your ears, sonny." Darlene wagged her finger at me.

"I'm just here to catch the bad guys," I assured her as we walked up the steps to the portico. The door was answered by a woman with black hair that probably should have shown a few grey streaks, judging by her age. She was wearing clothes that were calculated to look casual while giving off a heavy whiff of money.

"Come in. We are just devastated by this invasion of our private space. Imagine someone having the nerve to steal my car. And right out of our garage!" Her accent was pure Alabama country club.

We followed her into the poshly furnished living room.

"Darlene, it's so good to see you again." Midge Cargill

leaned in and gave her a quick hug. "Wow, that uniform looks perfect on you. Andy will be right down. He's still unpacking from our trip." No sooner had she said it than we heard him coming down the stairs.

Andy Cargill waltzed into the living room with his chin up and a broad smile on his face. His hair had been allowed to go grey and was swept back in a deliberate attempt to look breezy, but it must have taken some time to get just right.

"We've got two of the best. Chief Marks and Deputy Macklin, the sheriff's own son," he said, looking us over. I was about to let my teeth start grinding when he added, "I was deeply disturbed by what happened to your father. We should all be proud to have a man of his integrity as sheriff." He held his hand out to me.

I wanted to ask him why he'd sued the department if he thought Dad had so much integrity. Instead, I took his hand and shook it, deciding to take his words at face value.

"We'd like to see the garage where the car was parked," Darlene said.

"Of course. We can go out the back. There's a little covered walkway to a door on the side of the garage." He turned to his wife. "Midge, you don't have to come along. I can give them all the information they need."

We followed him out through a back hallway. Every foot of the house's interior seemed designed to impress. I wondered what the money from the county's settlement had paid for. *Maybe it was the BMW*, I grumbled to myself.

The garage was large enough to hold two cars, but neither spot was occupied. There were a few expensive tools hung on the walls and a compressor and car lift in one corner, suggesting that Andy might work on his own cars on occasion.

"This is the spot." He waved toward a car that wasn't there.

"Do you have surveillance cameras?" Darlene asked.

"Like I told your officer, I do, but they all mysteriously failed the day after we left on vacation. I guess I need to get some of those that I can monitor with an app on my phone. Who knew?"

"When did you leave?"

"A week ago. We went to Charleston. Midge wanted to meet up with her sister and do some Christmas shopping."

"Is anything else missing?" Darlene asked.

"Your officer asked us to look around. From what we can tell, only the car was taken."

"What would it take to steal this car?" I also waved toward the car that wasn't there.

"Okay, let me think. The side door was locked and the garage door needs the remote to open it. So you'd have to figure that out. We don't have the garage hooked into the burglar alarm. We're going to get that fixed on Monday. Once you got in, all you'd have to do is figure out how to get the car started."

I'd have to check with someone to see how hard it would be to start a BMW M6 convertible.

"You said the car was worth one-hundred-and-sixty-thousand dollars?" Darlene asked.

"That's what the adjuster told me on the phone."

"Does the car have GPS tracking?" I asked and he looked at me like I'd wanted to know if had a steering wheel.

"That's the first thing I thought of. According to the tracking, the car has been in Germany, China and New Zealand over the past five days. I think it's safe to assume that the car's system was hacked."

"Can they tell you when they got the first anomalous reading?"

Cargill looked thoughtful. "I see where you're going. Yes, they should. I'll ask them to email me the record."

"Knowing roughly when it was stolen will be a big help when we're trying to find witnesses or checking other security cameras."

"I'll get them to send it today," he promised.

We spent another half hour going over the garage. I didn't see the point in calling in Shantel and the crime scene team since Darlene assured me that her guy was good at collecting evidence. And we both agreed that anyone who was as slick as these guys apparently were probably hadn't left any traces behind anyway.

"We'll come back and talk to the neighbors when we have the data from BMW," Darlene said when we were back at our cars.

"We should be able to get some camera footage if we get the time of the theft narrowed down."

As I was driving home, something told me to go the long way, which took me past the businesses out by the interstate. I sometimes chose that route when I wanted a few extra minutes to think on the way home. As I drove by the industrial park, I noticed Southeast Express on the sign. That reminded me of something… or was it someone? Eduardo Alverez! I was pretty sure that was where he worked. I hit the brakes and headed back to the industrial park. Would they even be open on a Sunday? Would Alverez be there? Stopping could be a wild goose chase, but it might be a way to catch him off guard.

As I approached the large warehouse complex, I saw several cars in the parking lot and trucks backed up to the loading docks on the side of the building. The office occupied the front left corner of the two-acre structure. I parked near it and walked up to the building. I could see folks moving around inside, so I figured I'd gotten lucky.

A bell jangled when I opened the door, causing the full-bodied woman in a sweatshirt behind the counter to turn and give me an inquisitive look.

"May I help you?" she said in a polite but skeptical voice.

I pulled out my bifold and showed her my star.

"I'd like to talk with Eduardo Alverez." I gave her my best just-the-facts-ma'am expression.

She looked around as though she expected someone else to step up and talk to me. As I approached the counter, I could see through a door into a small office behind her where a man was hunched over a monitor. He paused, no doubt listening to us.

"Eduardo's not working today. You're a detective? I hope nothing bad has happened?" She made everything into a question.

"Let's start over. I'm Larry Macklin, an investigator with the Adams County Sheriff's Office. I just want to talk to Eduardo about an incident that happened to him. He was the victim, not the perpetrator," I assured her.

"He's all right, isn't he?"

"Your name's...?"

"I'm Freda Maynard. I'm the receptionist, cashier and sometime dispatcher." She smiled at me, but her eyes stayed distant as though she'd had her own run-in with the law at some point in her life. "You said he was the victim. Is he okay?"

I noticed that the man in the office had turned his head ever so slightly so he could hear us better.

"It happened over a week ago."

"Oh, that's a relief. I was afraid something else had happened." I half expected to see her fan herself as though she'd just managed to avoid the vapors.

"When is he scheduled to work again?"

"Let me check." She went into the office and disappeared into a corner of the room that I couldn't see from my vantage point. I watched, but didn't see any interaction between her and the man at the monitor.

"Tomorrow. He's got a full shift starting at seven in the morning," she said when she came back to the counter. "I'm sorry that you made the trip out here for nothing."

"I was out this way looking into an auto theft. I just thought I'd stop by on the off-chance he was in."

I was used to people being leery of law enforcement, but I was certain that Ms. Maynard gave a sigh of relief when I left. I wondered why.

That evening, Cara and I put up the Christmas decorations

while a couple of classic Christmas movies played in the background.

"Mom ran hot and cold on Christmas. She wanted to turn it into a winter solstice celebration, which fit in well with Dad's Viking tendencies. I was the one who was enamored with Santa Claus," Cara confessed, "though I always felt guilty about wanting presents. I would try so hard to think about everyone else and try to find or make them the perfect gift. But deep down in my little black soul I wanted that Furby or sparkling pair of roller blades."

"You were truly a demon child," I kidded her as we put up colored lights around our small deck.

"In one of the communes we lived for a while, all the other selfless little kids thought I was evil for wanting toys for Christmas. It didn't help that Dad's favorite tradition was to tell Krampus stories around the campfire."

"You're kidding."

"I'm pretty sure that a few of those kids are still wetting the bed and sleeping with the lights on at the age of thirty." She laughed.

I thought about my own Christmas traditions growing up and realized how lucky I'd been.

"Mom and Dad kind of spoiled me. I got one big present every year, and a few other lesser toys and some staples like clothes and books. Some of my classmates got more than I did, but I'm sure many got a lot less. Dad always took me with him to pick out a few toys for the Toys-for-Tots drive that we do every year. Which reminds me, we still need to put our gifts in the box at work."

Finished with the outside of the house, we put up the Christmas tree. When it was done, we turned on Christmas music and sat down in front of the sparkling tree. I had a beer or two while Cara sipped wine. It was one of those moments that I wished could go on forever. Even the snoring of the dogs, Ivy's prickly claws in my lap and the idiot Ghost batting at ornaments only added to my feeling of contentment.

Then there are other moments. I was probably snoring loudly myself when my phone jarred me awake in the middle of the night. Pete was on call that weekend, so it shouldn't have been dispatch. I looked at the number and didn't recognize it. Unfortunately, I knew that if I didn't answer it I'd be wondering who it was for the rest of the night. Not happy about it, I hit the green button.

"What?" I mumbled, making sure that I sounded properly irritated.

"Mr. Macklin? Is that you? Deputy?"

The voice had a Hispanic accent and was vaguely familiar.

"Yes, yes," I assured whoever it was. A glance at the digital clock told me it was almost four in the morning.

"He's having a big party! Eduardo Alverez. I can see it from here."

Oh, hell, it was Lenny Morales. My irritation clicked up a notch, but so did my interest. Could he have something useful for me?

"Tell me what's going on."

"They have a huge bonfire! The flames are making the trees glow!"

"Alverez is having a party with a big bonfire?" My sleep-fogged brain was trying to make sense of what he was saying. "How many people?"

"I can't see no one. The fire is behind his trailer."

Sleep was leaving me quickly. "But you can see people at his place?"

"No, I think there was a car earlier. Now I just see the glow of the fire."

"How do you know it's a party?"

"I can hear music."

"But no people?" I asked. Cara was awake now, sitting up beside me.

"No."

"No cars?"

"No."

"Just some music and a fire behind his house?"

"That's right."

I wanted to tell him that I'd have patrol come take a look, but the hairs on the back of my neck were standing on end. "I'll take care of it," I told him as I rolled out of bed, giving Cara an apologetic glance.

I dressed quickly and headed for my car. On the way, I called dispatch and asked them to send a deputy out to meet me at Alverez's place.

Less than a mile away, I could see the glow in the distance. In Adams County, it wasn't unusual for rural neighbors to have bonfires, especially on weekends when the winter nights were chilly, so I understood why no other neighbor had reported anything. But by the time I rolled into Alverez's front yard, I heard Deputy Sykes call over the radio for a fire crew.

As I got out of the car, I wasn't surprised when Sykes told me, "We've got a body in a burning car."

CHAPTER SIXTEEN

Even through the smoke, I recognized the Toyota Highlander that had appeared in the ATM video behind Alverez. For some reason, I wasn't surprised to find it in his yard. I watched as the fire crew worked to extinguish the flames. Music, some type of Hispanic rap, was playing loudly inside the trailer.

"From the looks of it, they used an accelerant. See the pattern on the hood? They were pretty liberal splashing it around," Lieutenant Tracy told me while we watched his men spray down the vehicle. "We're trying to be as careful as we can, but you know how that goes."

"I saw the body when I arrived, but there was no way I could get to it," Sykes said.

"You'll be able to approach it in a few more minutes. The body's slumped over in the passenger seat," Tracy said.

"Probably dead before the fire even started," I muttered. "I'm pretty sure I know who it is."

Who had decided that Eduardo Alverez had to die? They'd obviously wanted to make a statement by using that particular SUV. Had he failed to heed their first warning? Did he steal money from them? Have sex with their wife or girlfriend? Maybe he was moving in on their territory. I hadn't found any evidence that he was involved in drugs, but who knew?

Half a dozen neighbors were watching from a discreet distance. The sirens and flashing lights had drawn them out of their houses, even at this early hour.

I saw Lenny Morales standing in his yard and walked over to him. I asked for more details of what he'd seen, especially anything he hadn't mentioned on the phone.

"No, it was just what I said. About an hour ago, I woke up and there was an orange glow in the room, so I got up and looked out the window. I was sure it was Alverez having a party. The music." He shrugged.

"Have you seen any strange cars around his place in the last day or so?"

"I can't remember any." He kept looking over my shoulder at the glow coming from Alverez's yard.

"We'll want to talk to all the neighbors. Do you know of anyone with a security camera?"

"Yeah, maybe. What happened over there, anyway?"

It was always tough to know how much information to give out. Too much and it could jeopardize an investigation. Too little and rumors could run rampant and jeopardize an investigation. I decided to tell Morales the truth, just not the whole truth.

"There's a burning car with a body inside."

"Alverez?" he said, with a nervousness in his response that made me wonder what he was worried about. Of course, he'd made it clear that he had a problem with Alverez, so maybe he was afraid I'd think *he'd* killed him.

"We don't know yet."

Morales frowned.

"We'll be in touch. In the meantime, call me if you hear anything."

I headed back across the street. A glance at my watch told me that it was a little after five. I'd wait a bit before I called for the crime scene team. The car would be too hot and too wet to do anything with it for a while, so why wake someone up just so they could stand around and wait? I *did* call the coroner's office, but I made it clear there wasn't any point in arriving before sunrise.

While I waited, I decided to take a look inside the trailer and see if I could turn off the music that seemed to be on an endless loop. I grabbed several pairs of latex gloves from my car and went to the front door, which was unlocked. I had just stepped into the musty-smelling trailer when I felt a hand come down on my shoulder. I jumped.

"Gotcha!" Pete said.

I turned and shined my light in his eyes. "It's amazing how a big guy like you can sneak around. If it wasn't for the damn music, you wouldn't have caught me." My heart was still pounding.

"You wound me. I can't help being a wee bit overweight." Pete didn't sound hurt at all.

"What are you doing here?"

"I'm on call. So what are *you* doing here?"

"You tossed this case at me, remember?"

"We haven't proven that this is related to the attack on Alverez."

"I got a hundred bucks that says it is," I shot back.

"No bet. Well, let's see what's inside." He made a shooing motion with his hands.

I found the light switch with my flashlight, then used the tip of a pen to switch it on. The living room looked like a dozen people had lived there over the last ten years and none of them had bothered to clean or vacuum the place. Surprisingly, there weren't any worse odors than the musty smell. I quickly crossed the room and turned off the old-fashioned stereo.

"How long had he lived here?" I asked.

"Long enough that it was on his driver's license, for what that's worth. I doubt he'd been here more than a year. Now a bunch of this crap has been here for at least *five* years. Look at that newspaper." Pete pointed to an old *Tallahassee Democrat* under an end table.

"Any idea who the landlord is?"

"No. Could be Scrooge."

Scrooge, whose real name was Daniel Frasier, was an infamous local slumlord. The county repeatedly hammered him with code enforcement violations, but his response was always the same. He'd drag his feet for as long as possible and then make the cheapest and most temporary repairs that he could get away with. Everyone at the sheriff's office was disgusted with him. Not only did his tenants suffer, but so did we whenever we had to enter his buildings. Only a month before, one of our deputies had broken his leg when he fell through the floor of one of Scrooge's rented houses. I'd encouraged the deputy to sue, just to stick it to Scrooge in the pocketbook where it would hurt.

"What a dump," Pete said.

I took out my phone and filmed as we walked through the trailer.

"Can you tell if someone has searched the place?" I was looking at an old desk. The drawer had been pulled out and it looked riffled, but I couldn't tell if it was recent or if anything in the desk even belonged to Alverez.

"Nope. Shantel and Marcus aren't going to be happy."

I nodded and led the way back to the master bedroom.

"Okay, I think it's safe to say that the place *has* been searched," I said once I'd looked inside.

The room was neater than the rest of the house, without all the clutter. The bed had been made before someone had pushed the mattress half onto the floor. The dresser drawers were open and had clearly been searched, but the clothes inside looked neat and clean.

"I haven't seen a phone or tablet or anything like that," I observed.

"Me either. The bad guy either took it or, more likely, tossed the phone into the SUV before he torched it."

"This might be my fault," I said as we made our way back through the living room.

"How do you figure that?"

"I stopped by where he worked this afternoon."

"So you think someone there thought Alverez was going to talk and killed him?"

"We already figured he knew the person who attacked him, right?"

"Yeah, I see your point. Which means that we're left with the same question we started with. Why was he attacked in the first place?"

"If we knew why, we'd be a lot closer to knowing who, and if we knew who, we'd probably have a good idea why. It's one of those chicken-and-egg things."

We did a quick pass through the rest of the trailer. The second bathroom hadn't been used in months, maybe years. There was no water in the toilet and everything looked dry and dusty. Of the two back bedrooms, one was stuffed with junk, while the other held only a mattress and box spring on the floor and a small chest of drawers. Like the master bedroom, it appeared that someone had done a quick search.

"Do you think they found what they were looking for?" I asked.

"Doesn't look like they even tried to go through the junk room," Pete said. "Maybe they did, or maybe the search was just on the off chance there was something to find."

We left the trailer for Shantel's crew to document.

"Let's check out his truck," Pete said, pointing to the red Ford pickup in the driveway.

We shined our flashlights into the windows.

"The door's unlocked and someone went through the glovebox and the console," I said.

"And they didn't care if we knew they'd done it."

"Maybe they were hoping it would look like a robbery gone bad," I speculated.

"Seems like a stretch."

"They'd have to think we were pretty stupid," I agreed. Since the bad guys had apparently been inside the truck, we walked away from it and added it to Shantel's list.

We walked back to where the car was smoldering.

Lieutenant Tracy came over to meet us.

"No doubt this is murder," I told him.

"Bodies in burning cars usually are. Unless they've wrecked. Though I did read a case study of someone who killed himself, but still managed to set the car on fire. Sorry about any evidence," he said, nodding toward the dripping SUV.

Pete and I walked closer to the vehicle. The stench of burned plastic, rubber and flesh was nauseating. Pete took out a handkerchief and cupped it over his nose. I just pinched mine closed and tried not to think of what kind of chemicals I was inhaling through my mouth.

The body in the passenger seat was lying with its head resting on the center console. The burnt and waterlogged corpse was unrecognizable.

"He's the right size to be Alverez, but we'll have to wait for Darzi's office to identify him."

"Any chance he had a local dentist?" Pete mused.

"If not, we'll have to hunt up a close relative." *Great*, I thought, *could be a month or two before we can even be sure who the victim is.*

"I'd say the odds are good that it's Alverez," Pete said. "But if he was trying to disappear and actually burned someone *else* up in his own yard, it would be a pretty good trick."

"Don't give me any more options," I groused. "Though, if anyone else turns up missing in the next couple of weeks, we might want to do a comparison. Also, when we have the DNA profile, assuming we haven't made a definite ID, we should run it through CODIS."

"I didn't come up with a criminal record for Alverez, but if it's not him…"

"Can you read the VIN number?" I asked, as Pete looked through what was left of the windshield.

He took a picture with his phone, enlarged it, then shook his head. "Any reason I shouldn't wipe it off?" he asked, taking his handkerchief away from his face. I nodded and he reached through to rub at the corner of the dash. He took another picture, then backed away from the car, gasping for a breath of fresh air. "Got it!"

We went back to his car and Pete ran the number on his laptop. It came back matching a vehicle that had been stolen down in Gainesville in early November.

"We actually learned something," Pete said, sounding amazed. "Someone will have to let Kendra Jackson know that we've found what's left of her car."

"That one was on Jessie's list of possibles. Pretty ballsy of them to keep driving it around for this long."

"From what we know, they might have only used it to commit crimes."

"Good point. Still, they would have had to park it somewhere that they didn't think it would be found."

"Probably not an apartment or a house where a nosy neighbor might be curious about the new SUV," Pete said.

I looked at my watch again. Dr. Darzi's people would be showing up in about an hour. Until then, there wasn't much for us to do but string up crime scene tape and wait. With nothing else going on, the curious neighbors had wandered back into their homes, leaving the cold morning calm and peaceful.

"I could almost enjoy watching the sun come up out here if it wasn't for the stench of burning car in the air," I told Pete, who was texting with one of his daughters.

"Just be grateful that the burned plastic and rubber cover up the smell of burned hair and flesh," he responded, not looking up from his phone.

"Which one are you texting?"

"Jenny. She's got work this morning. Wants to know if she should get her car's oil checked, which is daughter speak for: Will I pay to have her car's oil changed?"

I heard the sound of an engine and looked up to see Marcus driving the crime scene van.

"I've got hot coffee and donuts in the van," he told us when he got out.

"Wow! What's the occasion?" Pete asked. Then he got a suspicious look on his face. "Where's Shantel?"

"She's at a seminar learning how to 3D map a crime scene with lasers," Marcus said nonchalantly.

"You don't have any help?" I asked, being a little slower on the uptake than Pete.

"Don't you get it? The donuts are bait," Pete told me.

"Just call them an incentive." Marcus smiled. "Come on, one of you can help me with the camera equipment." Shantel and Marcus had been working together for years and were the perfect team. But when Shantel was around, her boisterous personality frequently overshadowed Marcus. It wasn't until you got him alone that he became as outgoing as Shantel.

"I'll help," I volunteered, following him to the back of the van. "Why is she taking a class on equipment we don't have?" I had a bad moment when I thought she might be educating herself to get another job.

"We're going to get the equipment," Marcus said with a grin as he took cameras out of their boxes.

"The hell you say! Where's she getting the money?"

"She's already got the grant. Federal money coming down through the state." He handed me a bag with extra batteries and equipment for the video camera.

"Lasers. Sounds hi-tech."

"We're also getting a couple of drones too so we can film crime scenes from above."

"Color me impressed."

The coroner's van showed up a few minutes later and I was shocked to see Dr. Darzi in the passenger seat.

"I'm impressed we got management out here," I told Darzi as he climbed out of the van.

"Burn victims are a challenge in the best of times." He looked cold, even in his thick coat. "I feel I should share the burden with my colleagues."

"So I'm a colleague now," Linda said as she jumped out of the driver's side and surveyed the scene. Frowning at the rivulets of water still running down the side of the trailer, she asked, "I take it the body's around back?"

"In an SUV. The fire department had to hose things down."

"I've never been able to make up my mind if it would be better to just contain the fire rather than wash everything away. I should do some controlled experiments to see what evidence is lost while letting a fire burn compared to that lost from drenching the body," Darzi mumbled.

"We'll get the car and body filmed and photographed as soon as possible so y'all can get started," I told them.

"There's donuts and coffee in my van," Marcus offered as we headed to the backyard.

Once Darzi and Linda were able to get to the body, Marcus and I spent the next hour documenting the rest of the crime scene outside the trailer. It was frustrating knowing that much of what we were capturing was evidence left behind by the firemen and not by the perpetrator. But we couldn't assume anything. A defense attorney would demand to know why we'd ignored a footprint, even if it was obviously from a fireman's boot.

"You all have any idea where the victim was killed?" Marcus asked when we took a break.

"Pete and I walked through the trailer and didn't see any obvious signs of violence. No blood or hair. We're pretty sure that the perp was inside the trailer at some point because it looks like it's been searched, but we don't have any clue as to where the murder was committed. The really bad news is that the trailer is filled with junk from previous tenants."

"We better get more bags, but you'll get some relief in about an hour. We have a new intern. She lives in Tallahassee and has a toddler, so she couldn't get here until eight," Marcus informed me.

"You want to film it first?" I asked, knowing the answer. Document first, collect evidence second.

Though we went through the trailer more meticulously

than I had with Pete, I didn't learn anything new.

When the new intern showed up at eight, I left her and Marcus to finish up while I talked to Dr. Darzi, who was stripping out of his protective clothing. He and Linda had finished loading a thick black body bag containing the remains into the back of the van.

"There is a fella from my graduating class who has always been fascinated with burned bodies. Two papers he's written on them. Me, not so much. I don't like the smell or the texture of burnt flesh." Darzi made a face.

"That's too much information." I grimaced. "Do you have any preliminary thoughts on our victim?"

"You'll be happy to know that part of his clothing on his backside that was protected by his body is recognizable. Linda, show him the pictures."

Linda finished loading equipment into the back of the van, then came around with the camera. She showed me the pictures she'd taken of the corpse. He'd been wearing cargo pants and a tan work shirt. I could see some intact hair around the base of his neck that looked brown. Nothing eliminated the possibility that the body was Eduardo Alverez.

"Could you tell if there was anything in his pockets?"

"I didn't feel anything when I touched them." Linda frowned.

"I guess it's too much to hope that he'd have his wallet on him." Though I couldn't understand why the murderer would bother to take the wallet if they were just making an example of him. Wouldn't it make more sense to announce to the world who you had killed and left to burn? Of course, they might have searched the wallet for whatever they'd been looking for in the house, then tossed it into the burning car.

Normally, I would have asked Darzi for an approximate time of death, but there was no point in doing that in this case. It wasn't possible to learn anything from a body's temperature when it had been cooking in a car for an hour.

"We'll do the autopsy tomorrow," Darzi told me. "I'll let

you know when we schedule it. We've had the usual increase in holiday suicides and homicides, so it might have to be after hours."

"Pete said to tell you that he went to canvass the neighborhood," Linda told me before they drove off.

I headed out to find him.

CHAPTER SEVENTEEN

I'd hardly started across the street when I saw Pete coming out of a well-kept, light blue little cinder block home. It had dark blue shutters which matched the dress of the small, frail old lady who was waving goodbye.

"Sweet and observant," Pete said as he joined me. "She's the first neighbor I've found who will even admit to being awake last night."

I looked from the woman's front yard over to Alverez's trailer, trying to judge what kind of view she would have had. From the windows at the front of the house, it was about fifty yards to Alverez's door.

"She see anything?"

"A car that left about half an hour after she started hearing the music. The music was why she looked out the window."

"Thirty minutes after it started?"

"She wondered if Morales would go over and say something to Alverez. She and Morales go to the same church. At the church supper yesterday, he was telling anyone who would listen that he was going to stop Alverez from ruining their neighborhood. He was getting a little vocal about it and the priest had to come take him aside."

"What'd the priest tell him?"

"She didn't hear because they went outside."

"We might want to talk to the priest. Was this Sacred Heart?" I asked, referring to Calhoun's only Catholic church. It was so small that they shared a priest with another church in Tallahassee.

"No, it's not a Catholic church. It's that one, two blocks thataway." Pete pointed off to the west. "The Church of the Holy Scriptures. I think it's some sort of Catholic-evangelical hybrid. Their services run for about six hours on Sunday. Sarah says they're very proactive in helping their members with any type of crisis and do a lot of outreach to the immigrant and migrant community. On the other hand, they're pretty aggressive with their evangelizing and quick to shame a member if they aren't following the church's doctrines." Pete's wife Sarah was active in the local religious scene, serving as a deacon in their church and on several community boards.

"I can't see Morales as the killer," I said. "In that case, it would have to mean that he beat up Alverez at the ATM machine. In what world does that make sense?"

"Maybe the SUV and the murder aren't related. Maybe the guy who beat Alverez came and ransacked the house, then left the SUV. Later, Morales got in a fight with Alverez, killed him and burned him up in the vehicle." Pete frowned, shaking his head at his own suggestion. "No, that's crazy. Why would the person who stole the SUV and beat up Alverez come search the trailer and *leave* the SUV?"

"Makes more sense that the ATM attacker didn't get what he wanted the first time or feared that Alverez would turn him in. Maybe the SUV was a message to others."

"Like a drug dealer or loan shark?"

"Not drugs. I've never seen a dealer or addict who wouldn't have left more evidence in their home," I said.

"I hear that."

"Getting back to Morales. We can't ignore a guy that has a grudge against our victim and is talking tough the day that

167

victim gets killed."

"One of us will need to talk to the priest," Pete agreed.

I filled Pete in on what Darzi and Linda had found.

"Darzi is going to play a big part in this one. Cause of death, definitely, and maybe he can tell us about any bad habits the dead man had," Pete said.

"And whether it's Alverez or someone else," I added.

"I've got a fiver that says it's Alverez." Pete acted like he was going to reach in his pocket and pull out his wallet.

"No bet," I told him. "By the way, whose case is this?"

"I think we'll call it ours. If that suits you."

"The more that merrier. While we're waiting for Marcus to get the car towed, we can start on the trailer."

"I'll grab some evidence bags and more gloves."

"Grab some trash bags too. We can dump the stuff that we decide isn't important so we don't keep searching the same junk over and over again."

"Good thinking. That's why they call you the brain."

I tapped my head. "And don't forget it."

I headed for the trailer. I knew we'd be searching through it for hours. In the movies, the hero could walk into a suspect's apartment and spend only ten minutes looking before turning up a crucial piece of evidence. In my experience, you looked for hours and, if you were lucky, you'd learn a month later that there had been an important piece of evidence in all the junk you sorted through.

I was still standing in the doorway, working up the courage to re-enter the cluttered living room, when Pete came up with the supplies.

"I told Marcus that we're going to get started. Should we search rooms together or each take a room?" he asked.

"I'm starting in the master bedroom. You can come with or not." I smiled and grabbed a few bags and gloves.

"I'll start here." He sighed deeply. "I like a challenge."

I sorted through everything in Alverez's bedroom. He hadn't had much. His clothes had been rummaged through. The closet and dresser held only three pair of jeans, half a dozen T-shirts, a couple of dress shirts and pants, socks and underwear. On the bedside table, I found change and receipts for lunch and beer.

I stepped over a wooden box that was lying on the floor. About the size of a shoebox, the lid had an ornate silver inlay that I imagined had been crafted in Central or South America. The box had apparently held letters which were now spread out on the floor. As I sorted through them, I noticed that almost all were from a Cristela Alverez, except for two from a man named Diego Alverez. They were in Spanish, which I couldn't read, so I wasn't sure if Cristela was Alverez's mother, sister or wife. Was Diego his brother? Father? Uncle? I slipped them into an evidence bag with the intention of asking Julio to translate them for me.

Under the mattress, I found a foot-long carving knife. *Was this meant for protection?* I wondered as I bagged it for testing.

When I was finished with the room, I still hadn't found a phone or electronic device. Disappointed but not surprised, I went back to the living room. Pete had barely managed to cover a third of the room.

"I started at the door and I'm working clockwise. Just leave me to it."

"Won't argue with you. I'll go hit the back rooms. The junk room should be fun."

"Chances are, that's the landlord's stuff. Which reminds me." Pete took out his phone and called Julio. "Hey bro, do us a favor and check the property appraiser's website and tell me who owns Alverez's rental." He gave Julio the address and waited. After a few minutes he said, "Figures. What? Really, that's interesting. Oh, we'll definitely follow up on that." He ended the call and turned to me. "First, we were right, Scrooge owns this dump. Second, Julio has been doing some background checks and guess what he discovered...?" He let the pause drag out.

I glared at him. "It can't be that exciting."

"You judge. Kyle, the guy who borrowed the car that

Terri then stole—you know, that guy—his father was arrested by *your* father."

"What was the charge?"

"Multiple, including attempted murder, resisting arrest and assaulting a police officer. Julio says there's some more interesting details in the report."

"Just a coincidence? When did the arrest take place?"

"Early nineties."

"Twenty-plus years is a long time to hold a grudge."

"I've heard of longer," Pete said.

"Still."

"Just sayin', we should check his alibi."

"He was supposed to be driving to Texas and back when Dad was attacked. If that's true, then he should be able to prove it." Changing the subject back to the matter at hand, I asked, "Who's going to call Scrooge?"

"We'll do it together. The old guy will be a little less likely to file a lawsuit if there are two of us."

As well as running the worst rentals in the county, Scrooge was also infamous for suing anyone who annoyed him, especially anyone who worked for the city or county.

"You know, if the guy was nicer then someone would have already told him that there was a fire behind one of his rentals," Pete said.

"We need to talk to him anyway and see what he knows about his tenant. I did find some letters that should give us the next of kin." I held up the evidence bag.

"All the sad tasks that have to be done."

"I just hope that no one ever has to notify our next of kin."

"Amen, brother."

I was halfway through the junk room when my phone rang with a call from Dad.

"They're letting me out after lunch."

"That's great!" I told him.

"I want you to get Mauser and meet us at the house."

"I can bring him by later. I'm in the middle of searching a

victim's house."

"I want Mauser to be at the house when I get there!" he shouted angrily. "Damn it! Is it too much to ask?" That was apparently directed at Genie, who took the phone away from him.

"Your dad's just a little worked up." Genie sounded more worried than anything else. I remembered how we'd been warned that Dad might have emotional issues on top of everything else.

"I'm sorry," I heard him grumble through the phone.

"I can be there by three," I told Genie. I wanted to make things as easy on her as I could.

"That'll be fine. I doubt we'll get there much before then anyway." I knew that she must have been exhausted.

With Pete working with me on the case, it wouldn't be a big deal for me to swing by and pick up Mauser, who was spending the day with Cara at the vet. I just hoped that Dad's volatility wasn't going to be an ongoing problem.

I called Cara to let her know that our overgrown houseguest would soon be going home.

"Dr. Barnhill won't miss him."

"Mauser still causing trouble?"

"Nah, he's just being his usual big personality. Let's just say he's a bit of a distraction around the clinic."

I didn't tell her about Dad's outburst. There wasn't any need to cause her to worry over something that might not be a problem.

Hanging up, I turned back to the junk room. Among the boxes nearest the door, I'd found six that had probably belonged to Alverez. These contained some work boots, old belts, tools and some Spanish-language magazines. I slid them out into the hallway, then plowed deeper into the room, where almost everything was covered in dust. I knew it was a giant waste of time, but I had to check the whole room to make sure no one had snuck a body inside the room or that a rat hadn't dragged a gun under a pile of boxes.

Half an hour later, Pete came to check on me.

"I'm done," he told me. Even in the cold trailer, I could see the sweat on his forehead.

"Nothing?"

"A dozen bags of evidence. Mostly suspicious drugs or cigarettes, including some butts that we might check for DNA if we get desperate. What are these?" He kicked the boxes I'd set out in the hallway and I explained why they were there.

"Let's look at what you've got." Pete got down on one knee and flipped back the flaps on the first box. "Junk," he proclaimed after spreading out an array of ball caps, belts and work gloves. "But certainly could have been Alverez's stuff."

"That's a bunch of magazines," I said when he opened the second box.

"I didn't even think that guys buy men's magazines anymore. I figured everyone gets their jollies from the Internet." He flipped through the titles. "*Tetas*," he muttered, holding up one showing a woman with unnaturally large breasts. The next magazine had sports cars decorating the cover. "*Automóvil Deportivo*—must mean fancy car or something like that." The rest of the magazines alternated between cars, girls and martial arts.

"It's like looking in a teenage boy's head. Girls, cars and muscles." I shook my head.

"For me it was girls, cars and guns," Pete said as he held up several magazines, letting anything inside fall out. Mostly there were just subscription postcards, but in two magazines he found Western Union receipts. He handed them to me.

"One for two thousand and one for fifteen hundred." I looked at the dates and grunted. "Only two weeks apart and both addressed to Cristela Alverez in Quetzaltenango, Guatemala."

"Was he making that kind of money?" Pete asked.

"It's a question." I nodded toward our surroundings. "But it's not like he was spending a fortune on his housing."

"Julio should be able to help us get in touch with Cristela

Alverez."

"I figure once he translates the letters, we should know if she's Eduardo's mother or wife."

"Could be a sister," Pete suggested.

"Don't complicate this. I'm betting it's his wife."

"We'll get with Julio this afternoon."

Finally finished with the trailer, we helped Marcus and the intern pack everything back up into the crime scene van. We were almost ready to leave when an ancient black Lincoln Continental pulled into the driveway, saving us a phone call.

Scrooge climbed out of the car. He was wearing beige slacks and a tan turtleneck sweater. His long grey hair flew in the breeze as he hustled toward us.

"Who told you you could take that stuff out of my trailer?" he shouted. "Stealing!"

I wanted to tell him to call the cops, but thought better of it. Swallowing my disgust at the way the man treated his tenants, I said, "Mr. Frasier, this is a crime scene. We need to collect any items we feel are pertinent to our investigation." My voice was as calm and soothing as I could make it without sounding patronizing.

His angry red face told me he hadn't heard anything I said. "Where's your warrant?"

"This is a crime scene," I repeated. "A man is dead. We don't need a warrant to investigate a murder."

"Dead! Who's dead?"

"We found a body in a burning vehicle in the backyard of the trailer."

"The backyard! Then why are you hauling stuff out of my trailer? I've already called my lawyer! I want you to put everything back in there!" He was within a foot of me now.

"If you want, I can get a warrant. I would think you'd be worried about who the victim is."

"He's paid up through the end of the month." Frasier waved away any concerns for Alverez.

"Mr. Frasier, save your money. You won't win this fight."

"I know you! You're that son of the sheriff. Nepotism." I thought he was going to spit, he looked so disgusted at the thought. "I contributed to the guy running against your dad and I'll do it again."

"Just let us do our job. There's nothing you can do to keep us from investigating the murder of a man on your property." I was being very careful not to make threats or get angry.

"Your dad got stabbed, didn't he? Ha, incompetence. The man's a fool."

My blood started to boil in an instant. Before I could do or say anything stupid, I felt a large paw grab my arm and pull me back. Pete stepped between Frasier and me.

"Mr. Frasier, you might remember me. I had you arrested for assault a couple of years ago when you hit that woman with a yard sign," Pete said, and was pleased to see Frasier turn bright red. "You sued me and the department and lost. Oh, yeah, and the judge in your criminal trial said that he would give you probation, but that if he ever saw your face again, you'd be sitting in jail for a year. Remember that?"

Frasier sputtered.

"I don't want to arrest you for obstructing justice." Pete paused. "But I will. And I'll make sure that your case comes up in front of Judge Greene."

Frasier looked like he was going to explode.

"Now, why don't you come over here and tell me about the man who rented this trailer?" Pete waved toward Frasier's Lincoln. Slowly, Frasier followed him while I tried to cool down.

Pete managed to get a little information from Frasier. He gave the man a receipt for the items we'd taken from the trailer, then sent him away in his boat of a car.

After we wrapped the area in crime scene tape, it was almost two. Pete followed the van back to the office to meet with Julio while I headed to the clinic to pick up Mauser. I'd need to switch cars with Cara. While it was a tight fight to get the Dane into her car, it was next to impossible to cram him into my unmarked.

"It was fun having you at work, but it's past time for you to go home," Cara told Mauser as she ruffled his ears. He leaned into her for one last nuzzle before jumping clumsily into the car.

"I should be home at something like normal time this evening," I told her, before giving her a kiss and climbing behind the wheel.

CHAPTER EIGHTEEN

I'd heard stories about pets who could obviously tell when their owners were coming home. Well, Mauser must have known that his dad was waiting for him because, as soon as we got within half a mile of the property, he started going crazy with excitement. I thought for sure that he was going to bust out of the door or cause us both to die in a fiery crash as he bounded from the back seat to the front, his legs hitting my arms and head.

"Don't make me pull over!" I warned him.

As soon as we were in the driveway, he hit the passenger window glass so hard with his paws that I thought it would explode.

I saw Dad and Genie on the porch of the house. "Go inside!" I yelled before I opened the door. I was sure that, if they stayed, Mauser would plow over both of them in his excitement. As it was, as soon as I opened my door, he clambered over the top of me and left bruises on my midsection that would last for weeks.

I watched him tear across the yard so fast I thought he'd rip a tendon.

"Stop!" I yelled as he approached the front door at full battleship speed. At the last second, his brakes came on and he skidded up onto the porch. Dad cracked open the door and Mauser managed to kick his mania up another notch, zooming in small circles up and down the porch steps.

I caught up with the dog and managed to slow him down enough to let Dad step back out through the door. Only the fact that Dad braced himself against the door kept him from being laid flat by Mauser, whose tongue was hanging almost to the ground as he spun around in joy.

"Enough, clodhopper!" I told him, trying to get ahold of his collar. Dad's smile was almost worth all the bruises. We finally got Mauser calm enough that we could go inside, where Genie was watching us from the hallway with a big smile on her face.

"Come on in and have a seat," she told me as I caught Dad swiping at his eyes as he wrestled a little with Mauser.

"Thanks, but I'm still on the clock. We had a vehicle fire and death this morning."

"Major Parks gave me a brief rundown. He said y'all didn't know much," Dad said, then added, "Sit."

I obeyed, proving that he'd trained me slightly better than Mauser.

"Give me the CliffsNotes version."

"The fire took place behind the rented trailer of a man who was assaulted at an ATM downtown a little over a week ago. He was also our victim. The vehicle was most likely the same one driven by the person who assaulted him at the bank," I told him.

"Any... umm." Dad looked puzzled, then embarrassed.

"No suspects at this time. The victim, Eduardo Alverez, had been refusing to talk about the attack at the ATM, so I'd been trying to put some pressure on him. I went to where he worked—a warehouse out by the interstate—on Sunday." I took a deep breath. "And I might have triggered the murder. He wasn't at work, but it seems like an odd coincidence that he's killed the night after my visit. I'm going to follow up when we have some more information. I should have said that we're *assuming* it was Alverez who was burned in the

SUV. The identity hasn't been confirmed yet."

"Okay." Dad looked exhausted. I caught a glance from Genie.

"I'd better get back to work," I said, standing up.

Dad stood too, but had to steady himself on the arm of his chair. He looked like he'd aged five years in the last week. "Thanks for bringing Mauser home," he said in a small voice. He was so unlike himself that I wondered if the doctors hadn't been premature in letting him come home.

Though I'd told Cara that I expected to be home on time, it was already four o'clock when I retrieved my own car from the clinic's parking lot. I knew I needed to go in to the office, but the fact that I'd been woken up in the middle of the night was catching up with me. With a sigh, I decided that I didn't have a choice and drove the few blocks to the office.

Inside, I bypassed my desk and went back to the evidence room to find Marcus.

"You know, we have other crimes going on in this county besides all the ones you scare up," Marcus said, grinning when he saw me.

"I just wanted to make sure that Lionel got a look at the SUV."

"Not going to get much!" Lionel yelled from the open door of his office.

I headed in his direction and saw Jessie working at her monitor. She gave me a quick glance and a nod.

"You don't think you can pull anything from its computer?" I asked Lionel, who was fiddling with a pair of cell phones.

"Someone made sure I couldn't. Looks like they took a blowtorch or something to all the main computer modules."

"Seriously? You don't think it was just the fire?"

"I can show you." He put the phones down and turned to his monitor. "I took a couple of pictures for the record."

Lionel pulled up an image that showed a melted area under the hood of the SUV. "See this?" He pointed to an area below the melted plastic glob. "And this." He pointed to an area above the glob. "The module was put under some intense heat, while the areas eight inches away, above and below, are just scorched by the vehicle fire. My guess is they used a handheld butane torch."

"Terrific. I hate smart criminals," I grumbled.

"Rumor has it that the cops only catch the dumb ones."

"We'd do better if we had decent tech support," I responded.

"Can't help you on this one," Lionel said, ignoring my gibe.

I turned to Jessie. "Want to take a break?" She seemed to think about it for a moment before standing up.

"We can go out back," I suggested.

She followed me to the door that led out to the small fenced compound where the crime scene department put the cars that they were dusting and checking for evidence. The burned-out Highlander was parked next to Alverez's truck. Off to the side was an old Toyota RAV4 with the windows shot out, the victim of a tussle between rival drug gangs.

"I'm going through all the footage that the chief dropped off," Jessie told me while keeping her eyes focused on the ground.

It took me a minute to figure out that she was talking about Darlene. I remembered a text she'd sent that morning saying that Andy Cargill had been able to give her a timeframe for the theft based on information from his car's GPS.

"Any luck?"

"No."

"Good news is: you don't have to look for the SUV from the ATM attack anymore." I filled her in on the events that had occurred overnight.

"I heard that you and Pete were at a fire. I didn't know it was connected. So that's what you and Lionel were talking

179

about."

I pointed to the Highlander.

"No kidding?" She started to walk toward it.

"Don't touch. I don't know if Marcus has gotten a chance to go over it."

"If he hasn't, I'd like to see what he does." Jessie had stopped a few feet from the SUV.

"Shantel's at a seminar, so I'm sure he'd appreciate your help."

She walked around the vehicle, looking in what was left of the windows. As she came back around, she looked up at me. "Eddie told me that he's going to start over with AA." She paused. "He doesn't know if we should keep seeing each other."

"He's probably got a point."

"I know. Besides, I'm going to start my classes at the academy after the holidays, which won't leave me a lot of time anyway." There was a surprising amount of melancholy in her voice. I'd always assumed that she'd been hanging out with Eddie because he was kind of quirky and fun. From the outside, it hadn't looked to be anything very serious.

"You're really going to miss him."

"I've never felt like I was... normal. I guess meeting Eddie gave me someone to hang out with who was an outsider too."

"I thought weird was in these days." I was only half kidding.

"There's weird because you're different, and then there's weird 'cause you want people to notice you." She looked in the passenger-side window where the body had been slumped over. "I guess they weren't trying to fake a suicide or anything."

"No. Whoever it was just dumped the body in the passenger seat and torched the car. And, at some point, they destroyed its computer module."

"Wow. They must have really hated him."

"They certainly wanted him dead." I wondered if they

also wanted him unrecognizable. Why burn the body if they weren't trying to hide something? "Maybe they just figured it was easiest to burn all the evidence in one big bonfire," I said, thinking about the fact that we hadn't found a phone or computer of any type in Alverez's trailer.

"You think the body was Alverez's?"

"I was thinking about that. If Alverez is the killer instead of the victim, then this makes a little more sense. He burns the body and all of the person's ID, phone and stuff, giving himself a couple of days to get away. Even the people who sent the man in the SUV might hesitate to send more goons after him. They couldn't be anymore sure than we are whose body was in the vehicle."

I waved Jessie back toward the door. "Let's go inside. We'll find out if Marcus has gotten to the car and, if he has, if he found any phones or anything in the ashes."

Marcus was boxing up packages to go out to various labs.

"I did an inventory of the vehicle. Those boxes over there are what I've found. There was a melted cell phone, looked like it had been taken apart. If there was a SIM card, I couldn't find it. Various coins and melted pens, lots of junk that's probably just parts of the car that fell off when the firemen were putting out the blaze. I'll have to take a closer look at all of it. The fire was intense, so there wasn't much left."

I thought about the scene around the SUV when I'd first arrived at the trailer. There hadn't been any sign of a gas can or other accelerant.

"I smelled gasoline," I said.

"Whoever torched it used a bunch. Everything I took out of the car smelled like it."

"If they brought a can, that would imply it was premeditated. If Alverez was the killer and not the victim, you'd think that he would have just used what was handy and left any container."

"If it was Alverez who did the burning, then who searched the trailer?" Marcus pointed out.

"The victim. Maybe Alverez came home and found the person in his trailer, killed him and then burned the body up in the guy's SUV."

"Possible. But where does that leave you?" Marcus asked.

"Gives us another avenue to pursue. We'll have to see if anyone is reported missing," I said. Pete had notified our dispatch and the agencies in the adjacent counties to notify us of any reported missing persons in the next forty-eight hours.

"Won't the autopsy tell you who it is?" Jessie asked. She'd been listening intently to our conversation.

"Maybe, maybe not. There's almost no chance of getting fingerprints off the body, and we don't have a positive sample of Alverez's DNA. From what we know, his relatives are all in Guatemala. It could take weeks or months to get a good sample from them." As if on cue, I got a text from Julio that he was in the building.

I signed the evidence log so I could take out the letters that I'd found in the trailer, then headed for Julio's desk.

"Can you translate these letters for me?" I asked.

He put on gloves and carefully sorted through the pile of twenty letters. Since he'd moved over to investigations, I'd noticed how meticulous he was when examining evidence. I watched him as he organized the letters by date and made notes of the postmarks. Only two of the envelopes had a different return address. Those were the ones from Diego.

Once Julio had everything arranged to his satisfaction, he opened the first envelope and pulled out the two-sided piece of notebook paper.

"Do you want it word for word?"

"Just the gist will do for now."

"It's from his wife. She says that someone named Saburo is no longer sick. I think it's their son. No idea how old he is. A man named Diego has been helping to keep the garden and house in shape."

"There are two letters from him."

"I think he's either the wife's or Eduardo's brother. She

also thanks Eduardo for the twenty thousand quetzals he sent. Cristela is amazed at so much money and is glad that Diego is there to protect them from banditos, who would surely steal it if they knew she had so much money. After that, there's a bunch of sentimental stuff, and she hopes that he can come home soon."

"How much money is twenty thousand quetzals?" I asked as Julio Googled a currency converter.

"A bit more than two thousand dollars at today's exchange rate," he told me.

"That fits with the Western Union receipts we found."

The other letters from Cristela followed similar lines with mentions of children, mother and brother. Also, every letter talked about the money he sent. While she seldom talked about how much money she kept for their family, the amounts sent to the mother were always close to a thousand U.S. dollars.

"This one is from his brother." Julio was holding up a piece of stationary with the name of a hotel on it. Unlike Cristela, Diego had only filled up the front of the paper. "He seems upset. Wants to know when he can come to Florida. Says that he can help Eduardo with his work. It's coming across as pretty desperate. Diego has a woman that he wants to marry and he needs money. Talks about how he's helped out Eduardo's wife and now Eduardo needs to help him. He says that he will do anything. That part is kind of vague. I don't know if he means it as a threat or that he is willing to do any kind of work to get the money."

"Luckily we have another letter from him. I wish we could read what Eduardo wrote back."

Julio picked up the second letter from Diego. "This one was sent three months after the first one. He wrote it in October." He read the letter, raising his eyebrows with every line. "You could have a suspect. He's angrier in this one and says that he would quit taking care of Cristela's and Eduardo's children if it wasn't for their mother. He insists that he needs more money for himself and his fiancée. If

Eduardo doesn't help him, he claims that he'll come to Florida on his own. There's one part where he also says that their mother wouldn't even want the money that Eduardo sends if she knew where it came from. I don't know all the local customs and such, but this sounds like a threat."

"Great." I frowned. That's all I needed, some out-of-country wild card. "The big question now is: do we call Eduardo's wife and tell her that her husband is missing and a body has turned up behind his house, or do we wait until we have a better idea who the body is?"

"I think the right thing to do would be to wait," Julio said.

"But I'd really like to know if Diego is in Guatemala. If he's there, then we can figure he didn't have anything to do with his brother's death. Of course, it might not be his brother in the car; it might be Diego."

"Which is going to be a problem if you have to test the body's DNA using a familial DNA sample," Julio pointed out.

"Exactly. You can see why I want to know where Diego is."

Julio turned to his monitor. "According to Wikipedia, Quetzaltenango has a population of one-hundred-and-eighty-thousand people. Smaller than Tallahassee. If we can get ahold of someone from law enforcement down there, they might be able to run a check on Diego."

"Aren't they in the middle of some sort of war?"

"No, just corruption and death squads."

"Yeah, I'm not comfortable calling in the authorities on someone in a situation like that. I guess we'll just wait until we know more and then call Eduardo's wife."

I took the letters to log them back into the evidence room. Darlene called after I'd finished.

"I was just wondering if Jessie found our stolen car on any of the footage I dropped off," she told me.

"She hadn't found anything when I saw her a little while ago."

"She seemed a little on edge."

"A situation with Eddie."

"Eddie, your crossdressing informant?"

"Long story. I'm checking with her now," I said and walked over to Lionel's office. Lionel was nowhere to be seen, but Jessie was sitting at her monitor making notes.

"Any luck?" I asked her.

"No. I was going back over a couple that I might have zoned out on, just to be sure." She didn't take her eyes off the screen.

"Did you hear that?" I asked Darlene.

"So the car is still in town, or was until this morning." Darlene sounded puzzled.

"They keep the cars in a garage until things cool down?" I suggested.

"How much safer could it be than taking the car out of town before anyone even knows that it's been stolen?"

"You've got a point," I admitted.

"There's something strange about all this." Darlene's voice was thoughtful. When we had worked cases together and she'd talked like that, I'd known that she was about to sink her teeth in so deep that she wouldn't let go until she'd caught a bad guy.

"I should call you Bulldog Marks," I told her.

"I kind of like that," she said with a laugh.

"Assuming Jessie doesn't pull a rabbit out of her hat, where do we go from here?"

"I'm going to have to think about that. Feel free to come up with your own ideas," she joked.

"My thinking cap isn't working too well right now."

"What's wrong, Buster Brown?"

"Just worried about Dad. On top of that, there are all these niggling cases with loose ends dangling. It's like a weaver's convention in my head," I complained.

"You've got a right to worry about your dad. He's a good man. I wish we'd had a chance to string up the person who stabbed him."

"That bugs me too. I can't get angry at some poor girl who must have been having some type of psychological break."

"I've had my share of perps who deserved more pity than disdain. And you're right, it isn't as satisfying as slamming those iron bars shut on a real bad apple."

We commiserated with each other for a few more minutes, then I rang off. I'd barely had time to return my phone to its case on my belt when it shrieked loudly with an alert from the county's emergency management department.

CHAPTER NINETEEN

Forecast calls for Significant Weather Event this Thursday, read the message on my phone. I stared at it, puzzled, wondering what the hell sort of event it could be this far on the safe side of hurricane season. A second text cleared that up with a report that the National Weather Service was predicting a severe winter storm from southern Alabama through North Florida.

I shook my head dismissively. Almost every year we had at least one oh-no-we're-going-to-get-snow forecast, but they almost never developed into anything more than a few bitterly cold mornings. I had enough on my plate as it was and decided to let this particular freak-out happen without my participation.

Back at my desk, I spent a little bit of time on the other cases that were keeping my inbox full. When it was almost six, I realized I hadn't heard from Dr. Darzi. Anxious for the autopsy and hopeful that we could somehow get a positive ID on our victim, I called the coroner's office.

"Bad news," Linda told me. "Even Dr. Darzi has people he answers to. We got a rush order from the State Attorney. They had a shooting overnight at a restaurant near FSU. A student was killed, then a police officer shot and killed the perp. The phones haven't stopped ringing and we had two news crews in the parking lot an hour ago. Bottom line, they're going to get autopsied tomorrow. Your victim has been pushed to Wednesday."

"Just my luck," I grumbled.

"Darzi knew you'd call and said to remind you that you've gotten your share of priority placements."

"Yeah, yeah. I just want to know for sure who the guy is."

"I can tell you that it *is* a guy. If that helps."

"Some. What about fingerprints?"

"No luck. I tried a couple of different methods. The hands were just too badly damaged. If you have dental records, that would help. His teeth are in pretty good shape. There's some gold work on one of the right molars that's pretty distinctive."

"Can you tell how old the work is? The guy we think it is has only been in the country for a few years."

"Looks older than that. I'm not a dental-work expert, but I'd say it looks like it might not have been done in the United States."

"That bad?"

"No. Kinda the opposite. There's some engraving on it. Pretty fancy."

"Can you send me a picture?"

"That I can do."

Her text came through immediately.

"That's impressive," I admitted, looking at the scrollwork on the gold cap. "Though I can't remember seeing it on Alverez."

"It's far enough back that, unless he smiled, you probably wouldn't notice it."

"He never smiled when I was around. I'll ask Pete if he noticed the gold cap. Thanks, Linda."

I called Pete, who reported that he'd never gotten a smile out of Alverez either.

"Think the hospital would have a record of it?" I asked.

"His face didn't sustain much damage in the attack," Pete said. "Worth trying, I guess. It's a shame he wasn't arrested for anything. That tooth would have been noted on his intake papers."

"At least it gives us a hook for talking to his wife. A gold cap like that isn't something she's likely to forget. We'll need to call her soon. I'll touch base with Julio and make sure he can translate."

"Funny thing," Julio said when he answered his phone. "I called that guy Kyle to check up on his alibi."

"Tell me it didn't check out."

"No, it checked. I just got an odd vibe from the guy."

"Odd how?"

"Nervous."

"You *were* calling to check on his alibi," I pointed out.

"That's true. And he gave me some names and numbers, which I called and everything checked out. He just left me with a feeling." Julio sounded unsure.

"Ahhh, you had the feels," I joked.

Julio ignored me. "It's probably like you said, he just didn't appreciate being checked up on."

"Did you ask him about his father being arrested?"

"I figured I'd wait and see if his alibi was solid."

"Tell you what, let's go around to his job site and see how he acts when we ask him about his father's arrest."

"He's a trucker so he might not be there."

"Good point. The boss seemed cooperative. I'll call him in the morning and see what Kyle's schedule looks like."

By the time I drove home, the sky was dark, reminding me how close we were to the longest night of the year. Feeling every minute of my very long day, I had to shake myself a couple of times to keep from zoning out as I drove. I was finding it annoying that, the older I got, the more my body wanted a full night's sleep.

I was pleased to find the house occupied by the right number of characters: Cara, Alvin, Ivy and Ghost.

"Bet you miss him," Cara said as I walked through the

door.

"Who?" I said disingenuously.

"Your more charismatic brother."

"Ha! It's nice to be able to walk across the room without being plowed into by the *Titanic* of the canine world. Isn't that right?" I asked the two cats. Ivy was cleaning herself while Ghost stalked an imaginary foe.

"Liar, liar."

"Maybe I'll buy him a Christmas present." I smiled.

"How bad is the storm going to be?"

"What?" I'd forgotten the text.

"Thursday they're predicting ice."

"I'll worry about that on Wednesday. They're just giving us the worst-case scenario," I said with confidence.

After dinner and a short nap, I settled in to make some notes about the body at Alverez's trailer. While I worked, Cara read a book by Jeff Meldrum called *Sasquatch: Legend Meets Science*.

"You don't actually believe in bigfoot?" I asked, closing my laptop and joining her on the couch.

"I could tell you stories." She smiled, the colored lights of the Christmas tree making her red hair glow around her face.

"What does that mean?" I chuckled.

"You know how Mom and Dad had us living out in the woods most of the time. Well, I've seen things."

"You have *not* seen a Bigfoot."

"Have too."

"Come on!" I tried to tickle her, but she sat up and looked me in the eye.

"It wasn't funny at the time."

"Seriously? You hadn't just eaten one of your mother's special brownies?" I said, and regretted my words when I saw the look on her face.

"I'm not kidding."

"How old were you?" I expected her to say that she was nine or ten.

"Fifteen. We were camping in the woods of northern

California." She saw the look in my eyes and put up her hand. "It was *not* a bear. I was with a friend and we both saw the thing."

"You've had some interesting experiences growing up with your crazy parents," I said, remaining noncommittal on whether she'd seen a Bigfoot or not.

"You don't believe me."

"It's more that I don't believe in Bigfoot," I said, trying to be diplomatic.

"We weren't hunting for a Sasquatch, we just bumped into him."

"What did you just say?" Something had clicked in my brain.

"I said we just stumbled on him standing there in the path."

"No, you said that you weren't hunting Bigfoot."

"That's right. It was something that just happened."

"If you want to find something, then you go to a place where they gather."

"What the hell are you talking about?" Cara looked at me, confused.

"I need to call Darlene. You just gave me an idea." I stood up and went to the counter to retrieve my phone.

"You don't want to hear how your wife barely avoided being abducted by Bigfoot?"

"In a minute," I said, hitting Darlene's speed dial button.

"Where would you go to see fancy sports cars?" I asked as soon as she answered.

"Is there a grand prize if I get the right answer?" she responded.

"I'm serious. If someone is stealing fancy sports cars that spend most of their time locked in garages, where did he first see them?"

"I've cross-checked all of them and the owners took their cars to different places to be serviced."

"Right, so where else do those mechanical road toys go?"

"Do you have an answer? Or are you hoping I'll come up

with one?"

"Adams County Golf and Country Club." I smiled.

There was silence on Darlene's end of the call before she said, "Yosemite Sam, you might just have a genuine idea there."

"First thing tomorrow, I'll call all the victims and see if they took their cars to the country club before they were stolen."

"I've got a good feeling about this," Darlene said.

I noticed the look I was getting from Cara. "I'll call you tomorrow. Right now, I've got to go listen to a Bigfoot story."

"A what?" Darlene asked as I hung up.

Tuesday morning was warm and damp as I drove in to work. Even with the constant text alerts from emergency management, I was doggedly ignoring the weather reports that predicted a new ice age beginning on Thursday.

Julio was talking to Dill at the front desk when I arrived.

"I'm going to call to see if Kyle will be at work today. I may need you to call Alverez's wife too." I explained to Julio about the dental work.

"I don't think anyone in this country did that. It looks... refined. All we see around here are dollar signs and stuff." Julio was looking at the picture Linda had sent.

"Probably not. I'm going to check with the warehouse where he worked, see if anyone there ever saw him smile."

I went to my desk and called AmMex Trucking Company first. The woman who answered told me that Kyle Whitten was out on a run and would be back Wednesday afternoon. I thanked her and debated what to do next. Calling all the victims of the high-end car thefts could take a while, especially if I had to leave messages and wait for return calls, so I decided to get started.

I managed to speak with three of the car owners and all of them confirmed being members of, or guests at, the country club. I was feeling good about my hunch and reported the results of the calls to Darlene.

"I've got an emergency management meeting at one o'clock this afternoon," she said. "Don't you have to be there?"

"Probably. I think I got a text about it." I wasn't thrilled about sitting in a meeting where most of what was discussed wouldn't involve me.

"I'll see you there, Chicken Little. You know, you need to take your responsibilities seriously."

"Don't call me Chicken Little. I'm not the one saying the sky is falling. Even if we get an ice storm, the burden is going to fall on the power company, road crews and the fire department."

"And lots and lots of car accidents," Darlene reminded me.

"This is much ado about nothing." An image popped into my head of me writing up accident reports in the sleet. I pushed it away.

"We'll figure out how we're going to tackle the country club after the meeting," Darlene said sternly.

"Yes, Mother Marks."

I had time to go out to the warehouse and talk to some of Alverez's coworkers before the meeting. When I got to Southeast Express, Freda Maynard, the woman I'd spoken to the first time, was at the front desk.

"I remember you," she said in a loud voice that was a bit confrontational.

"I spoke with you about Eduardo Alverez," I said, showing her my ID to make sure she understood that this was a professional visit.

"He hasn't shown up for two days in a row." She made it clear that this was my fault.

"That's exactly why I'm here."

"He's a good man. We're having the devil of a time keeping up without him."

"Can you tell me if he had a gold tooth?" I decided to be

blunt and get to the point.

"What?" I'd managed to knock the starch out of her bloomers.

"Did you ever notice whether he had a gold tooth or not?" I repeated.

Her eyes shifted over to the wall on my right. Hung on the wood paneling were two dozen pictures with small plaques that read: *Employee of the Month*. The third one from the end was a picture of Eduardo Alverez, wearing a big grin. Sure enough, on the left side of his mouth I could see a shiny gold tooth. The identity of our body was confirmed. I pulled out my phone and took a photo of the image as Freda watched with a shocked look on her face.

"What's going on?" she asked with less bravado and more concern in her voice.

I walked back to the desk.

"When was the last time that you saw him?"

"I guess it was on Friday. He didn't work this weekend. Has something happened to him?"

"We believe that Mr. Alverez is dead."

Her hand flew to her mouth. "Believe?"

"A body was found and… couldn't be easily identified. However, the victim did have a gold tooth that looks like a match for the one in the picture."

"Why'd you think it was him?" I ran into three types of witnesses when conducting investigations. There were those who didn't want to answer any questions, those who were cooperative and those who asked their own questions. Freda was one of the latter.

"The body was found at his house."

"Oh. When?"

"Did Mr. Alverez have any friends at work?" As soon as I asked the question, she got a look in her eyes like someone who'd just realized that they were walking through a minefield.

"Friends?" Like she'd never heard the word before.

"Anyone he hung out with?" I pushed.

194

"I work here at the front desk. Why would you think I know who his friends are?" she asked defensively.

"We just want to talk to everyone who knew him."

"What did he… die from?"

"We don't know yet."

"But you need to question his friends?"

She was beginning to annoy me.

"We just want to get a picture of his last days. It could help us understand what happened to him." I thought I was going above and beyond by explaining this.

"I guess."

"Ms. Maynard, I really need your help. We'd like to find out what happened to Eduardo. Now, I know that you're in shock over this, but I need you to answer my questions as best you can." I was impressed with my own patience.

"I liked him. He was a nice guy. Some of the dimwits we have here won't even give you the time of day, but Eduardo always said hello and was real nice. Never got any complaints from his supervisor."

"I'd like to speak to his supervisor."

"I…" She hesitated. "Sam. Yeah, sure. I'll go get him." With that she hurried through a set of double doors leading into the warehouse.

As I waited for her to come back, I heard movement in the small office that was directly behind the receptionist counter. Through the clear door, I could see the computer station where I remembered seeing a man working the last time I'd been there.

I looked at my watch. It took Freda ten minutes to come back with the elusive Sam. He wasn't what I had been expecting. He looked like a lanky teenager half concealed in a yellow hard hat. The only thing that spoke to his authority was the stern expression on his face. He put his hand out slowly.

"Sam Hubbard." The hand shook mine with slow deliberation.

"Deputy Larry Macklin with the sheriff's office. Did Ms.

Maynard tell you why I was here?" I was trying to get a feel for what the relationships in the warehouse were like.

He glanced over at Freda before answering me, which told me something about the hierarchy.

"She said that something had happened to Eduardo?"

"We think he might have died early Monday morning."

"Damn! I'm sorry to hear that. He was one of the most dependable guys I've got."

"What exactly was his job?"

"He mostly drove a forklift and loaded up the trucks."

"What do you all do exactly?"

"We're a hub for small shipping companies," Sam explained. "There are a lot of guys that want to get a hook in the shipping market, but don't have the money to maintain a warehouse. To compete with some of the big companies like UPS or FedEx, you need to have a network of warehouses. We're the small guys' network."

"You own a bunch of these warehouses?"

"I don't." He laughed. "Actually, the company doesn't own that many either. Southeast owns about a dozen, but we're part of a larger group that covers the rest of the country, forming a large umbrella." I could tell that this was a pitch he'd given multiple times. He paused and seemed to remember why I was there. "Eduardo was great because he could be trusted to do more than drive a forklift. If I needed a truck moved, he could do that too. Flexible."

"When was the last time you saw him?"

"Friday. He had the weekend off."

"Did you notice anything… different about him?"

"Like what?"

"I don't want to suggest anything. Think back to Friday. Did he come in on time? Work a full day?"

"Yeah, I don't think he ever missed a day of work. Like I said, dependable. You know, we don't talk much in the warehouse. All the noise. You pick up your loading slip when you come in and go to it."

"I guess you all have breaks, lunch?"

"Sure."

"Did he sit with anyone? Go out to lunch with anyone else?"

"No. I'm pretty sure he usually went to the truck stop for lunch like a lot of the guys, but he stuck to himself. I considered that a bonus. When guys start palling around is when the trouble starts. Give me a guy that comes in, does his work and goes home when the whistle blows."

"He ever have any visitors?"

Sam seemed to think about this for a moment. "No."

"Ever hear him mention his family?"

"I'm sorry. Like I said, he kept to himself. I do too. We said good morning, good night, have a great weekend or see you tomorrow." He shrugged.

"You must have seen him talk to someone else that works here?"

"He talked to Freda." He glanced over at her. I tried to catch the look she gave him in return, but I wasn't quick enough. By the time I looked her way, she had turned to answer the phone.

"Okay, thanks." *For nothing*, I thought, but took out my card and handed it to him. "If you think of anything else, give me a call."

"Sure thing." Sam was already turning back to the double doors. I didn't even get a good-talking-with-you handshake.

I turned back to Freda.

"I'd like to get a copy of Eduardo's employment information."

Her face, which had been getting ready to smile and, no doubt, wish me out the door, froze into a grimace.

"Those aren't public." Her words were hard and cold.

"I'm not the public," I reminded her.

"Yes, well. I'll have to check with our HR department."

"It might speed things along if I talked to them directly."

"No," she said, and I thought for a moment that she wasn't going to give me a reason. "I mean, they aren't here. They're in another office."

"Okay. I could call them."

"Really, just let me talk to them and get back with you. I promise I'll call you as soon as I can." I could see that we were getting very close to the limit of her nerves.

"I'll expect to hear back from you by this afternoon." I handed her one of my cards. "My email is on there. Best thing would be for them to go ahead and send them to me. Save us all a lot of time and aggravation." I turned without waiting for another dodgy response.

As I walked out to my car, I wondered what they had all been so nervous about. Was someone connected to the warehouse responsible for Alverez's beating... or even his death? Because of the shady behavior, I'd moved the entire company up high on my suspect list.

CHAPTER TWENTY

I grabbed a quick lunch at the taco stand, then headed over to the emergency management operations center next to the jail.

"I knew you didn't want to miss this." Darlene gave me a smile.

"Major Parks sent out a text that anyone who wasn't actually on patrol should attend." I looked around to see who'd managed to come up with a good enough excuse to miss the meeting. I didn't see Pete, but Julio was in the corner talking to some of his firemen friends. We'd never had a bad cold spell when someone didn't manage to burn their house down.

Five minutes before the meeting was scheduled to start, I heard a spattering of clapping that started at the back and spread throughout the couple hundred people filling the room. Darlene and I stood up to see what was going on.

I saw Dad walking slowly toward the front of the room between the rows of folding chairs. He was wearing his uniform and walking very stiffly. A concerned-looking Genie stood by the door, watching him carefully. Everyone was on their feet, giving him a standing ovation. Looking at him walk and trying to look tough, I thought ungraciously, *Idiot.* I moved to intercept him.

He saw me coming and gave me a look that said, *Don't be a pain in the ass*. I just frowned at him and kept moving.

"What are you doing here?" I asked *sotto voce*.

"My job." It wasn't quite a hiss, but the hiss was implied.

"You need to be resting."

"You and Genie can rest," he grumbled without slowing his pace. He wasn't doing too badly, but when I looked closely I could see a slight wobble. I gave him an eighty percent chance of making it to his usual chair at the front table.

I followed at his elbow without touching him. If he'd thought for one minute that I was reaching out to support him, I'd have gotten a punch right to the eye. When we were two rows from the front, he gave me a look that told me I'd come as far as he'd let me. I stopped and waited another minute until he was within reach of the front table, then I joined Genie at the back of the room. I passed a guilty-looking Pete sneaking in late.

"I couldn't stop him from coming," Genie told me, frowning.

"At least he's reverting to type." I shook my head. "How's he really doing?"

"Good moments and bad. I gave him an ultimatum. If he came here, he'd have to take some pain medication."

I gave her hand a squeeze. "Let me know what I can do," I told her before heading back to join Darlene. Everyone had stopped clapping and retaken their seats.

Chief Hatcher from the fire department was the current head of our emergency management team. The job shifted between him and Dad about every other year. He gave us a breakdown of the current predictions from the National Weather Service, which certainly sounded dire. I thought back to the last winter storm six years before when half an inch of ice had fallen from the sky. The county had seen a hundred accidents, most of the residents lost power for a day and there'd been three house fires. *Surely we can do better than that*, I thought, also remembering that we'd had at least five winter storm false alarms since then.

"Florida and ice don't mix," Hatcher said. "We know that folks aren't going to take us seriously when we tell them to stay home, so we just need to be prepared. I think..." The chief hesitated, looking from Dad to Major Parks.

"Major Parks will still be in charge," Dad said and then, before everyone's attention had moved on, he added at full volume, "Through the rest of this week."

"That's fine," Hatcher said and gestured to Parks.

"I've talked to the highway patrol, who have assured me that they will shut down I-10 at the first sign of ice, whether it's falling from the sky or freezing on the road. The sheriff's department will have all of our deputies on duty or on call starting tomorrow."

I managed to keep my eyes from rolling.

"Chief Marks?" Hatcher said, looking our way.

Darlene stood up.

"My officers are going to be on call twenty-four-seven, assisting where needed. I've talked to Major Parks and we've agreed that, in this emergency, we're not going to worry about jurisdiction. My officers will serve where they're needed."

"Suck-up," I muttered under my breath after she sat down.

"You're going to be the epitome of the unprepared grasshopper," she admonished.

"Grasshoppers are a lot more impressive than ants."

"I'd rather be a live ant than a dead grasshopper." We went back and forth long enough that we missed most of the power company's presentation.

"Where are you on the cremated body?" Darlene asked as we got up to leave.

"We at least know who he is. Crap, I got so wrapped up in the sketchy way his coworkers were acting that I forgot to tell Pete or Dr. Darzi's office." Pete was waving at us from the back of the room.

As soon as we got close, I told him that I had a positive ID on the body. I showed him the pictures and gave him a feel for how suspicious Freda and Sam had been acting.

"We can go ahead and let his wife know," Pete said solemnly. He was a great family man and always had empathy for other people's familial connections.

"Julio said he'd do it for us."

"Now that we know he was the victim of a crime and is deceased, we can get his phone records."

"And GPS information from his truck."

"Changing subjects, we need to find a way to put some pressure on Kyle Whitten. You said he's going to be at AmMex tomorrow?" Pete asked.

"That's what they said."

"Let me know and we'll go out there together. Maybe having two of us show up will rattle his cage a little."

"We could make it a twofer and hit Southeast Express. They're both right there."

"Sounds like a plan. I'll practice my bad cop impression."

"You don't have to practice being a bad cop," Darlene ribbed him.

"Hey, you're supposed to just pick on him," Pete said, nodding in my direction.

"Come on, let's head out to the country club and leave this riffraff behind," I said to Darlene.

The Adams County Country Club always struck me as a bit sad. The building and grounds were selling more than they had to offer. Like a kid from the sticks getting married in a blue tuxedo, the club fell short of the elegance that it was striving for.

"Are they going to let us in?" I joked as we drove through the iron gates and up the crepe-myrtle-lined drive toward the brick building and its six white columns.

"Hell, I was invited to join. A perk of being Chief of Police."

"Yeah, Dad's a member too, but he never comes up here unless he's giving a presentation. He told me that the couple of times he's been here for dinner, everyone came up and wanted to talk about their neighbors and what they thought they might be up to."

"Yep. I get some of that. Trouble is, I'm not elected so I need the city commissioners' goodwill. So I do a little schmoozing." Darlene's attitude was very matter-of-fact.

I turned in my seat and looked at her. "I never pictured you as a game player," I said honestly. She had always been so blunt and out front with her opinions.

"Oh, please. You either play the game or sit it out."

"That doesn't sound like the Darlene I know."

"You must not have been doing a very good job of listening to me. How long were we partners?"

"Not sure. Too long or not long enough."

"I'm a get 'er done gal and sometimes the way to get 'er done is with a heaping bunch of honey."

"You never used anything but vinegar with me," I pointed out.

"You're just special."

The club's parking lot was almost full, which explained by a banner that announced the Third Annual Holiday Golf Tournament, which apparently was today. *My invitation must have gotten lost in the mail*, I thought. Darlene pulled into a space toward the back of the parking lot between a Cadillac and a Lexus.

"You old hound dog, I think you've got us on the right trail," she said when she stepped out and looked at the cars parked in the lot. "Now all we need to do is figure out what job he has. You know, I was up here for the Halloween ball in October and they had valets."

"You were at a ball? I don't even know who you are," I said with mock scorn.

"I was dressed as an alien."

I shook my head. "Let's go find someone to talk to."

"I called a woman I know on the board. She said we

should talk to Heidi Evens. She's the manager."

I followed Darlene to the club's office, where we found Heidi discussing an upcoming wedding with a bride and her wedding planner. From the looks on their faces, they weren't getting the answers they were looking for.

"I can't change the date. Our calendar is full a year out. Like I said, I can put you on a waiting list for a cancelation." Heidi held up her hands.

"That won't do us any good! We need to know when so we can plan everything. This is a *big* wedding," the planner said forcefully.

"I'm sorry that the groom is not going to be able to get the time off that he'd hoped, but there's nothing we can do." Heidi was standing up and trying to get them to follow her to the door.

"Fine! We'll just move the wedding to Tallahassee!" the bride screamed.

"Of course, you'll need to do what you'll need to do. Just remember that you only have a week to let us know before you'll forfeit half of you deposit."

"This is unfair!" The bride stomped out with the planner on her heels.

Heidi sighed before turning to us and smiling. "Chief, it's so good to see you again."

"Heidi, this is Deputy Macklin with the sheriff's office," Darlene introduced me.

"Nice to meet you," I said, trying to go along with the genial air.

"Oh, yes, you're Sheriff Macklin's son. I thought I recognized you. I hope your father is okay." She looked genuinely concerned.

"He attended an emergency management meeting today." *Though he probably shouldn't have*, I couldn't help thinking.

"I bet it was about the storm. Hard to believe when the weather is so nice today. Anyway, take a seat and tell me how I can help you." She waved toward the recently vacated chairs facing her desk.

"We're here on a rather delicate issue," Darlene said, sitting in the chair closest to the desk. "There's a possibility that a recent string of car thefts might be linked with the club."

Heidi's face fell. "Surely not." The words were spoken like a command. She leaned forward and put her hands on the desk. "What exactly are we talking about?"

"Several expensive cars have been stolen over the last six months. We have reason to believe that the person who stole them might work for you."

"Expensive cars," she repeated thoughtfully. "Simon Ridgeway mentioned that his car was stolen from his garage... I guess that was about a month ago. But I don't see how a car stolen from his garage could be linked to us."

"We think the thief might be using their job here at the club to scout out the cars he wants to steal."

"We do thorough background checks on everyone we employ," Heidi said as though that should be the end of the discussion.

"I'm sure you do. The person might not have a record. Someone could be using them. Maybe a man whose wife works here, or a father whose son parks cars for you."

"Of course, anything is possible." She sounded doubtful. "We're on shaky ground with this. The club feels a responsibility to its employees. Part of that covers protecting their privacy and their reputations."

"We feel the same way," Darlene assured her. "What we'd like is a chance to look over your employment records. Once we've done that, if there's anyone who we feel needs to be looked at more closely, we'll discuss it with you first."

Heidi didn't look convinced. "Opening up our human resource records is not something that we take lightly." She frowned and shook her head. "I hate to sound like a TV lawyer, but this appears to me like a fishing expedition."

"We have good reason for our suspicions. I know you don't want to harbor someone who is preying on your members."

"No. That's true. However, you don't have any proof. At least none that you're willing to share with me." She was digging in her heels.

Darlene and I had talked about our options. I decided to go with our good cop, bad cop backup plan.

"Chief, I think she's right. We'll just have to go back to the members who've had cars stolen and ask them if they noticed anyone here at the club who was acting suspicious or taking an unhealthy interest in the cars before they were stolen." Of course, we knew that this would start the members wondering if that was the case, and also start them talking to *other* members. In three days, the club's whole membership would be talking about the possibility that there was a car thief working at the club.

I could tell from her grinding teeth that Heidi instantly saw all the implications of what I was proposing. "If I let you look at the records, would you promise me that, if you don't find anything to back up this suspicion of yours, you won't go any further?"

"Scout's honor," I said, holding up three fingers and earning a dirty look from Heidi.

She took us to a smaller office where the walls were lined with files. She sat down at a computer station, punched a few keys on the keyboard and brought up a folder marked *Employees*.

"In here are subfolders for all the different positions. Inside *those* are two more folders, one each for past and present employees. In the present folder, you'll find records for each current employee… including mine. I'll also make you a list of the companies we contract with for special events. You can pick it up when you're done."

Before we could say anything more, she'd stomped out of the room.

"I should have asked her for a second computer," I joked.

"I don't think you made a new friend today." Darlene was already digging into the folders. "You can take notes."

It took more than two hours to go through all the records. The background checks looked legit, with notes made by the HR person who'd called the contacts. Only two employees had criminal records. One was for a bad check with the employee having explained the extenuating circumstances. The other was a minor charge for marijuana possession when the fifty-year-old employee had been nineteen.

We also made notes of all the married employees and the names of their spouses so we could run background checks on them later.

"No giant red flags," I said when we got up from the desk.

"Were you expecting any?"

"I can always hope."

"We're more likely to find something in the companies that they contract with, like the decorators or the parking attendants," Darlene said.

We picked up the list of contractors from Heidi, whose parting words were, "This better be the last I hear of this." She sounded like a high school principal giving a warning to truant students.

"I don't think your membership is going to be renewed," I told Darlene.

"I couldn't afford it anyway."

When we walked out of the club house, the parking lot was filled with golfers heading to their cars. Most were smiling and glad-handing each other while pulling their golf bags across the pavement. I recognized a dozen people, mostly businessmen, lawyers and politicians. There was one person who looked familiar, but I couldn't place where I'd met him. I figured I must be seeing him out of context, but couldn't nail it down.

I was still running through my mental rolodex as I got into the car and heard Darlene's phone vibrate, which it did frequently. When she looked at the caller ID, she answered it and, from the way she talked, it was clear that it was an old friend.

"Yes, I know the investigator handling that case," Darlene said, giving me a look that told me *I* was that investigator. "Sure, no problem. Come up here? You don't need to do that. You know that it was torched? Of course. I understand. You're staying at my place. I insist. You know where the key is. In the morning. I'm sure he'll be available." I got another look from Darlene. I nodded reluctantly.

"What?" I asked when she'd hung up.

"An old friend of mine. The burned-out SUV? It belonged to one of her friends. There were some personal possessions in it when it was stolen that her friend wants to get back."

I thought for a minute. "You know, that might be useful information. If we find any of the items at a suspect's house, it would be gold. You said she's coming up tomorrow?"

"Her name is Kay Lamberton. She's driving up from Gainesville this afternoon and staying at my place tonight. She'll meet you at the office in the morning," Darlene said as she pulled out of the country club's parking lot.

"Do you think she'll bring a detailed list of the items?"

Darlene laughed. "Honey, she's the closest thing to Sherlock Holmes you're going to meet in your lifetime. Okay, maybe Miss Marple. Or possibly a mix of the two."

"She's an LEO?"

"Mortician."

"Huh?" was the most intelligent response I could come up with.

"Long story. She and her brother own a funeral home near Gainesville. They've helped solve a few murders down there. I met her years ago when she helped out a friend of my family. In fact, she pushed me to become a police officer."

"How old is she?"

"Mid-seventies with the energy of a thirty-year-old."

"A mortician?"

"Don't get hung up on that. Before she was a mortician,

she was a nurse in Vietnam. Tough bird. I wouldn't suggest you cross her."

I held up my hands. "Don't intend to."

Back at the office, I went to my desk to organize my schedule for the next day. I was going to be busy, especially since I knew I'd be dragged into prep for the storm that was supposed to hit on Thursday. Thanks to Darlene, I already had a meeting first thing in the morning, plus I wanted to go to Alverez's autopsy, whenever it was. I still hadn't gotten a message from Dr. Darzi's office. Pete and I were also going to try to catch Kyle at AmMex, assuming that he was keeping to his schedule. I still figured that his dad being arrested by my dad was just an odd coincidence. Still, the idea that Terri Miller had stabbed Dad nagged at me, and I wanted to follow up on any other leads.

I got home to find Cara singing Christmas carols and baking cookies.

"You can have a couple if you help do the dishes," she told me as she spread icing on a gingerbread snowman. "The rest go to the clinic or friends. Oh, and I'll do up a box for your office. Just don't let Pete eat all of them."

"Fair enough." I picked out three cookies and started the water in the sink. "Dad came to the emergency management meeting."

"Was that doctor-approved?"

"He's as likely to follow doctor's orders as *your* parents," I reminded her.

"Good point. Still, he has to be in a lot of pain."

I touched my side where I'd been stabbed myself over a year ago. "I'm sure he is. I remember how it felt. I can still feel the spot where the knife went in."

Cara glanced at me with a worried frown. "I don't like to think about it. What will you be doing during the storm?"

"I'm still not convinced that it's going to be as bad as what they're predicting. Regardless, I'll be in uniform and on call for traffic accidents and any other emergencies that come up."

"Like what?" she asked with a grimace. She knew that on-the-road dangers could be a bigger threat to my safety than a crazy criminal with a gun.

"A couple of years ago during a bad cold snap, one of the nursing homes lost power and their generator was venting into the building. We had to help the EMTs and fire department with evacuation of the patients. Who knows, maybe this time I'll get lucky and just spend the night sleeping at the office."

Somehow we managed to put aside our fears of the future to enjoy the evening together. In my line of work, it was important to live in the moment.

CHAPTER TWENTY-ONE

Kay Lamberton met me at the door of the office on Wednesday morning. Her clear hazel eyes were sharp and seemed to take in everything around her. Despite her age, she was still quite attractive. Her grey hair was pulled back and braided into an intricate weave that complemented the pattern of her blouse. She carried a manila envelope in her left hand and stuck out her right hand to me as I approached, smiling politely.

"Let's go down to the conference room," I said after we'd introduced ourselves.

Once we were seated across from each other, she said, "Darlene said you could help me."

"I'll try. The car and everything in it was destroyed by the fire."

"Kendra Jackson lost her son back in May and there was a box of his belongings in that SUV. I don't have to tell you what those items mean to her."

"Of course. The vehicle was used for several weeks after it was stolen, so there's a chance that the items weren't in the vehicle when it was burned. And they could be as important to us as they are to your friend."

"I imagine that they could form a link between the thief

and the crimes you're investigating."

"Exactly. You said they were personal items?"

Kay pulled out two pages of printed notes from the envelope and slid them across the table to me.

"I worked with Kendra to come up with this list. She had pictures of a few of the things and I've included them here in black and white. But I can email you color images that will be a lot more use in identifying them."

I looked the over list. There were two rings—a high school class ring and one bearing the Marine Corps seal. The high school ring was engraved with *Proud of You!* The Marine Corps ring had *Even more proud!*

The list included a number of photos, including family shots, baseball team photos and scholastic team group pictures. There was also a University of Florida Gators ball cap, T-shirts of various types, a pair of athletic shoes and a belt.

"He was killed in a car accident in North Carolina on his way down to see her," Kay explained as I looked up from the list.

"Several items, the rings in particular, could provide us with valuable leads if we can find them."

"That was the conclusion that Darlene and I came to. She said that Kendra's car was involved in an assault and a murder?"

"Probable murder at this point, but yes. The victim was the same man in both incidents. I'd like to talk to Kendra and ask her a few questions."

Kay was already tapping her phone before I finished.

"Kendra, it's Kay. I'm here in Calhoun talking to the investigator who recovered your Toyota. He's going to try to find your son's things. He'd like to ask you a few questions." After a pause, she handed the phone to me.

I introduced myself and asked where the car had been stolen.

There was a long silence before Kendra said, "The Playpen."

"Where?" I wasn't sure I'd heard her right.

"I'm not a dancer, if that's what you're thinking. I was there having a drink. I used to work as a bartender at the Playpen when I was younger."

I remembered seeing the sign for the strip club off the interstate south of Gainesville.

"What time was your car stolen?"

There was another long pause. "I'm not sure. I got a ride home that night. When I went to pick it up the next day, it was gone... I've been drinking a lot since... I guess you're gonna judge me."

"I am not in any way going to judge you. I want to find the items you've lost. That's my only goal." Since she was being honest, I thought I should do the same. "I'm really being a little selfish. I want to solve the case that involved the burning of your car. Finding your son's items could be a big help to me."

"I just want them back."

"Tell me what you know, and I'll do my best to find them."

"If Miss Kay trusts you, then I guess I can."

"Tell me everything you can about the night your car was stolen."

"Not much to tell. I got to the Playpen about nine. I wasn't planning on going that night, but I got off work and had dinner. I guess things around my house were too quiet. So I drove over and parked in the rear like I always do. Like I said, I worked there about ten years ago, but I'm still good friends with everyone and I always come in the back door."

"Was it dark or are there lights behind the building?"

"There's a big streetlight back there. I wouldn't park there if it was dark. All the employees park there."

"Did you see anyone when you parked your car?"

I heard her chuckle. "There was a couple in a car, but I don't think they were interested in stealing cars."

"I take it they were lovers?"

"I don't know about that, but they were having sex."

"Did you recognize either one of them?"

She laughed again. "I'm not a peeper. I just went inside."

"Did you see your car after that?"

"Yeah, yeah, I did. I went out to get my coat. I got cold inside."

"When was that?"

"I guess it was maybe eleven. I wasn't too drunk then."

"Was the couple still there?"

"No, they'd done their business and were gone."

"Did you see anyone else?"

"There were fewer cars then. It was a Tuesday night. If it'd been Friday, there would probably have been more cars. But Tuesday is one of the slowest days."

"And that was the last time you saw the car?"

"Yep, that's right. I was pretty far gone when they wanted to close up, so Angel asked if someone could drive me home. Nice man offered to help."

"Did you know him?"

"Nope. He walked me to the door like a gentleman. Made sure I got in."

"Do you remember anything about him?"

"No, just that he had just got to town and came to the Playpen. Said he liked to have a drink sometimes. Nice guy. Wish he'd left his number. I asked the guys at the Playpen, but they didn't know him either." I heard a sniffle.

"Do you still have your keys?" I asked and she assured me that she did. A lot of car thefts happen in bars where someone takes advantage of a drunk to steal their keys and take the car. No experience necessary. Though I didn't think that had been the case here, since I'd noticed that the ignition had been punched out. That was an old-school method of stealing a car. Kids would use a screwdriver and a hammer to punch out the ignition, while professionals had developed specialized devices to do the same thing. Car manufacturers had made it more difficult, but for every better-built mousetrap there was a better-built mouse.

I talked with Kendra for another twenty minutes without

picking up anything that set off alarm bells. After I hung up, Kay nodded and reached her hand out to touch mine.

"Thank you. If you can find anything, it will mean the world to her. I guess you could tell that the world hasn't always been kind to Kendra. Her son was an amazing person and the bright spot in her life."

"I'll do what I can."

I walked Kay to her car while she shared a couple of the more interesting cases she'd been involved with. It was easy to understood how she had inspired Darlene.

Julio pulled into the parking lot as I was walking back to the building, wearing his uniform greens.

"You needed me to make a phone call for you?" he asked as I waited for him at the door.

"Alverez's wife. The one that wrote the letters."

"It's early in the morning there."

"Is there ever a good time?"

We used the landline at my desk to make the call. I didn't want to take a chance on my cell phone's reception going bad. We didn't have any luck finding the wife's number on the Internet, so the first call was to an information number in Guatemala. Two phone calls later and Julio was pretty confident that we had Cristela Alverez's number.

I listened as Julio talked to Mrs. Alverez. Sadly, I knew most of the conversation by heart. It didn't make any difference whether it was in English or Spanish—the emotions were the same.

Julio and I had worked out a list of questions for him to ask once he'd told her the bad news. I was particularly interested in getting access to Alverez's phone records and finding out where his brother was.

When Julio was done, he put the phone down and turned to me.

"I don't even know what is good news and what is bad news in a situation like this. The brother, Diego, is still there in Guatemala, at her house. The wife broke down crying and screaming, so Diego took over. He sounded surprised to hear that his brother was dead. I could hear his voice breaking as he talked about him. According to him, he's been in Guatemala since his brother left. No trips. He admitted to wanting to come to Florida, though he didn't want to say that his letters had been threatening. He said that Eduardo could be very stubborn. Liked to do things his way."

"What about the phone records?"

"He doesn't know anything about the records. Said that the bills never came to the home in Guatemala. He did give me these." Julio handed me a piece of paper where I'd watched him write down a couple of numbers. "These are the numbers that Eduardo called them from over the last couple of months."

"That'll help." I could trace them back to the service provider.

"He'll also get Cristela to fill out a request that the records be given to you. She has the Guatemalan equivalent of a power of attorney that Eduardo filled out before he left."

"It would take me a month; she might get it quicker. I suppose the phones were pay-as-you-go anyway."

I was a little disappointed that Diego Alverez had been eliminated as a suspect, even though I'd put him on the longshot list anyway.

"Do you want to come with me to talk to Kyle Whitten?" I asked Julio.

"You and Pete can handle it. I'm on patrol from now through at least tomorrow."

"Explains the uniform."

"High winds and severe storms tonight, followed by sleet tomorrow. Should be fun out on the road."

"I'll probably get the call sooner or later."

"I saw the list. You're on the second shift."

"Great."

"They're setting up bunks at emergency management for us."

"Better and better," I said, thinking about how nice the previous night had been, listening to carols with the smell of cookies in the air. I sighed.

"Could be worse. My buddy is a lineman. Chances are he'll be on the top of a pole keeping the power on."

"I'm not sure which would be harder, being a lineman or a fireman. I'd rather face being shot or stabbed than burned up or fried."

"You and me both, bro," Julio said and headed down to patrol to get his assignment from the watch commander.

At ten o'clock, I finally heard from Darzi's office that the autopsy on Alverez was scheduled for three. Which gave Pete and me time to run by AmMex first to see if we could talk with Kyle Whitten.

"I can't go to the autopsy," Pete told me when I called him. "The SWAT time is meeting to discuss how we'll respond if we get called out during the next couple days of bad weather."

I was having less confidence in my prediction that the winter storm wasn't going to be as bad as everyone was saying. A cold chill ran up my spine. I still remembered the hurricane and the months of cleanup that followed. I also wondered if I needed to do anything around our house to prepare. *Too late*, I told myself with a little kick to my own ass.

"Do you have time to interview Kyle Whitten?" I asked Pete.

"I'll be driving right by there in about five minutes if you want to meet me there."

"Perfect."

I grabbed my coat and headed for the door. Outside the air was wild and wet. I could feel the storm coming as I watched fast-moving dark clouds blowing across the sky. I looked at my watch and wondered how much time I had before the weather got really rough.

Major Parks was walking back from the emergency management center and waved me down before I got to my car.

"I walked over to check on preparations," he told me. "How's your dad? He looked like he might have been pushing things yesterday."

"You're not wrong. I think he wants to do more than he can."

"I understand that. I had to have surgery on my elbow... I guess it was ten years ago now. Drives you crazy, not being able to do what you think you ought to." He paused, and I wondered why he'd really stopped me. "I think you should check in on him. I got a call from him this morning and he sounded... upset."

"The concussion was pretty severe. His doctors said it would take months for him to get back to normal."

"He accused me of trying to take his job," Parks said bluntly. "I'm worried that he'll say the wrong thing in public and we'll all be in trouble. I'm just an old guy, but I've figured out that this social media crap can kill a career like your dad's in a heartbeat." Parks's concern was sincere.

I sighed. "I'll talk to him and Genie. I know he didn't mean anything he said."

"I know that too. But would everyone? Doesn't mean anything to me. I wanted to retire a year ago, but your dad talked me out of it. It's him and the department I'm worried about."

"Thank you. I'll see what I can do."

I left him feeling guilty that I hadn't checked in with Dad's doctors recently to make sure that his behavior was still in the range of expected recovery difficulties. The conversation hadn't helped my anxiety level.

Pete beat me to AmMex. I saw his car and was just pulling into the space beside it when Pete came out of the building.

"Wasted trip. Kyle's stuck in Alabama and won't be back until morning."

"Great," I muttered.

Promising to let Pete know what I learned at the autopsy,

I headed for Tallahassee. Once at the hospital, I hoped I'd be able to talk with Dr. Burke, Dad's consulting neurologist. Luck was on my side. I had to wait in her office for almost an hour, but Dr. Burke was able to squeeze in a few minutes to see me.

"I reviewed the charts and scans before your dad was released. I'll pull them up so I can show you the areas of concern." From a computer stand in the corner of her office, she used a short series of clicks to pull up Dad's scans on two large monitors hanging on the wall.

"There's the site of the original bleeding. You can see it clearing up in these images here."

I explained his recent behavior. She nodded and gave me a small smile.

"Normal. I said it would take a while for him to reacquire his emotional equilibrium based on where the trauma occurred. Memory loss and mood swings are part and parcel for this type of injury. You and your mother will need to be patient with him." I didn't bother interrupting her to explain that Genie wasn't my mother. The doctor didn't have time for the unimportant details. "I would suggest humoring him when possible. Getting upset with him won't help and there's no point. I have to explain to families all the time that the behavior patients are exhibiting isn't their fault. Not the family's fault and not the patient's fault. Given time, they will revert to their old selves. Battling with them will just lengthen the recovery time and be hard on everyone."

I nodded and prayed that she knew what she was talking about. Her demeanor and her reputation said that she did.

I left feeling better about the long term, but wondering how we were going to deal with the short term.

"The body is that of a Latino male who has been identified by a gold crown on his third molar with distinctive scroll work. See attached image," Dr. Darzi dictated as he began his exam of Alverez's body. Linda was assisting him today.

She'd explained to me that she wanted to follow through on the case.

I cringed when I saw the charred body on the stainless steel examining table and realized that I didn't mind the usual blood and guts as much as I thought I did. His lips had been burned away, exposing blackened teeth, and one of his arms grasped vainly at empty air. The body looked like it was still suffering through its death agonies. Dr. Darzi didn't bat an eye. He poked, prodded and carved all bodies with the same calm, professional manner.

"How bad do you think the storm is going to be?" he asked me as he examined the body. He started at the and examined every square inch of the burned flesh.

"Our emergency management team sent out an update about an hour ago. There are two fronts. The first one should move through tonight with wind, rain and possibly tornados. Sometime early tomorrow morning, the second front will come through with an Arctic blast that could give us sleet or ice... maybe both."

"Not good," Darzi said, feeling one of Alverez's knees.

"Something wrong with his knee?"

"No, I meant the weather. I did some of my graduate work in Wisconsin. I do not like ice."

"Not to mention the car accidents," Linda said.

Darzi went back to dictating his observations while I tried not to watch too closely.

"There is not much trace evidence that we can hope to retrieve," he said. "The fire burned the entire front of the body, and the fire hoses washed away anything that might have survived. Now, his buttocks and back did survive relatively intact. Still..." Darzi wasn't leaving much hope that we'd learn anything from the body. Then his hands cupped the skull.

"Ahh, here's something though. The back of his skull is cracked. Let me finish examining the mouth and nasal cavity, then we'll turn him over."

Once Alverez's body was on its stomach, Darzi examined

the back of the skull.

"This damage wasn't caused from the heat. If our workload had been closer to normal, we would already have the X-rays up." He shrugged as Linda swung the digital X-ray machine into place. "You'll want to stand behind that wall with us."

They took a number of X-rays, then displayed them on the monitors hanging from the ceiling.

Darzi turned to Linda. "What do you see?"

"He was struck on the back of the head at least three times," she said.

"Correct." He turned to me. "I should be able to give you some idea of what type of object was used when I have time to do all the measurements."

I stayed for the rest of the autopsy, though I didn't learn much other than that Alverez had eaten about an hour before he'd been killed. The lack of damage to his throat and lungs made it clear that he'd been dead before the fire was started. So now we had a murder with a blunt object and a fire to cover up the evidence... and perhaps to put the fear of God into anyone else who might threaten the murderer.

CHAPTER TWENTY-TWO

It started to rain as I drove back to Adams County. I decided to swing by Mr. Griffin's place and talk to Eddie. He'd been working at AmMex when I'd first met him and I'd been meaning to pick his brain on the off chance he might have met Kyle Whitten. But with all the drama between him and Jessie, I'd kept putting it off.

Though I wouldn't admit it to myself, I also really just wanted to check on Eddie. As annoying as he sometimes was, I wanted him to succeed.

I found him home in his apartment reading a book that his sponsor had recommended.

"I never thought much about self-help books, but reading it is kinda like talking to my sponsor," Eddie said, carefully putting a bookmark in place.

"What can you tell me about AmMex Trucking?"

He looked up surprised. "Why are you interested in them?"

"The woman who attacked Dad… the car she was found in was stolen from there," I told him and watched his eyes go wide.

"Really?"

"Yep. What do you know about the place?"

222

"They were pretty good until the kid took over," he said cryptically.

"What?"

"The boss's son. A real asshole."

"You mean that guy…" I searched the back of my mind for the name. "Glen Shaw?"

"No. I don't know who that is. The owner is Rudy Manning. Good guy. Didn't have to give me a chance, but he did."

Now that Eddie mentioned it, I remembered Glen having said that the Mannings owned the company.

"And the asshole?"

"Neil Manning. Scrawny little jerk. I went to school with him. He was creepy."

"The manager now is a big, hardy-looking insurance salesman kind of fella who was very cooperative," I said.

"Guess the owner got tired of having his son screw things up."

"Did you know a guy who worked there named Kyle Whitten?"

Eddie shrugged. "Nope. I think a bunch of the guys who worked there left when Neil took over."

I decided that I'd mined Eddie for all the information he had on AmMex.

"How's Mr. Griffin doing?"

"Excited about the storm. I brought home pizza for lunch and all he could talk about was storms. He told me about dozens of different storms that have hit Adams County, going back to snow in like 1900-and-something. Crazy what he remembers."

"I don't think he was alive then," I kidded.

"I don't mean personally remembers. Duh! I mean from all his work with the historical society." Eddie looked directly at me for the first time since I'd arrived. "And, yes, I'm sober. He makes me feel guilty, just like you. He doesn't say anything either. I know I've got to do better. Blah, blah, blah."

I raised my hands in surrender. "I'm not giving you a hard time. Remember, I know what you grew up with."

"Thanks for that. I can do this. What I really hate is that I got Jessie messed up."

"She's an adult. What's going on with her now has more to do with Terri Miller than you."

"Yeah. You know, I've tried to remember Terri. She was, like, two years behind me in high school. Of course, I mostly snuck around trying not to make eye contact with anybody."

"Were you picked on?" I hadn't ever thought about what Eddie's school life would have been like.

"Never. Everyone knew who my father and grandfather were. The worst of the bunch bought their drugs from them."

"Guess that makes sense."

"The bad part was that I had to tell them that I wasn't involved in the business when they'd try to use me as their contact." He smiled.

"You keep an eye on Mr. Griffin during this storm. The power will probably go out."

"We got it figured out. A friend of his brought over a generator, so we can run an electric heater if we need to."

"Where's the generator?" I thought about all the people who died of carbon monoxide poisoning in the winter.

He showed me where they had the generator set up in the carport. There was plenty of ventilation and I left feeling reasonably confident that they'd survive the night.

Genie called as I was heading back to the office. "I hate to ask you, but can you come over and talk to your dad?"

"Sure. What's going on?"

"He's all wired up about this storm. Says he needs to be in town."

"I'm on my way," I said, thinking about what Dr. Burke had said about humoring him.

I checked in with Cara on the way to Dad's.

"I'm heading home," she told me. "Everything is secure at the clinic. Scott will be spending the night in case the power goes out and we need the generator to heat the kennels. We ought to give that kid a raise."

She was probably right. The young kennel tech had done similar duty during the hurricane.

"I'm sorry I won't be home tonight."

"Don't worry about us. Me and the cats will be fine. Alvin will take care of us. Just keep yourself safe."

I gave her my love and hung up as I pulled into Dad's yard. The rain was coming down harder now and the wind whipped through the trees.

I entered the house through the garage. When I opened the door to Dad's kitchen, I could hear him telling Genie loudly how he wanted to go to the emergency management center. Mauser came barreling into the kitchen to find out who was invading his house and threw himself against my knees. He was hyped up more than usual and I was sure that Dad's unpredictable behavior was partly to blame.

"We're in here!" Dad shouted as though I hadn't already heard him yelling.

I walked into the living room and found Genie looking exasperated as Dad sat in an overstuffed chair, wearing his uniform.

"I guess Genie asked you to come talk me out of going in to the office," he said.

"If you mean, did I come to talk sense to you, then, yeah," I said, realizing immediately that I wasn't taking the placating route. "Look. We'll do whatever you want. I just want you to think about things."

"I'm not stupid. I know I haven't completely recovered from the... attack. I just want to do my job."

"Your job is to protect this county and its citizens. Don't you think that the best way you can do that is by letting the people you've chosen for their particular skills do *their* jobs?" I tried not to put any snark into my tone.

Dad pursed his lips. "I just want to make *sure* they're doing their jobs," he said quietly.

"No, you don't," I said in a gambit that I hoped would

pay off.

"What the hell do you mean?" His green eyes flashed angrily.

"The truth is: you want to feel like you're doing your duty. I understand that!" I felt like I had to shout to get his attention.

"Well!" was all he could come up with. He was simmering, trying to think where to take the argument next.

"I'll take you in with me," I offered, watching his eyes grow suspicious as I wondered at the wisdom of this particular bargain.

"What?"

"You heard me. You can come with me. I'll be spending the night at the management center like everyone else." I still hadn't checked the schedule, so I wasn't sure exactly where Parks had assigned me

"Okay."

"Do you think it will undermine Major Parks?"

"No."

"Do you think you're fit to go back to work?"

"I told you I just want to—"

"Supervise your employees," I cut him off. "That's what the job of the sheriff is. So what you're saying is you want to go back to work."

He looked both irritated and defeated. Then he stood up.

Where's this going? I thought.

"You're right," he stated, and I knew he had found a way to trap me.

"What?" I asked hesitantly.

"I won't go to emergency management."

"Good!" I thought I might have won a surprise victory.

"Instead, you and I will bunk down in my office."

"Huh?"

"You're right. If I show up at the emergency management center, then I'll be undermining Parks's authority. So I'll stay in my office where I can keep an eye on things without causing a scene."

Round one to Dad.

Mauser came over and leaned against me, his tongue lolling out as though he was laughing at me. I thought about what Major Parks and Dr. Burke had both told me and decided that maybe it wasn't the worst idea.

"Fine. Pack a bag."

"I've got everything I need at the office," he said.

I looked at Genie, who just shook her head.

Dad pulled her into a hug. "You've got the generator if the power goes out," he said, then gave her a kiss before letting her go.

We were quiet on the drive back to the office. At one point during the drive, I looked over to see Dad leaning against the door with his eyes shut. I could only shake my head at his stubbornness.

Dad looked happy to be back in his office. He stood behind his desk for moment, seeming to savor the experience of being "home." Then he went to the storage closet and pulled out a sheet and pillow and laid them out on the couch against the wall.

"Go across the street and let me know how things are going," he ordered.

I opened my mouth to remind him that it was pouring rain, but let it go. *This must be my penance for some evil done in another life*, I thought.

I was sopping wet by the time I made it to the management center. I'd driven across the street, but with the rain coming down sideways it didn't make much difference. Just walking to and from the car had turned me into the classic drowned rat... a very cold drowned rat.

I shook off as much of the water as I could and looked around at the first responders sitting at tables, talking and drinking coffee. I saw Major Parks with the dispatchers at a long table covered with monitors.

I was halfway across the room when everyone's phone, including my own, screeched with an automated tornado warning.

227

"They have a circular cloud formation, but don't believe that the funnel has touched down," the fire chief reported to the room.

Parks saw me and stood up. I motioned for him to join me in a corner, then told him about Dad.

"That's fine," he said. "Is he okay?"

"I'd say so. Just querulous."

"That sounds like the Ted I know. And I'm glad to hear it. He's my friend as well as my boss. As far as I'm concerned, you have your assignment. Assist your dad. I'll take you off the duty list so dispatch won't call you."

"I didn't bring him over here to get out of being on the road," I said.

Parks waved away my concerns and pointed me back across the street. I waited half an hour until the weather service issued an all-clear before heading back to the sheriff's office. We were still under a tornado watch, but there wasn't anything on radar.

I found Dad going through some papers on his desk, looking tired. He made me tell him everything going on at the emergency management center.

"You should lie down," I said.

"You're right. And I hate it." He stood up and walked over to the couch, reluctantly letting me help him settle in. Once he was comfortable, I wandered down to CID and sat at my desk. I browsed through my email, doing a little housecleaning, then I thought about what Eddie had told me. Bored, I decided to see exactly who owned AmMex Trucking.

I didn't have access to business licenses, but I could search the property appraiser's website. I used their map to identify the property and saw that it had been sold two years ago, from Rudy Manning to Neil Manning for one hundred dollars. That amount was typical for a transfer of ownership that was not so much a sale as an exchange of paperwork.

I clicked on Neil's name and saw that he owned three other properties—a modest house in a residential area, a large tract of land by the interstate, vacant except for some old warehouses, and another large lot near the interstate. I did a double-take at the location of that last one. Clicking on the map, I confirmed that it was the location of Southeast Express, where Eduardo Alverez had worked. Did the Mannings own both companies?

I had to work through more than a dozen websites to track down all the connections, but in the end it was obvious that a company called the RM Group was the umbrella organization controlling a dozen shipping companies, including AmMex and Southeast. I didn't need to use too many brain cells to figure out that RM stood for Rudy Manning. I wondered why I didn't know who he was, as he was obviously a bigwig in county business.

I went back to the property appraiser's site, but couldn't find any property in the county under his name. I switched to Leon County's site and hit the jackpot. The man owned a dozen properties around Tallahassee, including a mansion northeast of town. Eddie had said that the son had gone to school in Calhoun, so at least part of the family had moved on to larger digs after he graduated. I wondered if Neil had followed his father to Tallahassee, but a quick check of his residential property in Calhoun showed a homestead exemption. He apparently still lived here and managed the businesses.

I yawned and checked my watch. It was just past one in the morning. I pulled up the radar on my phone and saw that it was still raining, though ice and possibly a little snow would be moving in by morning. I read through the emergency management text messages and saw that so far there had been three accidents, several power outages and one tree down on a car, but no serious injuries.

I slipped quietly back into Dad's office and made myself a nest on the mattress he kept there for Mauser, dropping off to sleep as soon as I closed my eyes.

CHAPTER TWENTY-THREE

When I woke up, I was startled by flashing red lights. Slowly I remembered where I was and realized that the red glare was coming from the emergency lights that kicked on when the power was out. They stayed on until they were reset, even after the generator restored power. If all the lights were on, I almost never noticed them. But now, in the gloom of a winter's dawn, they cast an apocalyptic glow around the room.

It was a little after five. I checked on Dad to make sure he was still sleeping peacefully, then stumbled down to the locker rooms and showers. I found a couple of our deputies changing clothes.

"Look who's hiding out in his office," Andy Martel quipped.

"We all had our assignments. Ours was getting soaked pulling trees out of the road," Robbie Sykes said. "Larry's been waiting for the next murder."

"Thanks, guys. Appreciate your support."

"Did you at least keep the coffee pot filled?" Martel asked. "What they're serving across the street is sludge."

"I'll get it going," I said, feeling a huge twinge of guilt for staying warm and dry inside the office.

Half an hour later, we were drinking coffee in the break room. We'd been joined by a few other deputies, including Matti Sanderson, and they were all sharing stories of close calls and miserable weather from the night before. I had my back to the door, so I was startled when everyone stood up. Turning, I saw Dad standing in the doorway.

"Ladies, gentlemen."

"Boss," they said in unison. Everyone was smiling.

"You doing okay?" Sanderson asked with real concern in her voice. She was looking at his chest, where a small stain showed through his shirt.

He looked down. "Still seeping a little. I guess I'll have to pay for the shirt," he said with a sheepish grin. "Is the coffee any good?"

Dad sat and chatted with everyone until they all headed back out into the rotten weather. When the last of them had left, he turned to me and smiled. "I needed this."

I knew he meant the camaraderie, not the coffee.

"I know." I was still thinking about Neil Manning and the connection between Southeast Express and AmMex. "Did you ever know a Rudy Manning?"

"Sure. He owns AmMex and Southeast Express too. Why?"

"Ever have any dealings with him?"

"Sort of. His rotten kid got into a bunch of trouble and Manning was always there to bail him out. Manning's a decent guy. Usually contributes to my campaign. Why the questions?"

"Just some weird connections. Eduardo Alverez was beaten up and eventually killed inside a stolen car. He worked at Southeast. A car was stolen from AmMex and the person who stole it is the prime suspect in your stabbing. And a probable suicide victim. Adds up to two stolen cars and two dead bodies."

"From businesses owned by the same person," Dad said, his eyes narrowing thoughtfully.

"Alverez was the victim from Southeast and Kyle

Whitten at AmMex. Is there a link between those two?"

"There's already a link," Dad said. "They both receive, or in Alverez's case *received*, their paychecks from the same parent company."

"Good point. You called Neil Manning rotten. What did you mean?"

"Lots of nasty things. He would tear up someone's garden if he didn't like them. I remember him putting sugar in a neighbor's gas tank, though we could never pin that one on him. All juvenile stuff." He closed his eyes and tapped his forehead lightly. "There was a stalking accusation against him. He was fifteen, maybe? A girl and her family testified that he'd been following her home from school and had even put a tracking device on the family car. Oh, yeah, and he was taking pictures of her without her permission. Just creepy."

"You remember a lot about him," I observed. Normally, Dad had a pretty good memory, but he didn't remember everyone he'd ever arrested. And I was particularly impressed now… I allowed myself to hope that maybe some of Dad's memory problems were starting to clear.

"I was supervising the school resource officers at the time. Neil was a real conundrum. Bad enough to get a lot of attention, but he was very smart and able to walk a fine line between disturbing behavior and something truly criminal. Like taking pictures of that poor girl. He always did it in public, where legally a person doesn't have a right to expect privacy. Fine. But he had dozens and dozens of candid pictures. I keep going back to the same word: creepy."

"I guess his dad had enough money to hire lawyers."

"Oh, yeah. Which kept the State Attorney on his toes. Who wants to go to court on an iffy charge when the other side is going to hire the best lawyers money can buy?"

"He's been clean since he became an adult, I guess. He's running both AmMex and Southeast now."

"I hadn't thought of him for years. Honestly, I didn't even know his dad was letting him run the companies. Isn't there a prevailing theory that most good CEOs are sociopaths?"

"I think it's something like ten percent fall in the range of psychopaths, not sociopaths."

"Guess that makes sense. Sociopaths are the hotheads, right?"

"And psychopaths are cold and calculating."

"So maybe Neil's channeled his psychopathic tendencies into the family business. Or he's just gotten more calculating."

"Julio *did* come up with a motivation for Kyle Whitten to have been involved in your attack. Do you remember arresting a man named Willis Whitten?"

"You'll need to jog my memory on that one."

"Twenty-five years ago. Arrested for assault and attempted murder. I read the report. Whitten used a knife during the assault. The judge gave him ten years and he died in prison from a heart attack after five."

"Still don't remember."

"You were the arresting officer. I guess you might have been on the force for about seven years."

Dad rubbed his forehead. "Maybe. Feisty guy. The assault took place at an old bar that used to be down by the tracks. Actually, it was a package liquor joint where everyone knew the owner let people sit around in a room in the back and drink while they played poker. That case closed the place down for almost a year before it opened up again. I haven't thought much about it. The case was pretty clear. Plenty of witnesses. I don't think he ever denied trying to stab the guy. Just kept yelling that they'd stolen his paycheck."

"That's pretty good."

"So you think Whitten could have been involved in my stabbing as a way to get back at me? After more than twenty years? Of course, if his father died…"

"It's just one more link in the chain that seems to tie all this stuff together." I leaned back in my chair and thought about it. "I still haven't had a chance to talk with Kyle about it. He's been on the road for a couple of days, but the dispatcher said he should get in this morning."

"What time?" Dad asked.

"I'm not sure."

"Why don't we drive over there before we start getting any sleet or ice?"

I looked at my phone. "They've already closed down the interstate." I pulled up the radar and could see pink mixed with blue about twenty miles away. "We don't have a lot of time."

"We'll be warmer with the car's heater going." Dad smiled, looking more like his old self than he had since the attack.

"What the hell."

We each grabbed a coat before leaving the warmth of the office. Winter assaulted us as soon as we opened the door. As the ice approached, the temperature was dropping like a rock in water.

"Are you sure you want to go along?" I had to yell over the wind that was plowing out of the north at close to twenty-five miles an hour.

"Lead on," Dad said, bowing his head into the wind and following me to my car.

The streets were deserted as we drove toward the interstate. As we got closer, we saw a long line of semis pulled off the side of the road, overflowing from the parking lots of the Rolling On Truck Stop and the Roads Best Motel. The drivers were stuck there until the highway patrol decided it was safe to reopen I-10.

AmMex's parking lot was also filled with trucks. I assumed that they were allowing other truckers to park there to wait out the weather.

"Kyle might not have been able to make it home from Alabama in the storm," I said as I maneuvered the car into a spot at the back of the building.

"We'll find out," Dad said, reaching for the door handle.

I hadn't thought ahead to this moment. My knee-jerk

reaction was to ask him to stay in the car, but then I thought about it. If Kyle *was* involved in the attack on Dad because of his father's arrest, then what better way to rattle his cage than to have Dad walk in with me to ask him a few questions?

"Let me do the talking. You just stand close and look menacing," I told Dad.

"I'm not at the top of my menacing game, but I'll see what I can do. I should have brought Mauser."

"I'm looking for menacing, not Hound of the Baskervilles."

As we got out of the car, something cold and wet, but thicker than water, started falling from the sky.

I could see folks moving inside the building as we walked up to the door. In the reception area, there was a large table set up with coffee and donuts. About a dozen men were standing around it and talking. Several of them interrupted their conversations to stare at us as we walked in.

I didn't see anyone behind the desk. I started to approach one of the guys standing around when a familiar face came out of the back. I froze as another image flashed before my eyes. Same face, but wearing a golf cap and pulling a bag of clubs. I'd seen Glen Shaw at the country club, but I hadn't recognized him out of context.

Now, my mind was flooded with what-ifs. We had come in there with two stolen cars and two companies. Darlene and I had gone to the country club because we suspected someone connected with the club might be reconning high-end cars to steal. We hadn't considered that it might be a *member* of the club.

My mouth was hanging open when Glen saw us, but I shut it quickly as he approached. Like before, his hand was out and a smile bloomed on his face.

"Sheriff Macklin! And Larry, right?" We both received generous shakes. "Sheriff, I'm glad to see that you're up and doing well. To what do we owe this visit? That bad weather? We're doing our part. Anyone stuck here is welcome to park in our lot. I might even be able to rig up some extension cables for RVs."

"We want to talk to Kyle Whitten," I said.

There was an obvious shift in his mood at the mention of Kyle's name. Glen recovered fast, but not before I noticed his hesitation.

"I don't think he's back yet." His voice was noticeably lower and less hardy.

Apparently it wasn't low enough, because one of the men drinking coffee said, "He's out back. Got in about forty-five minutes ago."

Glen managed to say, "Thanks, Timber." He turned to me. "I guess you're in luck. I'll call him in." He turned and walked behind the counter, picking up a phone, pushing some buttons and speaking into it. "He'll be right up," he said to us after a minute. "Excuse me, there's a few things I need to check on."

Glen started to go through the door behind the counter, but stopped at the last minute and turned back. He stood there awkwardly, fiddling with a computer. Through the door, I could just make out someone sitting in the office behind the counter. I remembered the last time I'd visited. A man had been sitting with his back to the door working at a computer. Was it the same person?

As we waited for Kyle, I looked around the room and noticed that everyone was discreetly watching us. I wasn't the only one who'd picked up on Glen's odd behavior.

Finally, I saw Kyle come through the back doors. He looked worse for wear. Maybe it was just the weather and the hard trip he'd had, but Kyle looked more haggard than the last time I'd seen him.

From the look on Kyle face when he saw us, it was clear that Glen hadn't told him we were there. He stopped with the door half open and I was sure that he was thinking about turning and running away. Instead, he slowly stepped inside with the icy sleet illuminated behind him. He looked hard at Glen, who didn't meet his eyes.

Shaking off the cold, he walked over to us, his face a grim mask.

"You wanted to talk to me?" He looked first at Dad and then at me.

"Is there somewhere we can talk in private?" I asked.

"No," he said, taking me by surprise.

"We want to talk to you about your father," I said, hoping that might make him more interested in a private conversation.

"My father was an asshole," Kyle said in a louder voice than was necessary.

I gestured at Dad. "This is *my* father. He arrested *your* father, who died in prison. I think it's a hell of a coincidence that the person who stole a car you were driving ended up stabbing my father."

"I don't care what you think," Kyle snarled. I was certain that the aggression was a fear response. It was written all over him. "I was out of town when your dad was stabbed." He looked at Dad as though he expected to receive support from him.

"That doesn't mean you weren't involved. Did you know a man named Eduardo Alverez?" I asked, throwing the curveball at him.

That did it. Kyle broke right before our eyes.

"I didn't do shit!" he screamed and ran out the back door.

I got out of the door right behind him. As the cold, wet sleet hit my face, I was aware of someone on my heels. I turned to see who it was, worried that it might be Dad. That was a mistake. The pavement already had enough ice to send me spinning down to the tarmac. I was run over by Glen, who couldn't stop in time.

We rolled over each other while I tried to decide why he'd been following me. I didn't know if he posed a threat that I needed to deal with or if he was just trying to slow me down so Kyle could make his escape. I couldn't make sense of it. I saw Kyle heading for a semi that was idling about fifty yards away. I kicked Glen and struggled to my feet. Slip-sliding, I started after Kyle again, who was having his own issues with the frozen sleet.

Again, there was movement behind me as I closed in on Kyle.

"Not him!" I heard Glen shout.

I assumed he was yelling to Kyle. Kyle heard him and glanced back to see me closing in on him. He veered sharply right away from the rig, then slipped and went down on one knee. I slowed to turn after him, sure that I would be able to close the gap. That's when I was hit by a freight train that sent me flying the last twenty feet into the grumbling semi rig.

Glen had attempted a flying tackle, but what really happened was that he slid at the last minute and simply plowed into me without slowing down. My right shoulder and arm slammed into the step on the cab. I fought to get to my feet before Glen, who had gone completely to the ground, managed to reach me. I'd lost Kyle and now my eyes were fixed on Glen. Whatever game he was playing, it was clearly aimed at stopping me.

Glen got up and I expected him to try to grab me. Instead, he ran up and shoved me out of the way as he climbed into the cab of the semi.

I had lost. Glen was already closing the door of the truck and Kyle was long gone. *What can I do? Stand in front of the semi and wave my hands for him to stop?* I thought as I heard the air brakes hiss.

"Get in the other side!" Glen yelled down at me. The words were so unexpected that my brain couldn't comprehend them. "Get in! He'll get away!" Glen was screaming over the truck's engine as he revved it up. "Kyle isn't the man you want. *He* is!" He pointed to an F-450 truck heading for the road.

"Get out of the truck!" I screamed up at Glen, not having any idea what he was talking about.

He slowly started edging the semi toward the entrance to

the parking lot. "Last chance!" he yelled back at me.

I couldn't say what made me do it, but on impulse I ran and hopped up on the passenger-side step of the semi. One foot slipped, and only my hand reaching up and grabbing the door handle kept me from falling. I managed to pull the door open and crawl in as Glen accelerated out of the parking lot.

CHAPTER TWENTY-FOUR

"Are you crazy?" I yelled.

"I'm not letting that bastard kill my family." Glen wheeled the big truck onto the road, which was a four-lane here near the interstate, but would quickly narrow to a two-lane road once we got away from I-10.

"Who are you talking about?" My mind was trying to play catch-up. I had a feeling I knew who we were chasing, even though I'd never met him.

"Neil Manning, that little dirtbag. He's behind all of this." The sleet was coming down harder as we whizzed through the glare of lights that illuminated the interstate exit. The dull glow of the sun rising above the horizon was just starting to color the frozen landscape.

"How?"

"He kidnapped that girl."

"Terri?"

"Yes, yes. He grabbed her off the road."

"Why?"

"He knew her in high school. One day five years ago, he saw her walking down the road. No one was around, so he clipped her with his truck and took her home."

"What?"

"He's crazy. He kept her and brainwashed her."

"You knew this?" I asked, appalled.

"No, no, not until about four months ago. He'd messed with her head so bad at that point that she thought she was in love with him. She was convinced that he was the only one who could protect her from the people chasing her. He showed her all of those missing posters to prove that people were after her. Totally screwed with her head."

"How'd you find out about all this?"

"Neil thought he didn't have to worry about her running away, so he kind of dropped his guard. I think the freak was proud of her. He introduced me to her four months ago when I went to his house to talk business. After that, he even brought her to the office a couple of times. In her own screwy way, she told me a lot of it."

"Why didn't you go to the police then?" I didn't know how much of his story I really believed.

"Because that man is insane. When I confronted him about what she'd told me, and I'd filled in some of the pieces on my own, he threatened to kill my ex-wife and children. It was not an idle threat. That's why I'm going to run his ass off the road and kill *him*." Glen's face was illuminated by the lights of the dashboard. From his expression, I didn't doubt that he was serious.

Glen was driving fast, but on the wet, slippery road the big rig couldn't keep up with the more agile pickup truck.

"So what the hell happened with my dad?"

"Neil was letting Terri out 'cause he was confident she wasn't going to run away. He had her that brainwashed. Terri didn't steal that car. We let her drive it. That day, she'd pulled off the side of the road 'cause she thought she had a flat tire. Your dad stopped to help. When he recognized her and called her by name, she freaked and stabbed him. Remember, she'd been told all kinds of crazy stories about what the authorities would do if they caught her."

"So who killed her?"

"Once we realized that someone might have seen the car

when your dad was attacked, we reported it stolen to cover our asses. When y'all came around and started asking questions, Neil got nervous and decided that he had to get rid of Terri. So he got her to kill herself." There were tears on Glen's cheeks. He wiped at them as the semi hit an icy patch. The trailer swayed unnervingly, but Glen kept it on the road.

"He convinced her to kill *herself?*"

"She thought she loved Neil more than life itself. All he had to do was make her believe that if she was caught, he'd be killed. You got to believe me. If I'd known he was going to do that, I would have stopped it. I didn't know anything about it until I heard that the car had been found with her body inside."

For some reason, I believed him. "How's Kyle involved?"

"Kyle is Neil's main flunky. He got him to do all kinds of crazy shit. He beat up Eduardo. I think he might have killed him."

"So Eduardo is involved in all of this too?"

"That was my fault. I had him helping me to steal cars. We were both going to use the money to get out from under Neil's thumb."

"You picked them…" I lost my train of thought for a second as I felt the semi's wheels lose touch with the ground as we went around a curve. A hundred yards in front of us, I saw the red glow of Neil's taillights.

"I got this," Glen growled and put even more weight onto the accelerator.

"You picked out the cars."

"Right. Expensive, but not singular. We didn't want to tear them apart. Found a middleman and shipped them out of Tampa to South and Central America."

"How'd you get them to Tampa?" I wondered how he'd evaded Darlene's network of private cameras.

"We'd drive them right into the back of a semi. That's why we always picked small cars. We had to tip the driver and hope they didn't get checked by the DOT."

"You weren't cutting Neil in."

"Exactly. But he found out and got Kyle to beat the hell out of Alverez. At that point, I would have quit. It was Eduardo who said he had to have the money. We did another one and would have gotten away with it, except you stopped by Southeast looking for Eduardo. Neil heard you mention a car theft and knew we were behind it. So he had Kyle finish the job on Eduardo."

"Why didn't he kill you?"

"Didn't have to. He couldn't touch Eduardo's family. Mine was within easy rea—" He stopped and I felt him put on the brakes. When I looked out the windshield, I saw an odd strobing effect. As we careened toward it, I realized that Neil's truck was spinning out in the middle of the road. First the headlights and then the taillights flashed at us. I felt the semi speed up.

"Stop!" I ordered. I took my eyes off the impending disaster in front of us long enough to see the grim determination on Glen's face.

"I have a son and daughter, ages five and ten," he said as we slammed into Neil's truck.

Glen held onto the steering wheel with an iron grip as we were tossed up and down, running over parts of the pickup. The F-450 was a massive truck, but was no match for the semi. We flipped it on its side and pushed it off the road. Unfortunately for us, parts of the truck were stuck under the semi's front axle. The big rig slid off the road right behind Neil's truck, which had been stopped by a line of pine trees. Luckily for him, we hit the trees behind him rather than plowing into his truck.

The weight of the trailer, which I was to find out later was full of pet food, pulled the semi over onto the passenger side. I'd had the good sense to snap on a seatbelt as soon as I'd figured out that Glen wasn't going to stop. Glen hadn't bothered and landed on top of me. I came out of it with only a black eye and bruises from one end of my body to the other, but Glen had clearly broken several bones.

I managed to climb up over him as he screamed in pain and crawled out through the driver's door. And, no, I didn't feel the least bit sorry for him.

"If you had any doubts, I assure you, you are under arrest. I'll read you your rights when I get back," I told him as I climbed down from the cab.

The sun was nearing the eastern tree line, but there wasn't enough light to see into the crumpled cab of the F-450. Amazingly, my phone had stayed in my pocket, so I pulled it out and turned on the flashlight app. The sleet fell in little balls of ice as I approached the truck, which had completely turtled before hitting the trees. When I shined my light on the exploded window of the driver's door, I could see a man hanging down at an awkward angle from his seatbelt. He was breathing, but I couldn't tell more than that.

I called dispatch for an ambulance.

"Chief Hatcher and Major Parks have ordered all emergency vehicles to stand down until the weather conditions improve," I was told.

"I've got a man in critical condition. He won't live if we don't get him to a hospital."

"I can patch you through to Major Parks."

I was about to request that when I heard a car approach. I looked up to see the car's lights shining through the falling ice. I decided to stop them and commandeer the vehicle if I had to. It sped up as it approached us and I figured it was going to run past us. Instead, it slewed around and stopped in front of us. That's when I realized that it was my car with Dad at the wheel. He jumped out of the car, slipping and sliding as he jogged over to me.

"Are you all right?" he asked breathlessly.

"I'm fine. The others aren't." I wanted to give him a hard time for following us, but I was too glad to see him. He was peering in at the dangling Neil Manning.

"He needs help fast." Dad stated the obvious as I heard the dispatcher asking through my phone if I still needed help.

"Here." I handed the phone to Dad. "Dispatch."

"This is the other Macklin," Dad said. "Get ahold of Martel. He's from Wisconsin and ought to know how to drive in this crap. Tell him to bring blankets, flares and a portable source of heat if he can find something. And let him know that it's more important to arrive than to arrive fast. Slow and steady. We'll be here."

I took the phone and called Hondo, my favorite EMT.

"We're grounded," he said when I told him the situation. "These ambulances have rotten tires on the best of days. I can't risk it in the ice." He paused for a minute. "No worries. My buddy Jack—you know him—he's got a mad four-wheel drive that can get there." I told Hondo where I was. "Let me call him."

Two minutes later, a breathless Jack called me. "Man, I'm loading my truck and will be there in twenty minutes. Hondo wanted me to pick him up, but where you are, it'll be a lot quicker if my wife and I just come straight there. Grab all that stuff," I heard him instruct his wife. "Call the hospital and have a doc talk you through until I get there. Just hang on, buddy. We'll be there in no time." And the line went dead.

Jack Ormond was a lanky country boy who'd had experience as a medic in Afghanistan. The thing most of his patients remembered about him was his wide grin and good humor as he kept their life from slipping away. While he wasn't officially employed as a medic anymore, he'd kept a good supply of equipment and often had the chance to keep his skills up-to-date by patching up various injuries received by his hunting buddies.

Dad had already retrieved a couple of flares from the trunk of my car and placed them in the road. I pulled blankets from my trauma kit and helped Dad get Glen as comfortable as he could be in the cab of the semi, then I got on the phone with the emergency room to see what I could do for Neil.

Thanks to the freezing temperatures, Neil wasn't losing blood as fast as he might have otherwise. His seatbelt and airbag had saved his life. I thought about what Glen had told me and what he'd tried to do. Could this guy really be that dangerous?

The ER doctor had me assess Neil for back and neck fractures, then instructed me to ease him out of the truck and into a horizontal position. Neil never made a sound, except for some gurgling as he tried to breathe through whatever internal injuries he had. His right side had taken the brunt of the damage.

Deputy Martel arrived to help Dad with traffic control, which was thankfully light due to the storm. Jack arrived soon after and I stood off to the side as he and his wife loaded Neil onto a backboard and slid him into the back of Jack's truck. Then they did the same for Glen Shaw.

I left Dad at the scene and rode with Jack in the back of the truck with the patients while his wife drove to the hospital. Luckily, there was a topper on the truck so that we didn't freeze to death. As she drove, Jack assessed Neil's and Glen's injuries and stabilized them as best he could. Once we had turned them both over to the emergency room staff, I called Cara.

"It's still coming down here," she told me. "The lights have blinked, but haven't gone out. Scott says everything is fine at the clinic, so Dr. Barnhill told the rest of us to stay home. Which is good, since I'm pretty sure the doors of my car are frozen shut." I could hear the childish excitement in Cara's voice at experiencing weather so foreign to our part of the country.

"How was your night?" she asked me.

"It was very quiet until about two hours ago," I said, then told her all about my morning with Dad.

"You two should never be left alone." While she meant it as a joke, I could hear the real concern beneath the surface.

"We're fine. Damn it! I still need to buy you a Christmas present... Do you think the storm will be over in time for the stores to open back up?" I joked, trying to change the subject away from my reckless behavior.

"Christmas is still over a week away. But come home safely, and I'll be happy regardless."

"Ha, I'll remember that on Christmas morning."

I settled in to wait on word about Neil and Glen. I wanted to be able to officially arrest both of them, then I'd need to con someone into picking me up from the hospital.

By noon, the ice had stopped falling and the temperature hovered just above freezing. The text alerts on my phone let me know that they would be reopening the interstate soon. I looked up from my phone, trying to get comfortable in the waiting room chair, and saw a stout man in his mid-sixties, wearing a tailored suit, approaching me from the emergency room entrance.

"Are you Deputy Macklin?"

"I am. What—" I didn't get to finish.

"You were in the truck that rammed my son!" The man's finger was jabbing at me. "Why didn't you stop that maniac?" Rudy Manning's voice was loud and aggressive, but I wasn't having any of it.

"Your son is going to be arrested on a number of charges, including kidnapping. You want to know why I didn't stop the driver of the truck? Well, I want to know why you enabled your son to commit some pretty heinous crimes." I stepped into his space. "I tried to stop the truck, but the man driving it was terrified that if your son wasn't stopped, he'd harm his children. That's a pretty strong motivation."

Manning was taken aback, but only for a moment.

"I'm going to file an official complaint." His voice was still aggressive, but his volume had gone down a couple of notches.

"Be my guest. I want everyone to know what your son did. The more publicity, the better," I told him, not backing down an inch.

He started to open his mouth and say something, but I

had one more point to get across. This one I delivered in a low voice with as much menace as I could incorporate. "One more thing. If my father had died from the knife that your son helped to ram into him, you would have some really big things to complain about."

Manning looked shocked. "Are you threatening me?"

"We're done here." I turned and left him staring at my back.

A week later, on December 21, with the sun out and the ice long gone, though winter had now officially started, life was back to normal. A dozen accidents, power out for a day in some places and one fire: those were the total damages in Adams County. Not too bad considering it was a Florida icepocaylpse.

At noon, most of the sheriff's office personnel, along with friends and family, were gathered in a large meeting room at the jail for our annual holiday luncheon. The folding tables along the wall bowed under the weight of turkey, casseroles and salads. Another table was loaded down with cakes and cookies.

Julio, Pete, Jessie, Darlene, Shantel, Marcus and I were seated at a table close enough to the dessert table that we could make more than one trip without being too conspicuous.

"So Neil Manning was manipulating everyone?" Jessie asked.

"Pretty much," I said. "The thing that drives me crazy is that I saw him at both Southeast and AmMex, but didn't know he was anyone I needed to worry about. He was always sitting in an office with his back to me."

"Listening. I know those kinds of people," Shantel said between bites of pecan pie.

"He's a little creep. He actually smiled when I was questioning him about Terri Miller," Pete said. While Neil was still in the hospital and would be for a while, none of his injuries had proved life-threatening.

Pete and I both saw Jessie tense up at the mention of Terri's name. Pete turned to her. "I blame myself for not being able to rescue her. I should have questioned everyone from her high school class. Several have told me since that they remember him creeping on her, even though he was a senior while she was a freshman. Apparently, he'd written her some notes, though we've never found them."

"I saw the container where he kept her," Jessie said in a low voice, looking down at her plate. I wished she hadn't mentioned that. For the first three months, before he'd worked all of his mind-whammy on her, Neil had kept Terri locked up in a large shipping container at his vacant property.

"Yeah, that was bad. But Terri was tough. Thanks to her, we're going to be able to put him away on those kidnapping charges for a long time," Pete said.

"Those notes she made will be nails in his coffin," I said. Terri had managed to make notes on pieces of paper she'd found in the cargo container, then had hidden them under the nasty carpet that covered the floor. I guess she'd forgotten about them by the time she'd convinced herself that she loved him.

Jessie was still staring down at her plate, pushing the food around disinterestedly.

"That girl never told the little troll about those notes." Shantel was talking directly to Jessie. "That means that somewhere, deep inside, she was still Terri and wasn't going to let him get away with what he was doing. I bet she's mighty happy that we're going to lock him away so he doesn't hurt anyone else. You helped us do that."

Jessie looked up and gave her a small smile.

"Y'all made a woman down in Gainesville very happy too. That box of personal items you found is going to make her Christmas a bit brighter," Darlene told us.

"It was in Neil's garage," Marcus said.

"We'll need to keep a couple of items as evidence, but we

should be able to send the rings and most of the pictures back to her in the next day or two," Pete said.

"How many people knew about Terri?" Marcus asked.

"When I took Glen's statement, he said that most of the people working at the two businesses were in the dark. All they knew was that Neil was an asshole and would 'hurt'—his word—anyone that crossed him, so they all kept their eyes down. Except for Kyle. He was Neil's biggest toady," I explained.

"Which reminds me. Kyle will be coming back to Adams County just as soon as the paperwork is done so he can be extradited from South Carolina," Julio said. We'd all been impressed that Kyle had managed to get that far in the awful weather.

"Enough talk about work," I said, though I needn't have bothered. Just as the words were out of my mouth, a cheer went up from the back of the room. We all turned to see Dad, wearing a Santa hat, coat and beard, enter the room leading Mauser, reindeer antlers in place. Genie stood behind him, smiling.

"Ho, ho, ho!" shouted Dad. "As always, there are no Christmas bonuses!" Loud boos mixed with laughter greeted this announcement. "The good news is: your right honorable sheriff should be back on duty by the end of January!" This was met with an extended round of clapping.

Genie and I had spent the better part of a day negotiating with Dad about when he would return to work. I thought we'd done well to get him to agree to a month of rest.

"I'm impressed there's still some food left."

I turned to see Cara standing behind me. I got up and gave her a kiss.

"Better hurry and get yourself a plate before I go back for my third round," Pete said, pointing at his own plate.

When the party was over, I walked Cara out to her car.

"Have you gotten my present yet?" She elbowed me.

"Maybe," I said, happy that the sapphire necklace was already tucked away in a hiding place at the house, waiting to be wrapped.

My text alert went off and I glanced at my phone. It was from Eddie. *Need to talk to you now! 911*

Cara was looking at me, no doubt worried by the frown on my face as I read the message.

"Eddie," I said, which was explanation enough.

I started to call him, but then I saw him waving at me from across the parking lot.

I pointed him out to Cara, who waved and received a shy wave back from him. I gave her a kiss before she got into her car. After I watched her drive off, I walked over to Eddie.

"What's the big emergency?" I asked, less then charitably.

"I need your help." He looked desperate.

I softened a little. "Okay, what's going on?"

"I want to get Jessie something for Christmas and don't have a clue."

I almost laughed. "And you think I can help?"

"I thought about... You know, some underwear or something. I know all about—"

I held up my hand. "Stop, stop, stop! I don't want to hear anything about your knowledge of women's underwear."

"That's not right anyway," Eddie agreed. "We aren't really... So I don't know. Jewelry is kind of out too."

"Okay. Let me think." *What would Jessie like?* I wondered. Then I snapped my fingers. "I have something. We'll take my car."

I drove a mile down the road to a leather shop in a small strip mall. The front of the shop was barely ten-foot square, but behind the counter was a large work area with dozens and dozens of boots and shoes lined up with paper claim tags on them, as well as racks of belts and pieces of cow hide waiting to be cut.

"Mr. Macklin, what can I do for you today?" Raul Spencer asked. People in town had tried to guess his age, but could never quite settle on a number. To me he looked like the same old man Dad had introduced me to when we came in to pick up my first duty belt almost nine years ago.

I pulled out my bifold. "My friend wants a badge case as a gift for a young lady."

"Okay!" Raul pulled out his order pad. "What color?"

The three of us went through all of the options of color, size and border.

"If it's a gift, you might want to have it engraved with something," Raul suggested.

"Maybe," Eddie said, and I was afraid he was going to start dithering again. But then his eyes lit up. "Put, *I believe in you.*"

The chill of winter seemed to melt away and I thought, *This is going to be a good Christmas.*

Larry Macklin returns in:

Valentine's Warning
A Larry Macklin Mystery–Book 17
Coming late 2021!

ACKNOWLEDGMENTS

As always, thanks to my wife, Melanie, for her editing skills and support; to H. Y. Hanna for her inspiration, assistance and encouragement; and to all the fans of the series. Larry never would have come this far without all of you!

Original Cover Concept by H. Y. Hanna
Cover Design by Robin Ludwig Design Inc.
www.gobookcoverdesign.com

ABOUT THE AUTHOR

A. E. Howe lives and writes on a farm in the wilds of north Florida with his wife, horses and more cats than he can count. He received a degree in English Education from the University of Georgia and is a produced screenwriter and playwright. His first published book was *Broken State*. The Larry Macklin Mysteries is his first series and he released a new series, the Baron Blasko Mysteries, in summer 2018. The first book in the Macklin series, *November's Past*, was awarded two silver medals in the 2017 President's Book Awards, presented by the Florida Authors & Publishers Association; the ninth book, *July's Trials*, was awarded two silver medals in 2018. Howe is a member of the Mystery Writers of America, and was co-host of the "Guns of Hollywood" podcast for four years on the Firearms Radio Network. When not writing Howe enjoys riding, competitive shooting and working on the farm.